QUANTUM FEELINGS, INC.

ROBIN JOHNSON

Quantum Feelings, Inc.

ISBN 979-8-9953813-0-3

Cover design by Bruce Scallon

We're at a unique point in history. Where what once required many people spending many years and many millions can now be done by a small group of inspired people from a dorm room, or in my case, a bedroom closet. Ideas can be proven before they need to be committed to. The revolutions of our generation—in business, education, social structure, and even politics—are not being catalyzed by generals or politicians, but by highly empowered individuals like yourselves—the wizards of our time so to speak—who can see with clarity how the assumptions of previous generations no longer apply. And the revolutions often grow out of nothing more than an intense hobby, an inspired attempt of seeing if things can be rethought a little better.

\- SAL KHAN, COMMENCEMENT ADDRESS,
MIT, JUNE 8, 2012

ONE

Jackson, sixteen and gawky, fidgeted in the chair, unsure what to do with his hands now that he wasn't holding his phone. His freshly cut fade—all clean curves and quiet confidence—was more than a hairstyle; it was one thing he got to choose about how he showed up in the world.

"Tell me about some of your device-free activities this past week," prompted Dr. Matthew Venable, mid-thirties, wearing L.L. Bean like a uniform. "What did you do? How did you feel?"

"I left my phone at home when I ran to grab milk for my mom. It's just the corner store, so I didn't totally freak. I kinda missed having my earbuds, but I guess it's safer not to be zoned out when you're walking around Cambridge."

"And how far's the store from your place?"

"Like, ten minutes each way."

"So that's twenty minutes without your phone, and you didn't feel lost or anxious?"

"Nope. It was chill."

Matthew smiled. "It sounds like you managed some decent

stretches without your phone. Any anxiety or panic episodes since we last talked?"

Jackson paused. "Yeah. In chem class. The teacher called on me and I blanked. My vision blurred. Everything spun, and my chest got tight. I couldn't breathe. My hands were shaking like crazy, and my heart felt like it was trying to escape. I bolted to the nurse's office. Took, like, half an hour to calm down."

"Did you try any of the stuff we've practiced? The three-three-three? Breathing work?"

"I couldn't. It hit too fast. Like, one second I'm fine, and the next it's like my brain's glitching out. There's no time to do anything."

"That makes sense. Panic can ambush you like that. That's why we practice these tools ahead of time, when you're calm. So this week, I want you to set aside five minutes a day—just five—to run the three-three-three. Doesn't have to be the same time every day, find a moment when you're chill. Practice spotting three things you can see, three you can hear, and three you can feel. Want to give it a go now?"

"Right now?"

"Yep. Right here."

"Alright. Uh ... I see you. I see the clock. And that weird animal on your shelf. What even is that?"

"That's a marmot."

"Seriously? Is it, like, alive?"

"Used to be. It's taxidermy. Someone cleaned it up and stuffed it so we can appreciate marmots forever."

"That's ... kinda gross. But also weirdly cool."

"Three things you hear?"

"You. The clock. And ... I guess my heartbeat. It's in my ears again."

"Do you usually hear your heart beating in your ears?"

"Not really. Only sometimes, like when I'm kinda on edge."

"Good observation. Keep an ear out for that this week. It might be your body giving you a heads-up. Now, up on your feet."

"Huh?"

"One last thing. We're gonna do the Labrador shake."

"The what?"

Matthew turned on the speaker. Arcade Fire's "Ready to Start" started playing.

"This? Really?" Jackson smirked. "Feels like vintage Spotify-core."

"From the Grammy Album of the Year when you were born. This is basically your theme song."

Matthew demonstrated a full-body shake, like a wet dog drying off. "Now you."

Jackson half-shook.

"Nope. Try again. Channel your inner golden retriever, go!"

Jackson laughed and gave a proper shake.

"There you go! That's what I want you to do when the panic starts. Reset the nervous system. Practice once a day this week."

Jackson snorted. "Okay, sure. See you next week."

Matthew exhaled as the door closed behind him. He thought: *It's a beautiful Friday afternoon, 70 degrees and sunny. Jackson should be at the park or riding his bike, not sitting in a therapist's office.*

He turned to his laptop to type up session notes, the image of Jackson's panic still fresh.

Matthew had enough success stories to know that somatic therapy helped, but the problem was scale. How to make somatic therapy available when every third teen was suffering like Jackson?

WALKING HOME THAT EVENING, Matthew felt twitchy.

He was on Massachusetts Avenue, threading the narrow strip of sidewalk between the Sloan buildings and Kendall Square—about as close as MIT got to a "campus." Unlike the manicured lawns of other elite universities, MIT sprawled in Brutalist fragments and glass cubes. Matthew thought his alma mater had always been more concerned with the future than the aesthetics of the present.

As uncomfortable as twitchy felt, it was still a *feeling*. And lately, he'd been moving through something flatter—a kind of emotional quiet that had less to do with calm and more to do with absence. *Depressive anhedonia*. The inability to feel pleasure.

He'd come back to Cambridge to feel again, knowing that many of those feelings would be painful. It's where he'd launched his early career, excited and engaged in a partnership with his best friend, Darren, that ended in a painful divergence —over method, over mission, over what counted as healing.

Matthew thought about his undergraduate years. Back then he had believed he could make technology-assisted somatic therapy widely available.

He loved his four years at MIT. He'd been thrown together with Darren Katsaros, a neuropharmacology student, and Maya Venkataraman, a computer science student, and others in Terrascope, a freshman course designed to nurture interdisciplinary teamwork in problem solving.

He remembered the heady feeling of being asked to work on real world problems.

MIT's Computer Science and Artificial Intelligence Laboratory, known as CSAIL, had hosted a series of guest speakers to anchor tech students in an ethical framework.

Matthew remembered one from 2009:

"Designing for Minds Under Pressure: Ethics, Tech, and the Adolescent Brain."

Dr. Amina Kassam, director of CSAIL, had moderated the session.

"Tonight we welcome Stanford professor, Dr. Lena Marwick.

"She is a scholar whose work on attention, attachment, and early digital culture is shaping how we think about technology's impact on the developing mind."

As applause swept the room, one of Marwick's early formulations had appeared on the screen:

When communication becomes effortless, connection becomes optional.

Matthew leaned against the wall in faded jeans. He enjoyed these ethics discussions. Next to him, Darren was already wearing the subtle gray-on-gray uniform of the tech founder he would soon become. Matthew could see that Darren was multitasking. He had subtle, sleek earbuds in—likely listening to the Harvard Business Review IdeaCast.

Maya sat cross-legged on the floor in a cotton tunic and loose pants, her sleek MacBook open, her long braid skimming the power strip but never quite touching it.

Marwick began with early data—faint but unmistakable upticks in adolescent anxiety beginning around 2008, trends so new they weren't yet in newspapers. She described "ambient disconnection," a state in which young people were constantly reachable but seldom reached.

The room stilled. "A generation fluent in contact," she continued, "but starved for presence."

She paused to let the idea land. "Too many of our tools

were designed for speed and throughput," she continued, "but not for emotional complexity. And young nervous systems take the hit."

Maya's hand shot up during Q&A. "Dr. Marwick—you describe face-to-face interaction as a kind of developmental nutrient. But what about neurodivergent or touch-averse students? Does stepping back always signal pathology, or can it be a boundary?"

Marwick nodded appreciatively. "You're right to name that. In my fieldwork, teachers tell me their students struggle with eye contact, timing, repair cues—things that used to be practiced in unstructured moments. But retreat isn't always pathology. Sometimes it's self-protection."

Marwick paused. "My concern isn't with choice. It's when buffering becomes default—when micro-moments of awkwardness, or curiosity, or repair get designed out. Those moments are where empathy takes root."

Matthew raised his hand next. "Do you think those of us building software need to be trained in neuropsych? In somatic literacy?" He wasn't trying to be provocative; he genuinely wanted to know whether cognitive science should be part of the engineering toolkit.

Kassam stepped in. "You're on the right track, Matthew, but can you find another way to make tech neuropsych-informed without cramming 2200 freshmen into the Intro to Psychology lecture hall?"

A chuckle rippled through the room.

Matthew joined the chuckle and suggested, "Maybe have people fluent in neurobiology on our interdisciplinary design teams?"

"Thank you—that is a realistic solution. If young people's nervous systems are already strained by the environments we build, resilience can't be an afterthought. We need to design digital and physical spaces that support reflection and regulation."

A hush fell. The students were listening.

Kassam continued: "You can't just think about what tech does. You have to be on the lookout for what it quietly displaces."

TWO

Maya craved coffee. The faculty meeting had drained her.

When she stepped in front of her graduate assistant's desk, Sam jumped out of her seat. "Yikes!"

"Uhm, sorry?" Maya raised an eyebrow.

"My bad. I was in algorithm mode. Social reboot in progress." Samira "Sam" Shahidi's hair—thick, dark, and full of motion—curled gently at the ends like it knew exactly where it wanted to go, even if she didn't always.

"It's all good." Maya chuckled. "That little adrenaline spike will tide me over until I get my hands on a cortado."

Then her smile faded. "New policy just landed. I have to write narrative evaluations for each of the eighty students in Computation in Problem Solving. Management says under-grads are flaming out from the pressure of grades."

Maya was the newest faculty member in MIT's Computer Science and Artificial Intelligence Lab, known as CSAIL. She carried a heavy teaching load, in addition to implementing research grants for TrailMind, a tech platform she was shepherding to reconnect anxious youth to nature.

"No problem," Sam beamed, already typing. "I can help you automate the inputs for narratives. I'm not gonna leave you holding the bag when I graduate. I'll build an ingestion pipeline and fine-tune a large language model on anonymized evals—it can scrape their coding logs, forum posts, and peer reviews, all of which were collected with students' permission. That should help you generate feedback about their strengths, their struggles, the whole arc. We've got this."

Maya breathed out a sigh of relief. Sam would automate the analysis of the student's work history, making it easy for Maya to synthesize into narrative. At least someone wasn't feeling overwhelmed.

"I've got to head out to meet Hannah. Is there anything you need from me today, Sam?"

"Nope. I'll have the algorithm in your inbox by this evening. We can pick it up tomorrow and take it for a test run."

"It can wait until Monday, Sam. It's a gorgeous Friday afternoon. Go out and enjoy the first 70-degree day of 2026."

Maya gave Sam a cheery wave good-bye, but the ache of impending loss tugged at her ribs. Graduation was just weeks away, and a recruiter from LoopWell had already taken Sam to lunch—twice.

Sam's rare gift for blending empathy with technical skill had shaped TrailMind's feedback systems into something truly human-centered. It was no surprise that LoopWell wanted to scoop her up.

Maya couldn't afford to put Sam on the TrailMind budget. Not after the platform's federal funding had been pulled back as part of sweeping changes in Washington.

MAYA HURRIED to the Media Center's Commons Café. She appreciated the soft space, a respite of warm light and soothing acoustic music nestled between the glass-and-steel walkways of the MIT Media Lab. She spent more hours in the cafe while earning her PhD than in her fourth-floor walk-up in Somerville.

Maya spotted Hannah's short, spiky, blond hair. Hannah Oak had been Maya's student and a TrailMind researcher a few years back. Now she was an influential blogger questioning whether Big Pharma was helping, or compounding, the growing teen anxiety epidemic.

Maya eyed the two steaming cups of coffee in front of Hannah. "I hope one of those is for me."

Hannah looked up from her laptop. "Natch. What's up? Why the emergency meeting?"

"No emergency. Just the usual hustle for those sweet, sweet dollars." Maya closed her eyes as she mindfully savored the first sip of coffee. "What are you working on?"

"Trying to land an interview with Darren Katsaros. There's a rumor that he'll be called to testify before a House Oversight Committee. Something about an AMC—an Advance Market Commitment?"

"He did get an AMC. It's the same mechanism the government used to accelerate production of the COVID-19 vaccines during the pandemic. Darren's AMC guarantees the federal government will purchase millions of doses of NeuroEase if he can accelerate development and production. It's a big deal. Sounds like your blog's making waves with the policy crowd."

"I mean ... maybe? But I'm not the only one out here side-eyeing Big Pharma's love affair with anxiety meds." Hannah leaned back. "We're throwing pills at a generation that's just ... drowning."

"Welcome to Tuesday."

"Exactly." Hannah sighed. "So what's going on with Trail-Mind and CSAIL?"

"Oh, juggling narrative grading for eighty freshmen thanks to the new flexible grading policy." Maya shrugged. "Plus writing grant applications to replace the grants I already won but got clawed back. So, you know, the new normal in academia."

"Wait—not the TrailMind grant?"

"Yep. The big one from the National Park Service. It was supposed to fund our TrailMind rollout to one hundred and twenty national parks. Adaptive anxiety support, indigenous narratives...the whole vision."

"Ugh, that's brutal." Hannah winced. "You've got a killer product, and the demand is so real. People are starving for something like this."

"Tell that to the states I'm now pitching one by one. I've got meetings with twenty different park departments next semester —and I'm speaking on a panel in Boston Common next week about why Massachusetts should step up to fill the funding gap for the Boston Harbor Islands Park."

"Whoa. A public forum in the Common? That's got colonial cosplay written all over it." Hannah smirked at the image in her head of Renaissance Faire meets Plymouth Plantation.

"Right? It's actually kind of poetic—did you know the Common is the oldest public park in the country?"

Hannah nodded in appreciation. "Send me the details. I want to cover it. Front row. I can't just blog 'Big Pharma Bad'–I need to tell the stories of real, scalable, effective solutions. Trail-Mind gives Gen Z an actual alternative—to break that loop of constant notifications masquerading as connection that feed the screen-induced cortisol spikes." Hannah grinned. "And honestly? TrailMind will play better on TikTok than a Substack policy deep dive. I could thread participants' stories into sixty-second reels—something hopeful, grounded, with enough spark to make the algorithm blink twice."

Maya nodded in agreement. "Back to Darren—what's the issue? Why won't he talk?"

"I did get him on the phone, briefly. I asked him about the congressional hearing rumor.

"He said, and I quote, 'I'm not here to knock anyone out of the market. But if they're serious this time, I need to know. Because I'm done slowing down for people who romanticize friction.' Does that make any sense to you?"

"Hmm." Maya's eyes narrowed. "Maybe you should talk to Matthew."

"Do I know him?"

"Probably not. But he and Darren were joined at the hip back when we were all undergrads. They were obsessed with solving teen anxiety—real idealist vibes. But then something blew up between them. Total falling out. Might be worth talking to Matthew if you want to understand Darren's trajectory."

"Interesting." Hannah pulled out her phone. "What's his last name?"

"Venable. Matthew Venable."

THREE

Matthew's client, Ava, arrived early on Saturday with a cheerful knock on the door. Her cheeks were a little rosier than usual, and her pin-straight black hair was clean and neatly combed—clear signs she'd actually slept the night before.

"Guess what?"

Matthew looked up, smiling. "You look happy. What's up?"

"No panic attacks in two weeks. And I kinda forgot to take my meds the last three days ... but I actually feel okay." She bounced on the balls of her feet, the energy unmistakable.

Matthew raised an eyebrow. "What made you stop?"

"I've been helping my friend Nia with this project on Spectacle Island. You know those islands in Boston Harbor? Total park vibes."

"I know them well. In fact, I'm meeting my parents out there this afternoon for a hike."

"Of course you are." She grinned, pointing to the L.L. Bean logo on his vest. "Anyway, Nia's like a citizen scientist. She's working with this MIT prof, testing these devices and apps along the trails. My job? Strap on this smart-watch thing, walk the trail, and listen."

"Listen to what?"

"Well ... trees. And sometimes park rangers. But like, not real ones—recorded voices. They tell stories about the trees, the birds, the bugs. Ecosystem stuff."

"That sounds incredible."

"It is. One tree said it's been on the island for three hundred years. It told this whole story—first Native peoples, then settlers, then fishermen. It was like history class but without the snore-fest."

"What else?"

"There was this tiny animal I never saw, but I could hear it describe its underground 'condo'. The voice was AI, but it played like a storybook—talking about its family and neighbors, like some furry homeowners' association situation. I actually want to go back at night and try to spot it in real life."

"That's amazing. I'm proud of you. I know being in the woods hasn't always felt safe for you."

"Nia made it easy. We took the T together, then the ferry. It felt like an adventure. And get this—I could still see the Boston skyline, but I was in the woods. And I was fine."

"Lit." Matthew used the Gen Z affirmation with a sheepish grin, earning him an eye roll from Ava.

He chuckled. "I'm glad Nia looped you in. Just—about the meds. If you feel any anxiety creeping back, promise you'll check in with me first? We don't want to yo-yo off and back on."

"I promise. But honestly? I feel stronger. Like, I'm connecting with something real."

"That's powerful. And hey, invite me sometime. I'd love to tag along. It's one of my favorite places on Earth, and now it sounds even cooler."

"I'll ask Nia and text you the deets. Therapy hike?"

"Therapy hike."

<hr>

THAT AFTERNOON, after his surprisingly upbeat appointment with Ava, Matthew caught the T to the ferry terminal to meet his parents.

Cambridge was home to his emotional safety net, Michelle and Jack Venable. His parents ... and his best friends, he had to admit, even if that made him a Millennial cliche.

As the train passed Charles/MGH station, dipping below the red-brick bulwark of Beacon Hill and into the tunnels, Matthew stared at the reflected blur in the subway windows and thought about when he would find his own path back to purpose. He knew himself well enough to be sure that purpose grounded him, and only from there would he find happiness and pleasure.

Was private practice the way forward?

A classmate from his psych program had already referred several private clients to him, saying: "Sadly, there are plenty more where those came from."

As the crackle of the disembodied voice of the conductor announced their arrival at the Park Street Station, Darren's words came back to him like static over a broken signal. *One-on-one therapy is to the Gen Z anxiety crisis what a teaspoon is to a person stuck in quicksand. Helpful, maybe, but lacking the necessary speed and futile at scale.*

By their senior year in 2012, Darren had developed the charisma to command a TED Talk–style stage in the Bartos Theater.

"We lose weeks waiting for calm to come naturally. What if relief could arrive in thirty seconds—measured, precise, molecularly tuned to your own cortisol curve?" he had asked investors as he pitched a cortisol-modulating sublingual strip on behalf of his Hacking Medicine team.

"This isn't escapism—it's optimization. A sublingual strip that dissolves the noise, gives your nervous system the reset it's been begging for, and gets you back in the game before anxiety steals another hour."

From the audience, Matthew and Maya saw clearly that the pitch was landing—the judges from venture capital firms, pharma reps, and Sloan MBAs were nodding, already mentally sketching the valuation arc.

Maya whispered, "He's not wrong about system delays. But he's prescribing absence."

"He's avoiding the mess," Matthew whispered back. "He wants to cure discomfort without getting touched by it. He doesn't see himself inside the problem."

Matthew and Maya didn't wait for the handshakes and LinkedIn swaps. They slipped out quietly and crossed campus to the Hayden Library.

Fifteen minutes later, Darren, humming with adrenaline, found them in the library. He asked Matthew, "What's your gut say about the pitch?"

Matthew smiled with a shrug. "It was ... slick. You had them. You owned that room."

Darren grinned. "You noticed I worked in the Terrascope slide?"

Matthew chuckled. "Every founder needs a fail-fast myth. But you made the community look like the obstacle. It wasn't."

Darren stiffened slightly. "It was inefficient. Too many perspectives. That village water plan took—what? Twelve weeks and three pivots. People drown while committees write memos."

Maya pushed back her chair and stood. Her tone stayed calm, but the edge was unmistakable.

"The friction is where the insight lives, Darren. That's how we get to root cause. You're designing relief from symptoms, not solutions."

She looked down at her notes strewn across the table; shook her head and walked away.

"I'm designing something that works." Darren waved her off and started pacing.

"If we can get this to market in under a year, we'll have the quals to fund your somatic R&D too."

Matthew should have seen the fractures with Darren sooner, but it took five years of trying to fit a nervous system into a business plan for the final break to happen.

FOUR

At the ferry launch, Matthew's mother, Michelle, tilted her Korean cheekbones toward the sun, wild black curls streaming in the wind. Matthew kept his own curls disciplined these days, freshly trimmed by an efficient barber who, like a good Lyft driver, knew not to chat.

Matthew's father, Jack, wore a tie-dyed Grateful Dead t-shirt and faded nylon hiking shorts he'd owned since Matthew was a Cub Scout.

Michelle radiated the kind of energy that came from years of yoga and green smoothies. Matthew understood that his parents prioritized spiritual and physical self-care not as indulgence but as endurance—tools to keep showing up for their values, which included environmental advocacy and voter rights volunteering.

They boarded the ferry for the 30-minute ride to Spectacle Island, skimming across the harbor under a sparkling sun. The chop was enough to feel alive, but not so much to turn anyone green. From the top deck, the skyline receded, replaced by the slow reveal of the island's two drumlins, those smoothly rounded, green oval hills that a glacier left behind when it passed through Boston 15,000 years ago.

Once ashore, they confirmed the return ferry schedule gave them just under two hours.

"What will it be, then?" Jack asked. "A leisurely loop around the South Drumlin Trail or a heart-thumper up the North?"

Michelle was already leading the way. "North Drumlin. I need to feel my quads complain a little."

As they ascended the hill, Deer Island came into view, and beyond that, the layered haze of East Boston. A few sailboats were already darting across the harbor, early-season skippers chasing wind.

Hiking the Harbor Islands stirred up old memories. During his years at MIT, Matthew had trudged these same trails wearing a clunky prototype vest loaded with biosensors and haptic feedback modules, as a research assistant for an experimental MIT project on human-tech-nature integration. The project was designed to help anxious students reconnect with the outdoors. He'd been part of the team that built it.

Back then, the data was messy, the tech was finicky, and the funding uncertain—but it felt like progress. Like something real. But then the split with Darren had derailed it all.

As his parents hiked on ahead of him, Matthew's thoughts turned to that moment in 2017 when the friction had finally won. Not the generative kind Matthew embraced, but the kind that splinters and tears. They'd kept brainstorming, adapting, and recommitting to advance their shared mission—until entrenched systems frayed the collaboration beyond repair.

Darren had pitched their full-spectrum vision to a Dutch venture capital firm. When Matthew jumped in to explain the therapeutic technology, Noa cut him off.

"The pill is scalable. Therapy isn't. Let's start with what moves. The rest goes on the back burner."

Before Darren could say anything, Noa was already at the white board, sketching out preliminary terms for her firm's investment in NeuroTech's fast-acting anxiety pill, NeuroEase.

Matthew waited until they were four blocks away from the VC's office before he stopped and turned to Darren.

"This was supposed to be a system, Darren. Holistic. Context-aware. Built from the nervous system out. You're prescribing escape instead of building resilience into the system."

Darren sighed. "Systems die without funding. You want change? Meet the market where it lives. Or don't."

Matthew raised a hand slightly. "Let's take a breath and talk about integrity."

"No." Darren shook his head, almost sadly. "Now it's time to talk about impact. You think your ethics matter more than helping a million people finally sleep through the night?"

"Forget ethics. What happens when people start sleeping through their own lives?"

"Noa said the somatic tools are on the back burner—not off the table." Darren threw up his hands. "But if you don't want to move forward? Fine. Stay behind."

Darren started to walk away, saying over his shoulder, "You're still waiting for the world to deserve the cure. I'm trying to get the cure to the world."

When Stanford offered Matthew a fellowship and sunnier skies, he headed West. But in Palo Alto, he found himself caught up in a similar vortex of speed and scale.

He had pitched a software development kit that offered pre-built components to integrate nature-focused grounding and somatic-awareness features into other apps or platforms. A venture capital firm licensed the technology and embedded him as a founder-consultant in another startup.

He signed on hoping to shepherd the soul of the project, but slowly watched it become unrecognizable. His "co-regulation" ethos got translated into "scalable calm tech." The nature focus evaporated. The haptics were now just notification nudges tied to productivity performance indicators. He earned hefty bonuses as the startup marketed corporate mindfulness packages, bundled into human resources wellness dashboards.

After two years, he wasn't just burned out—he was numbed by the grief of watching meaning get monetized.

Michelle brought him back to the present.

"Nothing makes me happier than having you back. Whether it's a pit stop or ... something more."

"I'm still figuring it out," Matthew admitted. "Private clients are rewarding. Watching them come out of shutdown— reconnecting to their bodies, their memories. That moment when someone breathes fully for the first time in weeks ..."

Jack grinned. "I'm sensing a 'but' coming down the trail."

"But," Matthew nudged his dad, "there are so damn many of them. I know that makes private practice a good business choice, but I always thought I'd work on a bigger scale. And twice now I've ended up on the wrong side of a false binary choice: drugs or therapy, nature or virtual reality. I'm not anti-tech. Hell, you don't make it out of MIT without absorbing the gospel of 'next-gen solutions.' But I keep seeing us miss the bigger picture."

"You're not anti-tech." Jack slung an arm over Matthew's shoulder. "You're a tech romantic. You want code to do what art and language barely can: map the tangled interactions of human grief, shame, joy, pride."

"Maybe I should learn quantum error correction coding—

might help with life too," laughed Matthew. Jack stopped and looked pointedly at Matthew.

"It's not so far-fetched."

"Scrap the couch and launch a startup called Quantum Feelings, Inc. The Food and Drug Administration might even fast-track it."

Michelle laughed but then turned serious.

"You know, your dad and I were idealists too.

"We used to say, 'think globally, act locally'. Still works—just swap leaflets for livestreams. That's why I'm glad the governor's relaunching a citizen advisory committee for the Harbor Islands. They're not just looking for donors. They want doers. Thinkers."

Matthew raised an eyebrow. "That so?"

"The governor told me herself." Michelle's activism and volunteer work had landed her spots on more than a couple of the governor's citizen advisory committees.

"They're trying to crowdsource ideas from real people. Interdisciplinary. Scientists, artists, social workers, volunteers. The park is losing a dozen federal funding partners. If the state budget is going to fill those gaps, they need community vision, not just policy wonks."

Jack chimed in, "Reminds me of your old MIT program. What was it—Terra ... something?"

Matthew stopped walking. "Terrascope. God, we were so fired up back then. Me, Maya, Darren. All of us. We thought wearable tech and civic apps could fix everything before we turned thirty."

"Don't knock innovation." Michelle nudged him back into motion.

"Your father and I heard Neil Howe on NPR. He's a historian, a demographer. He said your generation is pragmatic, collaborative, and tech-savvy—the right stuff to break our political stalemate and build more effective civic institutions.

"Get us back on track by 2032 so Dad and I can sit back and enjoy our golden years."

"We read his book," Jack added.

"It said your mom would undergo a transformation and willingly pass the generational torch. And look at her—she's practically glowing with institutional optimism." Jack caught her in a one-armed hug and kissed her temple.

"Seriously though, Amina Kassam has been saying the same thing. This isn't a crisis, it's a design challenge. You Millennials see complexity differently."

Matthew shook his head slowly. "It's not the tech I question —it's our ability to implement it in systems addicted to short-term fixes. Like Darren's Advance Market Commitment to push millions of doses of anxiety meds. Without therapy, those pills are just Band-Aids."

Michelle laid a hand on his shoulder. "Which is why we need you at the public hearing in Boston Common next week. They're gathering ideas to replace defunded federal programs —mental health, elder care, public education. The Harbor Islands Park has taken a big hit."

"Interesting. One of my clients has been testing a wrist wearable for an MIT professor. She says it makes her feel connected to nature instead of fearing it. She's even weaned herself off her anxiety meds. I wondered if it's Maya's project."

"Maya did stay at MIT. She's a professor on Amina Kassam's team," Michelle confirmed.

"Whoever is building those wearables, I'd be keen to meet them."

Matthew hesitated.

"Maybe I should look into that advisory committee for the Islands.

"If walking the trails on Spectacle Island could help one kid stabilize enough to rethink meds, maybe it could be scaled to support more kids."

Michelle smiled and pulled an envelope out of her pack. "I took the liberty of submitting your application for the governor's advisory committee. The deadline was the day you were driving across Utah."

"Of course you did." Matthew accepted the envelope with a roll of his eyes. "OK. I'll take a look at it. See if I can live up to your pitch."

FIVE

Later, jogging back to the T station, Matthew felt lighter. His parents' meddling came from love—and from faith.

On the train, earbuds in, Matthew tapped a podcast he'd bookmarked on Substack.

Unprescribed, Ep. 237
Saturday, May 16, 2026
"Pushing Pills with No Exit Ramp"

A beat of static, then a woman's voice, steady and unhurried.

Hello people. Hannah here with some news to share. Monday evening I'll be in the front row for a public discussion that has the potential to shift how Massachusetts—and maybe the nation—thinks about public space, mental health, and the legacy systems we're too scared to update. Spoiler: it's not just about park maintenance.

Matthew tilted his head slightly, the way he did when something unexpected sharpened into focus. Her delivery was even, precise. No theatrics. No wobble. This was someone used to being listened to.

It's about the unspoken contract we made when we started handing out pills instead of purpose. Treating symptoms instead of rethinking the systems that produce them. Traded walks in the woods for doom scrolling. When we stopped asking what Gen Z needs and started asking how to keep them "productive."

Matthew felt a frisson run up his spine and send little pops of hope and excitement through his brain, as if Hannah were picking up on his conversation with Michelle and Jack.

Before we unpack that thought, let me take you back a few years to the COVID pandemic. A new-fangled federal funding mechanism, the Advance Market Commitment—or AMC—successfully incentivized the development and distribution of several effective vaccines against a deadly virus. That made sense.

Post-pandemic, Congress threw an AMC at the production and distribution of a new, non-addictive anxiety medication—NeuroEase—to address another emerging public health crisis.

But anxiety is not a virus. It's not something you "catch" —it's tied to deeper stressors like economic uncertainty, social isolation, and climate fears. Medication can mute symptoms, but it won't help people understand and overcome their stress triggers.

Four years into distribution, some are claiming that getting daily doses of NeuroEase to millions of youth is a success story, while others are asking 'shouldn't those numbers be going down by now?'

Take a close look at the NeuroEase AMC and ask yourself—are we funding a pill pipeline with no exit ramp?

The seminal question is: should a neuroregulating drug —designed to stabilize anxiety symptoms—be given to youth for free with no therapy required? What are the social and ethical costs of frictionless care?

The National Park Service used to fund a non-pharmacological program, TrailMind, to mitigate anxiety. TrailMind uses augmented reality to help kids get into nature—a high-tech way to lower anxiety by reconnecting with the outdoors. It has real promise. But the federal money's gone now, clawed back—suddenly, and messily—with all the subtlety of a bear in a trash can.

Meanwhile, the pharmaceutical pipeline remains wide open in the current draft of the federal government's 2026 budget.

Full disclosure—several years ago, I had a work-study job on TrailMind as an undergraduate at MIT.

But the team behind TrailMind isn't backing down. They're stepping up. And the Massachusetts State House might just be listening.

In my next post, I'll take you inside the evolving fight to

reclaim nature as a first-line mental health tool—and what a federal Advance Market Commitment has to do with it.

And yes, I'll spill the tea on NeuroTech.

Stay tuned, citizens.

As Hannah's podcast wound down, Matthew realized he'd been holding his breath. He stared out the dark window and saw only his reflection.

As he ascended the escalator to Kendall Square, Matthew wondered what it would've taken to find the middle ground—to design a system where pharmacology and therapy didn't just coexist, but actually collaborated.

***

TWENTY-THREE FLOORS ABOVE, in his Kendall Square penthouse, Darren Katsaros was also thinking about how pharmacology and therapy might converge. His lobbyist, Audrey, had warned him to expect a summons to testify before the House Oversight Subcommittee.

"They're going to ask how your pill got priority while community mental health block grants and the National Park Service TrailMind grants are being defunded," she had informed him.

"Shouldn't they be asking Evie Chen that question?" Darren asked. "It's the CDC that pushed the AMC through."

"Evie left CDC. Took the severance package when the funding cuts started in 2025," Audrey told him. "The summons is coming from the office of the ranking Democrat on the Oversight subcommittee. This is what his staff told me, 'The AMC was designed to de-risk innovation, not fast-track social dependency. The public's patience for private-sector saviors is thinning. They want tools, yes. But they want tools that work with communities—not replace them.'"

For Darren, having the AMC in the federal budget meant a projected $1.8 billion for NeuroTech. He had to be ready to offer complementary, community-informed, non-pharma solutions, if pressed.

A Slack message flashed across his Peloton Tread monitor as he passed mile six.

Trending on Substack.
Hannah Oak's Unprescribed.
"I'll spill the tea on NeuroTech."

"Damn it." He punched the cool-down button six miles ahead of schedule. He'd never heard of Hannah Oak.

He pulled up Substack, found her feed, and opened the episode. The woman's voice was calm, measured. And then:

It's about the unspoken contract we made when we started handing out pills instead of purpose. Treating symptoms instead of rethinking the systems that produce them...

The words landed like a blow.

Was this Hannah Oak talking to congressional staff, Darren wondered. *Feeding the narrative?*

A FEW BLOCKS AWAY, Maya's laptop glowed in her otherwise dark apartment. Evening had crept up on her as she pored over a color-coded Gantt chart. At a glance she could see how soon the funding would end for each of the dozen Trail-Mind field pilots she was currently running.

As a young faculty member, Maya had secured a multi-year National Park Service grant. Her proposal had aligned perfectly with NPS's emerging strategic priority: mental health and wellness —not just for the public, but for overstretched park staff grappling with wildfire trauma, staffing shortages, and rising visitor tension.

TrailMind offered exactly what the NPS needed: low-friction tools that enhanced the restorative benefits of outdoor spaces without adding burdens on rangers.

Designed for reflection, nervous system regulation, and quiet recharging, TrailMind married leading-edge augmented reality tools and biofeedback with the lived wisdom of park rangers and indigenous interpreters.

Within the first two years of the MIT-NPS partnership, TrailMind's impact was measurable—reducing stress and fatigue, elevating mood, and boosting users' sense of awe, purpose, and connection.

Now a series of red bars stretched ominously across her Gantt chart. "The timelines are tight," she moaned.

"Oh, not Nia, too," she murmured as her cursor hovered over a cell, looking at her field-based co-designer's funding for the Boston Harbor Islands Park: *Pilot – Spectacle Island – Aug. 2* now flagged orange for risk.

She opened a tab titled *AltFunding_Prospects_v3.xlsx*. It displayed a table of over thirty rows.

Maya sorted by the submission deadlines. Some deadlines were in ten days. One in seventy-two hours.

Maya sighed. She understood the math. Since January 2025, the federal cuts had come fast and ruthless, gutting public research with no warning. But when the National Park

Service canceled her TrailMind grant, it felt personal—a break in the social contract she was raised to believe in.

Her parents had come to America on H-1B visas, two computer scientists who believed in a nation that invested in ideas for the public good. That faith had guided her work, but the world had changed. The old institutions were rudderless, sinking under the weight of deepening inequities.

Maya faced a hard new truth: she needed a new trail map for social innovation—one that showed how communities, not federal institutions, would hold the future together. Funding proposals for TrailMind would need to mirror the fractured optimism of states and cities—red, blue, and purple—each with its own idea of how to address the inequities the federal system could no longer balance.

For a moment, she slipped into old habits—imagining long nights drafting grant applications alone at her screen. That version of Maya—solitary, overextended, closed off—wasn't going to save this project.

She had learned to catch herself in the spiral. When her thinking narrowed and her shoulders curled in, she would pause, breathe, and tap into the loop she'd trained herself to run —*Remember the team.*

Not the product, not the specs. The room. The radiator. The team.

AS MAYA RECALLED, the radiator had hissed every few minutes in the basement lab in MIT Building 12. It had been early March 2009 and the sun was still setting before seven p.m.

The prototype that Maya's interdisciplinary Terrascope

team had built wasn't working. The climate modeling had kept crashing, and everyone was snapping at each other.

"Let's call it a night." Maya held up a hand. "I'll fix the backend, isolate the rendering error, and we can patch the rest tomorrow."

"We're not asking you to fix it alone." Matthew met her gaze before continuing. "Let's just make sure we all understand what the point of the tool is. Right now, it's just a map with some flashing data."

Maya bristled. "It's not just a map. It's a dynamic interface."

"It's a dynamic interface that tells us what?" he asked softly. "We keep adding features, because we have MIT's best systems architect on our team. But our design should be demand driven, not supply driven. Can you describe why a real person would use the tool?"

Maya crossed her arms, jaw tight. "The why is obvious," she muttered. "Climate data, ecosystem risks, visualized in real time."

Matthew shook his head. "That's what it does. Not why someone would use it in their community to advocate for policy based on what it shows. Until we know that, we're just churning data."

Maya hated how much that landed.

Darren sat cross-legged on the floor, having pushed Red Bull cans aside. "The American Psychological Association has a Task Force on the Interface Between Psychology and Global Climate Change. They published some recommendations for addressing climate grief. I can share the relevant findings. Bottom line—we could design an interface for teens that offers empowering toolkits for lobbying their local government for mitigation policies."

"Civil engineers will use it. When you're designing for the

1oo-year event, the data is right there." Kris Barsa's warm baritone voice inspired confidence.

"I can see parents and teachers using it to help kids who are scared," offered Alex Kim, a student from the Scheller Teacher Education Program. "So many students are afraid of the future, of climate change, of failing. What if this tool helps them not just learn—but feel capable again?"

And something shifted. Not just in the project—but in Maya's appreciation for the power of being part of a team moving together with purpose.

SEVENTEEN YEARS LATER, Maya had a new team now. Not age peers, but decidedly design peers.

Maya thought of Nia, already prototyping new features in the field. Of Aiden, who had a gift for explaining the tech to high schoolers and park rangers alike. And Xander, who always made sure the onboarding process worked for neurodivergent co-designers—looping in visual scripting tools, offering stim-friendly field kits to support repetitive, self-regulating behaviors, and refusing to treat accessibility like a box to be checked.

They weren't just competent interns. They were co-designers with energy, voice, and real stakes in the work—more fluent than she'd ever been in the language of embodiment and collective care, designing for neurodivergent accessibility.

They asked better questions than she had at their age. They laughed without irony. They flagged blind spots in the user experience—UX—but also in her thinking. They knew that nervous system regulation wasn't just neural—it was political, cultural, ecological.

Let them help draft proposals, she thought. *Let them take the mic at public hearings. Let them tell the story.*

She added a new column to the Excel sheet in which she tagged the relevant co-designer. She hesitated, then added two more cells: *Alexis K. – school pilot advisor* and *Kris B. – Ranger Assist peer support model.*

She sent a WhatsApp to Alexis and Kris. *Sharing the current known universe of TrailMind funding opportunities. I welcome your insights, ideas.*

Then she sent out a Slack message to the team.

@trailcore: 8:47 p.m.
New grant doc in the drive—column added to flag lead co-designer by use case. If you've got field data, lived experience, or an angle you want to own, claim it. This is your story too.

SIX

On Monday evening, Maya arrived early for the public meeting in Boston Common. The turnout was large, but it looked more like a concert at the Hatch Shell than a civic engagement. People sat on picnic blankets, eating cheese and crackers while waiting for the program to begin. Among the crowd were uniformed park rangers and parents still in office clothes, wrangling children.

She spotted Alexis Kim—Alex had transitioned after graduation—and Kris Barsa. They were sharing a plaid blanket, sitting cross-legged and laughing softly over steaming takeout containers.

"""

"Well, this is unexpected. A Scheller scholar and a Marine sharing ramen under the elms?"

Alexis grinned and waved her chopsticks in the direction of Back Bay. "We just bumped into each other at Totto." She lowered her voice in a conspiratorial tone, "I told Kris not to sleep on the spicy miso."

"She ain't wrong." Kris winked. "Also—I think I owe you one, Maya. A veteran buddy of mine linked up with Jackson out in Glacier, thanks to Nick's network. Says it's the first time he's felt useful in years."

Maya's expression softened. "That means something."

Alexis gestured at the surrounding crowd with her chopsticks. "And for me? This meeting matters because kids don't just need therapy—they need parks as part of the learning ecosystem. TrailMind gets that. It translates nature into nervous system literacy."

"And honestly? If we can train rangers and veterans to be co-regulators in that system, then we're not only rebuilding trails, we're rebuilding civic trust," Kris added.

Maya smiled. "Remind me to quote both of you next time I pitch this to a skeptical funder."

Nia came jogging up, slightly out of breath. "Hey, Dr. V— glad I made it in time!"

"Perfect timing, Nia. Meet my friends Kris and Alexis. MIT alums—and both keen to hear what you've been doing out on the islands."

She turned to the blanket.

"Nia, like Jackson, is a field-based co-designer for Trail-Mind, working out at the Boston Harbor Islands. She's also an incoming MIT freshman."

Alexis scooted over, patting the blanket. "Congratulations, Nia! Please, join us."

"Have some noodles," Kris offered, holding up a cardboard box and a paper-wrapped set of disposable chopsticks.

A chime sounded over the speaker system. Maya gave a tired but genuine smile. "I'd better get up there. Save me a dumpling?"

Maya found her seat in a section of folding chairs facing the stage, while the state and city officials shook hands, caught up with constituents, and everyone waited to get started.

Hannah came up from her picnic blanket to say hello. "So, it's very interesting that they have you on a panel tonight with Matthew Venable after we were talking about him."

"What? Matthew Venable? Dr. Kassam's assistant didn't tell me that when they asked me to come tonight. How did you find that out?"

"I have my sources."

Just then, Matthew himself walked up and took a seat several spots away from Maya.

"Well, there he is." Maya pointed. "Your sources were spot on ... as usual. Did you get in touch with him about your podcast? Do you want me to introduce you?"

"Sure. I haven't reached out to him yet, no time like the present."

Maya walked over. "Matthew?"

"Hello, Maya." Matthew offered his hand. "Great to see you."

"This is Hannah Oak. Producer and host of the Unprescribed blog, and keen to meet you."

"Hannah. Pleased to meet you. By coincidence or serendipity, I stumbled across your blog this weekend, and I'm a fan."

"I imagine AI had more to do with pushing the blog at you than fate," Hannah laughed. "Unprescribed's got your digital residue all over it. That's why I'd like to interview you for one of my future episodes."

"Me? Why?"

"You've drawn a line in the sand when it comes to prescribing pharmaceuticals for anxiety without accompanying them with therapy."

"That's true. But not a unique position."

Hannah nodded. "Fair. The story I'm really after, and the story I hope you're ready to tell, is how did you and Darren Katsaros part ways?"

"Huh." Matthew pressed his lips together. "You're going to have to give me some time to think about whether that is a story that I'm willing to tell. It is a story."

"I'm sure it is," Hannah held out her phone to tap Matthew's phone. "Here are my deets, and I'll wait to hear from you. I'll leave you to catch up with Maya." She turned to Maya. "Later, babe."

Matthew gestured to the seat next to him. "How have you been?"

"I have had my good times and my bad times, as one can imagine, given that it's been, what? Twelve years or more?"

"Yikes, that makes me feel old. Since the program is about to start, why don't you tell me what was the best good time and what was the worst bad time."

Maya smiled. "That's easy. TrailMind."

"TrailMind—was that the best or the worst?"

"Both." Her smile faded.

BOSTON'S MAYOR drew the crowd's attention as she stepped up to the podium.

"As Bostonians, we know that green spaces aren't just nice to have—they're essential. They're where kids play, where neighbors connect, and where we protect our city from the impacts of climate change.

"Through our Open Space and Recreation Plan, we're working to weave parks and natural areas into the very fabric of our neighborhoods, making sure every resident—no matter their background or ZIP code—has equitable access to nature. That means expanding our urban forests, investing in solutions like floodable parks and rain gardens, and continuing to transform spaces like the Boston Harborwalk into vibrant, welcoming places for everyone. It's about building a healthier, more resilient, and more inclusive city for generations to come."

She introduced the Governor of Massachusetts, acknowledging her leadership amid challenging times.

"Let's be clear—these federal funding cuts are devastating." The governor swept her gaze across the audience.

"Massachusetts is facing the potential loss of up to $16 billion, and that threatens not just numbers on a spreadsheet, but the essential services our families rely on—health care, education, infrastructure, and more. But even in the face of these challenges, we are not backing down. My administration remains firmly committed to investing in the places that define who we are—our public lands, our state parks, and our natural resources.

"Places like the Boston Harbor Islands aren't just beautiful —they're vital. They drive tourism, support public health, offer educational opportunities, and remind us of our responsibility to protect this planet. We are doubling down on efforts to keep these parks accessible, resilient, and thriving—for our kids, for our communities, and for the future of our planet."

The MC thanked the governor and then ran through the agenda for the program and explained the logistics of where attendees could access microphones to participate in the discussion.

An usher came to escort Maya and Matthew to the stage as the commissioner of the Department of Conservation and Recreation spoke about losing federal funding for the Boston Harbor Islands National Park.

Then, Maya was surprised to hear her boss, Amina Kassam, introduced. *I'm going to have a word with that assistant,* Maya thought.

At the podium, Dr. Kassam spoke with the calm authority of a respected environmental sociologist and MIT faculty member.

"We're here today not just to debate jurisdiction, or budgets, or app permissions. We're here because parks are about people. And people need healing spaces—especially in times like these."

Kassam's framing carried the gravitas of someone famously known for having worked on reforestation with the Nobel Peace Prize laureate Wangari Maathai during the early days of the grassroots Green Belt Movement in their native Kenya.

She gestured toward the two panelists seated on either side of her: Maya looking poised, professional, but visibly tired; and Matthew looking like a textbook Bostonian in L.L. Bean.

"I'm proud to introduce two MIT alumni, Dr. Maya Venkataraman and Dr. Matthew Venable. You've both asked what these islands can mean for young people facing an anxious future. But your approaches diverge. So I'd like to begin there. Maya, would you start?"

"My work centers on designing tech tools that reconnect young people with nature through the digital language they already speak. These kids aren't addicted to tech. They were born into it. We have a responsibility to meet them there with tools that can gently guide them out." She glanced at Matthew, who avoided eye contact.

Kassam asked, "And Matthew?"

"I agree with the diagnosis. But I've seen too many students relying on digital tools that mediate experience," he said.

"That reinforces the very neural loops we're trying to break. TrailMind has promise—don't get me wrong—but are we just polishing the glass between them and the real world? Or are we teaching them to put it down?"

Matthew paused before turning to Maya. "I know we want the same thing. I just don't think the answer can be more digital interface, no matter how well-designed."

"So we should demand they cold-turkey their way into transcendence?" Maya raised a brow.

Dr. Kassam interjected, "Sounds like both of you are craving the same thing: presence. But one of you wants to light a digital lantern along the way. The other wants to blow out the screens entirely."

A soft laugh rippled through the audience. "So let me ask this: what did the islands teach you when you were out there? Not the app users. You."

Maya's lips parted, then closed again. She looked back at the projection of Spectacle Island. Her voice softened. "I went out there to test a tool. But as I sat on a rock and watched a crab disappear under a tide pool ledge, I forgot to look at my device. For ten minutes. Maybe longer. I felt like ... that's what stillness tastes like."

"Yeah. Mine was on Peddocks Island," Matthew grimaced. "After a bitter argument, I hiked a trail that dead-ends at this scrubby overlook. No signal. No plan. I was angry. I just sat. The island let me be. Like a parent who doesn't try to solve everything."

Dr. Kassam leaned in. "And now we're getting somewhere." She folded her hands, looking from one to the other. "I think our task—yours, mine, all of ours—is to stop arguing about whether the bridge is made of code or moss or memory. The question is: does it help them cross over?"

Maya exhaled. Matthew nodded, slowly.

"We all agree that we need human hands guiding artificial intelligence. I'm asking you both, Maya and Matthew, to lead this quest. Let's not pit wonder against wisdom. We can have—we need to have—both."

AS THE LIVE audience on Boston Common applauded Amina Kassam's proactive framework, Darren Katsaros' eyes flicked across the four television monitors mounted above his desk. The Boston stations, WBZ, WCVB, WHDH, each had slightly different shots of Matthew Venable, Maya Venkataraman, and Amina Kassam. "Live from Boston Common" read the banner at the bottom of the WBZ screen.

Darren had learned, long ago, that emotions couldn't be debugged. Not really. Back in Terrascope, Matthew and Maya had treated him like a sellout for wanting scale and speed. They didn't see that he was just trying to keep the system from crashing. Watching them now on WBZ, Darren couldn't help but wonder—had they changed? Or was he still the only one willing to name the cost of doing nothing?

Darren glanced out the window of his Kendall Square penthouse. The Common was discernible in the distance, a dark patch in a grid of engineered light. He'd sent an intern to report back to him on the meeting, equipped with a GPT app that would spit out a sharper, shorter report in two minutes than the kid could write even if he pulled an all-nighter.

On the WBZ screen, Darren spotted Dr. Thura Aung, health policy advisor to the senior U.S. Senator from Massachusetts, standing at the back of the stage. Respectfully known as Ko Thura, Aung was a principled health expert exiled by dictatorship, now quietly shaping U.S. health policy from a tiny back office on Capitol Hill.

Darren wondered if he should have put in an appearance himself. The Senator's recent op-ed—undoubtedly shaped by Aung—framed youth mental health as "a national debt we cannot afford to leave unpaid." It emphasized that Massachusetts should lead the way by piloting non-pharmaceutical alternatives before leaning heavily on federal Rx.

He made a note to reach out to Ko Thura.

SEVEN

The next morning, Maya came to in a fog.

Damn Matthew Venable.

She winced remembering how he'd avoided her eyes as she talked about tech tools.

When they'd worked together on the Terrascope project as undergraduates, they were so easy together. They would linger after the group broke up, trying eccentric ice cream flavors at Toscanini's or sharing scallion pancakes at the now-defunct Steam Café. Collaboratively, enthusiastically, they refined project milestones by aligning tech inputs to user outcomes.

But last night he'd sounded skeptical about using tech to mitigate the void affecting so many young people now, the void of not having grown up in nature. Ubiquitous devices were part of the problem, but Maya was sure the absence of nature in their overprotected, coddled lives was equally, if not more, responsible for climate grief and chronic anxiety.

Maya thought back to her childhood. She spent her school year in a vortex of tech, probably more than most in her peer group. Her parents, both computer scientists, had her coding in

Python before she turned ten. But for two weeks each summer, they'd all unplug and head to Yosemite to visit Leo, her father's best friend and her honorary uncle.

"Uncle Leo, do you ever get lonely out here?" nine-year-old Maya had asked on one trip as she built a morning campfire with ease.

"Not really, kiddo. Out here, I'm never alone. You hear that?" Leo had gestured toward the forest. "The trees are talking. You just have to slow down enough to hear what they're saying."

Maya listened. "It's just wind." She shrugged as she mixed cocoa, sugar, and milk in the familiar dented camp pot.

"Maybe. But the Ahwahneechee would tell you it's more than that. That breeze winding through the pines? That's the breath of Tutokanula—the Great Spirit Chief. They say he carved these cliffs so his people would always have shelter."

Maya looked up at El Capitan. "Really?"

"Really. And when you walk this valley, you're walking through his memory. Every stone, every whisper of water—it's part of the story. You don't need a screen to understand the world, Maya. Just your senses. Your attention. Your presence."

Maya's father joined them, accepting a cup of cocoa from Maya.

"That's Leo for you—still the same poetic soul who once turned our dorm room into a Zen garden with nothing but a rake and a carpet remnant."

Leo laughed. "And you called it a fire hazard."

"I like Yosemite better than coding camp." Maya looked from her father to Leo.

"That's because out here, you're using a different part of your brain." Leo tapped her temple gently. "The part that listens more than it calculates. You're not just a visitor in nature, Maya—you are part of the warp and woof of a natural world that will give us everything we need, if we let it."

"So you're saying Tutokanula remembers me?"

"Only if you remember him."

STILL RAW FROM last night's confrontation, Maya headed to MIT.nano to test the new neural interface she'd designed to simulate the sensory immersion of being outdoors.

The building gleamed like a spaceship, buzzing with grad students and machines. She bypassed the bustle and slipped into the sensory pod, a translucent cocoon meant to erase the outside world so the device could measure her baseline.

She clipped the band around her temples, settled back, and tried to still her mind. Within minutes, her chest tightened. Her pulse spiked. The silence was suffocating. This was supposed to be neutral ground—but her body was rebelling. She yanked the headset off and stumbled out, palms damp.

Baselines, she thought bitterly, *were for people without fault lines.* Institutions wanted clean data, clean outcomes. What she had were panic attacks and workarounds.

By the time she reached the Stata Center, she was already dialing her Uncle Leo, who had remained her most trusted source of advice throughout college and beyond.

His face appeared against the soft glow of a California morning, redwoods swaying behind him.

"Hey, hija. Still rewriting the future from that sci-fi building of yours?"

"Only when I'm not chasing federal grants. Or explaining to freshmen why grades aren't life itself."

Leo chuckled, then tipped his ranger hat back. "What's going on?"

She hesitated, then spilled it. "TrailMind's biggest grant got clawed back—National Park Service budget cuts. I keep rewriting proposals, chasing new requirements. It's like trying to code while the operating system keeps rebooting."

The smile eased from his face. "In the field we say: if you're aiming for ecosystem change, turbulence isn't a bug—it's the habitat."

"Give me some good news, Leo."

"I don't know. That's a tough one."

Leo sucked in air through his teeth. "The California Parks' budgets are thin. We can't conjure more staff, but we can give the rangers we do have new senses—early-warning systems, community stewards, tools that help them read the land in real time. Not a moonshot. A ground game. Community-first."

Maya nodded slowly. Processed what he was saying. *Federal foundation collapsing. Local ground holding.*

The words hit harder than comfort—they felt diagnostic.

"I read about the Boston Common meeting." Leo studied her for a moment. "How did it feel seeing Matthew again? After all this time?"

Maya exhaled. "Disorienting. During our panel discussion he said anxious teens don't need apps in forests, they need therapy. It stung. But it was also ... familiar. At MIT he was always chasing perfection. Never comfortable with anything incremental."

Leo's brow softened into a thoughtful crease. "Matthew chased purity: the immaculate model."

Maya echoed, "While Darren was all velocity: scale, funding, momentum at any cost."

Leo nodded. "But they both end up fragile. You can't touch the real world if you never let your feet meet the ground."

Maya let the quiet hold them. "And me? I'm the one scrambling in the middle—trying to prop things up while the system is rotting."

"Not rotting—transforming."

Leo shook his head, that ranger-philosopher calm settling around his words.

"If you're looking for something more than a friendly ear, I'd tell you: be the one who can feel where the old wood is turning back into soil. Notice the first hints of renewal, like a forest after a burn."

"That..makes sense." Maya soaked it in. "I'm pretty sure my Gen Z co-designers are already planting in its place."

"There you go." Leo smiled. "You're learning to build with the community. And it grows because younger hands and older hands are making it together."

Maya felt her shoulders ease. Leo had reframed it: not a triangle of rivals, but three different models of response.

Darren—scale. Matthew—perfection. Maya—bridge.

All three reaching for the same thing—to calm a raging sea of anxiety.

AFTER DISCONNECTING FROM LEO, Maya ran a GPT query through the lens he'd just pressed into her. Within minutes, the AI had synthesized dozens of field reports from TrailMind's young co-designers across the Harbor Islands, the Rockies, and the Sonoran Desert.

She carried the printout to the Chancellor's Garden, settling near a clump of Columbine whose red-and-yellow bells reminded her of Yosemite summers.

To her surprise, the analysis wasn't about design metrics. It revealed a framework—language the next generation had given her.

Nia's line leapt off the page: "One student said it felt like their first 'green light' day."

These weren't products of her control, but proof of what emerged when she stepped back.

Her phone buzzed.

Hannah: Dinner and a debrief?
Maya: Yes. Kismet? My treat.

She glanced again at the Columbine, let the calm settle, and whispered aloud, "Yes."

THAT AFTERNOON, Matthew's phone also chimed with an incoming message. It was from his parents.

Michelle: Dinner and a debrief?
Jack: Your mother can grill you, and I'll grill the halibut. :)
Matthew: Can't wait ;)

He took advantage of the May sunshine and walked toward his parents' house, aware of the lift in his mood these past three days. Ever since Ava had come into his office—bright-eyed, rested, telling him about her day with Nia on Spectacle Island —something in him had been lighter.

And now, wondering if Nia might be collaborating with Maya added an unexpected thread of hope he wasn't quite ready to tug on.

It stirred memories of his time walking trails on Spectacle Island wearing Maya's early haptic devices. He recalled the late nights they had spent dissecting and debating their findings. It had been a rare instance when he felt a romantic connection to a peer.

Matthew knew that desire came slowly for him, rooted first in trust. Years earlier, he'd underlined Stephen Mitchell on how libido takes shape through safety, recognition, and mutuality—well before *demisexual* had found its way into the literature.

Seeing Maya again reminded him that she had once slipped past his emotional defenses—not through charm or proximity, but through purpose. They had shared momentum, intellectual chemistry, a kind of mutual reverence for the work.

Seeing her now, grounded and still building, stirred something both old and unresolved.

Not desire, exactly. Possibility.

A quiet recognition that someone else saw the world's fractures the same way he did—and wanted to repair them.

EIGHT

When Matthew arrived at his parents' house, his mother gave him a hug and his father handed him a beer.

"A hug and a beer—life is good," Matthew laughed.

"Come perch by the grill while your dad cooks."

"Gladly." Matthew rested a hand on her shoulder as he followed her through the garden. "And hey, thanks for encouraging me to join the Boston Harbor Islands Park Advisory Committee."

"Honestly, I think you're perfect for it."

"Well, I appreciate the vote of confidence. It feels meaningful to be part of something that might actually change things."

"Good. As you heard last night, this is a big priority—not just for city leaders, but beyond. The Harbor Islands have become a symbol, a test case. Proof we can shift away from the status quo without losing what matters."

"Hear, hear," Jack called from behind the grill.

"I heard that urgency loud and clear—from Dr. Kassam, the mayor, the governor. But what landed for me was this deeper challenge: how do we build something that helps the next generation handle anxiety in a way we haven't figured out yet?"

"Exactly." Michelle pointed at him. "That's where you come in. Let other folks handle the budget. Let someone else worry about maintenance contracts or negotiating with the federal union reps. Your focus should be on what these spaces can do for the future—emotionally, socially. Our parks have saved us more than once."

"Truth."

"Now—tell me more about this program that Maya designed. Or do I call her doctor now?"

"Dr. Venkataraman. We were on the same Terrascope team as undergrads and continued to collaborate as research assistants. So, it's OK to call her Maya."

"Right. So what's she working on? I'm curious about where she's taken the project. And hey—if it's private, feel free to shut me down."

"No, it's not private. Actually, it's something I've been thinking about a lot. One of my clients was describing how much calmer she's felt after spending time on Spectacle Island —working with a researcher who I think is probably on Maya's team."

"That's exactly what this is about, right? Reconnecting young people with nature in ways that actually make a difference."

"Yes. She's going to try to get me invited out there next time she goes.

"If it's as promising as it sounds, I'll definitely want to report back to the committee. We meet on Thursday."

"Tight turnaround. But probably worth it."

"Yeah. It kind of is." Matthew smiled.

"I'm done grilling, Michelle. Are you?" Jack quipped, gesturing with a spatula like a mic drop.

"Yup. Let's eat." Michelle carried the fish to the table.

The scent of the halibut mingling with her hydrangeas made Matthew think back to another fish dinner in the garden.

It had been June 2016 and Michelle's hydrangeas had been in bloom. Matthew had been home for a visit from his graduate program at Stanford. Jack had grilled fish for Darren and his parents, in town for Darren's graduation from the Sloan School of Management.

Michelle topped up Lena's wine. "Congratulations, Lena and Nick. You raised quite a force."

Nick shook his head with a smile. "I still don't understand what our boys are working on exactly. But I know it matters."

Lena smiled shyly. "Darren talks about systems like they're living things."

Michelle raised her glass in a toast. "To our fine young men. We're proud of both of you. Different paths, but the same fire."

Darren accepted the toast with a sip of wine, then looked at his watch. "Please excuse me. Sloan graduation party. Everyone pretending we're not already pitching each other startups."

"Don't let them talk you into anything too permanent," Jack counseled. "You've got momentum. Use it."

Darren grinned as he stood up. "That's my exit cue."

Lena accepted Darren's kiss on the cheek as he left. Matthew saw him out.

When he came back, he found his parents sitting in the garden. Nick and Lena had gone to bed.

Matthew sat with his parents. "We're close, I think. The data's coming together. The UX build is solid. Darren's got the investor side humming. He's ... good at it."

Michelle sighed. "The data and the UX may have to catch up to the hype. Darren's ambition is still a step ahead of his self-awareness."

Jack tapped a finger on the table. "Problem is those funders just want a piece of the next ten-bagger."

"That's why I'm there," Matthew put a hand over his heart. "To shape the ethics. The design layer. I think he wants that balance."

"But it's his nature to avoid messiness, to take the cleanest route." Michelle slid the pepper mill across the table like a chess piece. "But you can't solve problems without immersing yourself in the messiness."

"He says I want meaning more than motion ..." Matthew admitted.

Jack chuckled. "Sounds like a euphemism for saying you're a drag."

Matthew looked away. "I'm just trying to hold the center."

Matthew's phone chimed, bringing him back to the present.

"Give me one second," Matthew held up a finger.

A minute later he joined them at the table. "Good news—my client just invited me to join her tomorrow at Spectacle Island."

He looked up beaming. "Guess I'm getting a firsthand look after all."

AT THE SAME time that Matthew was eating halibut with his parents, Maya was snagging a window table at Kismet, a new Turkish restaurant she'd been meaning to try.

Hannah blew in just moments after Maya. "Hey, glad you picked this place. It's been on my list."

"Well, your message popped up. I was about to ask you to dinner, so—kismet," Maya grinned.

Hannah laughed, then waved over the waitress. "Bring us your favorite meze to share, and a bottle of Çankaya, please."

She turned to Maya. "Okay, so last night was intense. I want to run my take by you before I post anything, but I felt this undercurrent—that protecting public spaces like the Harbor Islands could be part of how we respond to the anxiety epidemic. Especially for Gen Z."

"Totally. That theme came through loud and clear. I reached out to Uncle Leo this morning. We had one of those mind-expanding convos, as usual."

Hannah laughed. "Did he tell you to look at the whole project through a different lens?"

"He did. Basically, I need to let go of the tech. There are plenty of engineers who can manage the backend. But what matters is how we position this for public health—not just cool features that get people back in the parks."

"I'm not trying to pressure you, but I do think you could be creating one of the only scalable alternatives to drug therapy right now."

"Too late—Leo already dropped that weight on me. So bring it. Pile on, guilt-free." Maya laughed.

"Okay, so ... I want to write about the possibilities we saw in the forum, but I want to ground-truth it with you. What's scalable? Dr. Kassam pressed you a little on the numbers, but that was public. Now you're off-mic."

"Right. So this morning, after I talked to Leo, I ran an analysis on the field reports from my team. Pulled the emotional data—how people were actually responding."

Maya paused, thinking it through. "And now I think we're sitting on something real. I haven't modeled the full cost yet, but my graduate assistant, Sam, can run the budget scenarios in her sleep. What I need to focus on is how to measure which applications actually help people regulate and reconnect."

"That's huge. Okay, can I tease that in the blog, or are you keeping it under wraps for now?" Hannah scribbled notes.

"You can hint. Two applications—"

The waitress arrived with the wine. Maya nodded for her to fill their glasses and after appreciating the first sip, continued:

"Two applications. One is right here—our team's been making great progress with the multi-sensory Indigenous Sounds app. It's getting attention for how it engages both auditory and tactile channels," Maya explained.

"Oooh. Do you think anyone on your field team would be up for a video blog?"

"That would be great. Nia, the lead field-based co-designer, is prepping for a conference this summer. Participating in the video blog will help her shape the narrative."

"And the second one?" Hannah pushed.

"From the West Coast. They're working with neurodiverse users as co-designers to shape the app around sensory and communication diversity. It's careful work—but it could be transformative."

Maya tilted her head. "What would this vlog look like— field footage, interviews?"

"Hair, makeup?" Hannah asked, already grinning.

Maya shook her head but laughed. "Guess I'd better pack my lip balm."

A THIRD DEBRIEF from the Boston Common forum took place in Washington.

Darren had jumped on the five p.m. shuttle to D.C. Dr. Thura Aung, health policy advisor to the senior Senator from Massachusetts, had agreed to meet him.

They sat at a small table near the window at Teaism in Penn Quarter—quiet enough to speak in low voices, public enough that half of official Washington could confirm they shared a tray of modest dishes: miso soup, naan sandwiches, and herbal tea.

"What did you think of the meeting on the Common last night?" Darren asked. "Big turnout. Press was good. The Senator even smiled."

Aung chuckled. "Massachusetts has savvy, progressive leaders. But some things still have to be driven at the federal level. Not every state is going to be as proactive. And we don't want to widen the gap between states offering solutions—and those offering dogma."

Darren exhaled. "I'm feeling the pinch. I got into this work to end suffering, but venture capitalists aren't mission-driven. We can't pretend pharma's going to work for free."

Aung nodded. "Yes. But we also have to ask whether pharma is a solution when it's being managed by a school nurse with a locked cabinet and no training or a community health worker walking door to door with expired gloves."

Darren looked at him, brow furrowed. "You think pushing distribution down that far was premature?"

Aung shrugged. "I think it was necessary. When you've seen a village wait two weeks for a mobile clinic that might not come—when you've watched a mother try to resuscitate her child with boiled water and prayers—you stop waiting for 'perfect'. You train whoever's willing to help. You adapt."

Darren nodded slowly. Then, after a beat, he said, "And yet ... we do have a responsibility to make the model sustainable. If the Oversight Committee tanks the AMC on optics alone, we lose the license to keep scaling—and the funding bridge to next-gen integrations. We're starting to see real progress on tech-enabled somatic and behavioral supports that can work alongside pharmacological treatment, maybe even lower long-term reliance on it."

Aung replied. "That's what I hope this hearing addresses—not just dollars and amortization curves, but the public health objective."

Darren gave a half-smile. "That's why I wanted your insight before I prep my testimony. Between elected officials' populist jabs and the pharma lobby's gold-plated charts, we need one damn person in that room who's actually touched a suffering child."

Aung set his tea down and looked at Darren. "Then write it like someone who still wants to end suffering. Not just balance the books."

BACK HOME AFTER her dinner with Hannah, Maya sat cross-legged on her sofa, laptop balanced on her knees. The printout of the field report analysis rested beside her like a map.

She pasted a note into the #TrailCore Slack channel—carefully setting it to Schedule Send so it would land in her team's feeds at 9:00 a.m. sharp. No midnight cortisol jolts on her watch.

@trailcore
Reading your field notes today was like watching a framework assemble itself. You named what TrailMind really is—therapeutic anchors, self-efficacy spikes, inclusive prompts, collective impact. This is not my invention. It's yours. I want us to honor that by building leadership pathways that reflect it. If you're willing, I'd like to see Nia step up as lead on therapeutic anchors, Aiden on self-efficacy spikes, Xander on inclusive

prompts, and Rajiv on collective impact. Think of this as moving from field notes to field leadership. The framework is yours; the next phase should be, too.

She hit send before she could second-guess herself.

Unprescribed Ep. 238, Tuesday, May 19, 2026, "Digital Healing or Distraction?"

HANNAH: Last night's public hearing at the Boston Common bandstand wasn't your typical dry policy affair. It felt more like a generational referendum—on therapy, on technology, and on who gets to define "connection" in an age of spiraling anxiety.

The mayor and the governor made it clear that state and local governments aren't just funding parks to boost tourism or tick boxes on environmental reports. They're investing with intent—expecting returns that show up in public health data, carbon drawdown metrics, and yes, even on the teen anxiety balance sheets.

Parks, they argued, must pull double or triple duty as spaces for healing, resilience, and climate adaptation.

It's a big ask, but there is already an immersive augmented reality platform being piloted on the Boston Harbor Islands. Think public parks meet open-source healing. The woman behind it—MIT's Dr. Maya Venkataraman—spoke with a kind of quiet conviction

that made even the skeptics sit up straighter. But not
everyone was sold.

Psychologist Matthew Venable, who specializes in Gen
Z anxiety, pushed back. His critique? That even well-
intentioned tech might reinforce the overstimulation it
aims to counteract.

"This generation doesn't need more pings and
prompts," he said. "They need a path back to their
bodies. To stillness."

It wasn't a fight, but it wasn't comfortable either. And
that's what made it matter.

What's Next: I'll be heading out to Spectacle Island
later this week to experience the TrailMind modules
for myself—no filters, no PR handlers. Just me, the field
kits, and the teenagers who helped co-design them.

Are these tools truly rewilding our nervous systems—or
just dressing up dopamine loops in national park
packaging?

Stay tuned for the vlog. As always, I'll show you what
I see.

NINE

At South Station Ava led Matthew to where Nia and her field team gathered. Matthew didn't see Maya at first. Didn't see her freeze before slapping on a smile as she stepped over to him.

"Hello, Matthew."

"Hello, Maya. Hello again, Hannah."

"Hey, I know you!" Nia grinned. "You were at the Boston Common thing, right?"

"Yes, I was."

Maya made a formal introduction. "Matthew Venable, meet Nia Elk. Nick Donnelly sent her to us from Montana," referring to their fellow MIT alum and Terrascope colleague, now working as a rural doctor.

"That's cool you made it out here," Nia enthused. "I've been wanting folks to actually see what we're building on Spectacle."

"Me too. Lead the way."

Maya whispered in Matthew's ear, "Nia has a hyper-sensitivity to sound Nick thought could be a design strength, not a liability."

Just then the ferry let out the required long blast of its horn to announce its departure. Nia flinched so hard she nearly dropped her data tablet.

Maya could only imagine how the blast reverberated through Nia's chest like a sonic punch. She saw Matthew reach out a steadying hand. Ava accepted his hand, grounding herself with long, slow breaths.

After a long exhale, Nia told Matthew, "Dr. Donnelly says it's hypervigilance. But my Blackfeet grandfather says it's not anxiety. It's memory. 'We listen to the land, but we also listen to threat.'"

Matthew nodded. "Your body's been trained to survive environments that don't give warning shots."

Nia smiled and let go of his hand.

Maya's smile softened as she heard Matthew lighten the mood, teasing Nia: "Be careful or you'll find the Pentagon wants to stick 'tactical asset' on your forehead."

Nia cracked a grin. "Too late. I already got pulled into secondary at the airport for making an app that listens better than most adults."

As they walked to catch the ferry to Spectacle Island, Maya felt the dissonance she'd been feeling about Matthew melt away.

That, she thought, *is the Matthew I remember.*

ONCE THEY WERE UNDERWAY, Hannah gently herded Matthew away from the group.

"So, what's your take on this rumor about a congressional hearing? Do you expect Congress will greenlight another multi-billion-dollar Advance Market Commitment for Darren's NeuroTech pill?"

"A little of both. The pill works. That's not the problem. The problem is acting like a pill is the solution." Matthew shrugged.

"HHS is framing it as a moonshot for mental health."

Matthew sighed. "And the irony? If the government continues to guarantee it will buy the pills through the AMC, more schools will start recommending it. Insurance will cover it. And suddenly, not taking it will look like you're choosing to fail."

Hannah looked up from her notebook. "Wait—say that again?"

"Think about it. Not taking the pill will start to look like negligence. Resistance. Non-compliance. That's the dystopia we're creeping toward—medicated conformity marketed as mental wellness."

Hannah nodded slowly, gazing out at the waves. "So what are we heading to Spectacle Island for, then? The resistance?"

Matthew smiled. "Let's go find out."

On the other side of the bow, Maya stood elbow-to-elbow with Nia to talk over the thrum of the ferry's motor as it sliced through the waves.

"Your field reports are awesome, Nia." Maya beamed.

"I loved your analysis of the story maps. I'm excited to see your research in action—what's the setup for today?"

"Thanks, Dr. V! We've got two micro-groups running in parallel this morning—TrailMind's Somatic Sync and the EarthBeat loop. Five participants in each. They're all teens from the Charlestown Youth Collaborative. Ages fifteen to seventeen. No neurodivergent diagnoses, but definitely anxiety-prone, based on intake."

"And the haptics?"

"Right. Group A—Somatic Sync—they'll be wearing the modified commercial sensor bands. Vibration pulses are synced to their breathing once they reach a steady cadence. The idea is to help them entrain with natural sounds and settle their nervous system. They'll follow the forest loop trail and stop at three biofeedback waypoints."

"And who's observing?"

"Sasha and Jay will be shadowing them—low interference, mostly observational. Jay's also audio-recording short reflections at each stop. Sasha will take manual notes on posture, engagement, and verbal cues. We've got consent for all that."

"Excellent. And EarthBeat?"

"EarthBeat's our control-ish group. They'll stop at the same waypoints. No haptics. Just short mindfulness cues through guided attention, one-minute barefoot grounding sessions and sensory journaling.

"Mira and Kareem are taking notes and offering the participants the opportunity to collect the soil swabs for the microbiome pilot."

Nia grinned at Maya. "And your noodle friend has a group of veterans on the Ironwood spur. It's set up as a sensory focus extension, shielded from the beach winds, and just a short dangle from the Coastal path."

Maya raised an eyebrow. "My noodle friend? Are you talking about Kris, the decorated veteran of two tours in Afghanistan?"

"Yeah. The soldier with the soft center. Fed me noodles on the Common. Developed this proprioceptive reconnection protocol for vets with phantom limb pain. It's good stuff. And he paid their ferry fare himself. Quiet about it, too."

"Good catch." Maya's voice tightened. "We budgeted for transport during the NPS phase, but once the grant got clawed back ... I've been kicking the access can down the trail. But it's real. A ferry in Boston, a bus in Montana—barriers still block the path to public spaces."

"I know, I grew up right next to Glacier National Park. But if I wanted to walk in the park, I had to pay twenty bucks like a tourist. My grandfather said it was like buying a ticket to your own memory. If Dr. Donnelly hadn't paid my entrance fee into Glacier, I would never have seen a vole."

"Or developed a kick-ass app to introduce the pine vole to your peers." Maya beamed with pride.

"I pre-loaded the ranger logs and last month's field patterns into the GPT query set." Nia looked down, shyly, at her tablet. "Should generate preliminary clusters on affective response—calm, tension, curiosity, etc.—by the time we ferry back."

"You're a machine!" Maya punched a fist in the air.

Nia held up her phone. "Speaking of machine. How exactly did you send me this Slack message at nine on the dot? It's giving robot energy. Do you have, like, a scheduling bot writing your pep talks?"

Maya arched an eyebrow, deadpan. "No bot. Just a manager who believes in not spiking cortisol with midnight pings."

Nia grinned. "That's ... actually kind of TrailMind of you."

Maya laughed. "High praise! OK—Let's give them something real to feel today. No filters. No scroll. Just sky and earth and data."

"On it!" Nia winked.

***

AS THEY DISEMBARKED from the ferry, Nia asked, "Does everyone want to stay together or should we break into two groups so everyone has a little more time to interact with the various apps?"

"Two groups. Smart thinking." Matthew looked at Maya, who nodded her concurrence.

Matthew went with Ava, who introduced Elena Ortiz, a graduate student in neurobiology, and Ravi Singh, a CSAIL student working in augmented reality.

Maya and Hannah went with Nia and another research assistant, Sarah Lin, who focused on environmental psychology.

Along the Coastal Loop, Nia stopped in front of a weathered cedar post with a solar-powered display panel marked "Pine Vole Listening Station." A small bronze plaque beneath the digital interface read, "Field Audio: Pine Vole (*Microtus pinetorum*). Reintroduced 2026. Touch to listen. Developed with TrailMind AR."

"This is the animal I was telling you about, Dr. Venable." Ava held out a set of earbuds to Matthew. "Do you want to listen?"

"No, you listen. I just want to get a sense of how it works."

Matthew stepped back as Ava strapped on the trendy smart watch that Elena handed to her. She stood in the designated spot, put her earbuds in, and began to listen intently.

Matthew looked over Ravi's shoulder as he opened an app on his tablet, monitoring Ava's heart rate variability, galvanic skin response, and neural activity patterns.

Ravi glanced at Matthew. "Don't worry. We re-consent every session. Data's anonymized, encrypted. No IDs."

Matthew nodded in appreciation for the rigor of the exercise, then turned back to Ava, buoyed by the expression of delight on her face as she listened to the vole.

ON THE SUMMIT TRAIL, Nia stopped in front of a carved granite bench nestled beside a windswept pitch pine. A small touchscreen was embedded in the bench backrest. The display glowed faintly, labeled, "Echoes of the First Light: Indigenous Sound Recordings." Nearby, a sign read, "These soundscapes were gathered in partnership with the Aquinnah Wampanoag and the Mashpee Wampanoag Tribes, honoring the voices and songs shared with permission."

"These recordings include ceremonial chants, oral histories, and ambient nature sounds curated by the elders," Nia explained as Hannah captured video on her phone. "The haptic vests allow users to not only hear but feel the sonic patterns—especially the low-frequency rhythms. It's part of our effort to create a multi-sensory connection to ancestral wisdom, with full consent and collaboration throughout the development process."

Nia helped Hannah strap on a lightweight vest with embedded actuators and sensors, while Maya put her own vest on.

Hannah handed her camera to Nia to get video of the vest in action.

On Nia's signal, Hannah pushed the activation button. A soft heartbeat-like pulse traveled across her chest, synchronized with a recording of a water drum rhythm. Then came the layered sound of waves crashing, wind through tall grasses, and a voice singing in Wôpanâak—low and resonant, almost like a lullaby.

Hannah's eyes closed briefly as the vibrations shifted gently up her spine and across her shoulders. Hannah and Maya each listened to three different indigenous sound recordings, then sat down on a nearby log with Nia to record the vlog.

"The water chant." Hannah closed her eyes then looked at Nia, just off camera. "I don't know how to explain it—it made me feel rooted and kind of ... mournful. But in a good way? Like a longing that belongs to everyone."

"I noticed your skin conductivity spiked right around that

time," Nia observed. "Suggests an emotional peak. Did that correlate with the haptic pattern?"

"Definitely," Hannah nodded. "It was like being inside the rhythm."

Nia turned the camera to Maya. "Technically the fidelity of the signal was very high. I think the real achievement here is the latency—we're getting under 10 milliseconds between audio and haptic sync. That's incredible in a field setting."

Hannah gave Nia the 'cut' motion with an audible 'ugh'. "High fidelity and latency? Really? That's how you're selling TrailMind to the masses?"

Nia snickered. Then she pulled up the data visualizations of Hannah and Maya's readouts, side-by-side.

Nia looked at Maya with wide eyes. "Uhm, Dr. V? You're like ... flatlining. That chant hit Hannah like ancestral déjà vu, and you're out here vibing at zero?"

TEN

If you find yourself arguing with someone whom you respect and love, try to surrender your own ego to the shared identity you have with that person. In the heat of an argument, do the opposite of what your pride tells you to do. If you have the self-control, stop talking and give your opponent a random, intense, minute-long hug.

—Sal Khan, Commencement Address, MIT,
June 8, 2012

Hannah looked at the data on Nia's screen. "I think my emotional response was stronger because I wasn't analyzing anything. I was just ... there, receiving it."

Maya raised an eyebrow. "You mean I was too analytical to feel anything?"

Maya looked up to see that Matthew and Ava had joined the group.

Matthew plopped down cross-legged on the ground opposite Maya and Hannah, as Nia and Ava wandered off discussing voles.

"Wow. It was eye-opening to watch Ava engage with the pine vole recording. I am grateful that Nia invited me to join her today. Tell me what you two are working on."

Hannah jumped in. "We've been listening to soundscapes recorded with tribal elders. Each one layered with ambient and ceremonial audio. The vest translates key frequencies into tactile vibrations. My biometric data showed an elevated emotional response."

Matthew asked if he could listen to the indigenous recordings.

"Only if we can record your biometric data."

Matthew laughed. "Of course. My biometric data is your biometric data."

Maya signaled to Sarah. "Do you have a consent form for Dr. Venable to sign? He'd like to listen to the indigenous recording, and we'd like to be able to capture and analyze his biometric data."

Sarah offered the requisite paperwork, which Matthew scanned and signed. Then she helped him into the haptic device and explained the menu of indigenous recordings he could choose from.

As Matthew began to listen, Maya sat on the log, peeling a pine needle apart between her fingers. Beside her, Hannah had the haptic vest still loosely draped over her shoulders, its sensors glinting softly.

"You didn't feel anything from it, did you?" Hannah probed gently.

"Not really." Maya shook her head. "I mean—I felt the vibrations. Technically. But it didn't ... land. It was like ... getting a massage through a winter coat."

"It's wild how different it was for me. I got goosebumps.

My chest tightened—like something old and beautiful was being stirred."

The two looked at Matthew whose eyes were visibly moist as he looked off in the distance.

Maya looked away. "That's what it's supposed to do. That's the design. Sensory resonance. Emotional feedback. I helped write the paper that hypothesized the outcomes." She sighed. "But when I put it on, it's like my body's reading it as … data. Not as feeling."

"You think it's the anxiety?"

"Maybe partly. Chronic hypervigilance can flatten interoception. I know the theory. But there's something else."

"I'm listening, not judging."

"I've always had a strange relationship to sensation. Not absent—just … filtered. I remember in college, people would talk about music giving them chills, or scents triggering memories. My body doesn't organize around longing the way other people's seem to. So these tools—built to stir connection, arousal, even awe—they miss me. Or I miss them."

"Maybe," offered Hannah. "Or maybe the map just needs more terrain."

They turned their attention back to Matthew, who had clearly moved on to the recording of a circle dance—low footfall rhythms layered with elder laughter and the distant rattle of seed pods. A faint smile tugged at his mouth and his shoulders visibly softened.

When Hannah approached Matthew to discuss his experience with the indigenous sounds, Maya set off down the trail.

"Let's get your thoughts on tape while it's still fresh." Hannah held up her camera.

Matthew sighed. "The vibrations traveled in looping pulses across my chest and down my arms. I felt like a memory had been set free—as if I had once been part of something ancient and alive. As a psychologist, I understand the vibrations stimulate my ventral vagal complex, the nerve system that promotes social engagement, calm, and emotional safety. That tells me this experience may amplify body-mind integration, fostering what we call interoception, our ability to sense what's happening inside our own bodies. It's a cornerstone in somatic therapy for anxiety."

"So ... real talk. Do you think what we did today—what we felt—could actually replace anxiety meds?"

"That's the question, isn't it?" Matthew chose his words carefully. "It has the potential to reduce the need for pharmaceuticals. For some people. In some situations. But replace? That's trickier."

"Trickier how?"

"Because medication addresses biochemical dysregulation —neurotransmitter imbalances, receptor sensitivity. It's not just emotional. For people with moderate to severe anxiety disorders, meds can be lifesaving."

Matthew continued.

"What these apps do—if they're working the way we think —is help re-pattern the nervous system's baseline state. That's huge. That's the core of what we try to do in somatic therapy, but this ... could scale it."

"So it's more like ... prevention?"

"Prevention, support, even re-regulation. If someone can use this tech to build interoceptive awareness—to tune into their body's signals, and learn how to work with them—they might not need medication long term. Or someone on meds might be able to lower their dose. Or come off gradually, with support."

Hannah turned off the camera. "I wish I'd had this fifteen years ago. When I couldn't tell if my hands were shaking because I was scared or because I hadn't eaten."

Hannah grinned sheepishly. "This would've helped me listen to my body, instead of just trying to shut it up."

"That's exactly it. Most meds mute the alarm. But this? This helps you learn where the fire is—and maybe even how to put it out."

Matthew rose, gestured to the trail, and offered his hand to Hannah to help her to her feet.

"But it's not one-size-fits-all." Matthew looked off down the trail in the direction Maya had gone. "Some people aren't ready to feel. For them, the haptics might be overwhelming. Or triggering."

"So we'd still need therapists. Interpreters?" Hannah coaxed.

"Therapists. Guides. And consent-based design," Matthew confirmed. "But we could reach so many people who've fallen through the cracks.

"Kids who don't want to talk. Veterans who can't. Teens who'd rather feel a vibration than fill a prescription."

Hannah smiled. "That's the Holy Grail, isn't it?"

"It is. You're good at translating this world. That matters."

MAYA HURRIED down the trail in search of Elena, hopeful that she had a framework for this. Elena was studying neurodiverse sensory pathways in response to sound-touch synchronization.

She passed a group of day trippers taking photos of the Boston skyline. She thought to herself, *would they vote to fund TrailMind—or dismiss it as an expensive gimmick?* Then schooled herself, *Stop asking if the state can afford it. Ask what it costs if we don't.*

Maya caught Elena near the shade shelter, and launched right in.

"Can I ask you something? The haptic audio—why does Hannah light up and I feel nothing? Same vest, same chant, but for me it's just ... data."

Elena tilted her head, intrigued. "That's multisensory integration. Some people's nervous systems route sound and touch through emotional pathways. Others don't. You may have lower responsiveness in your C-tactile afferents—the fibers tuned for gentle, affective touch. They're not about force, they're about meaning."

Maya paced, agitated.

"So my body's reading signal as telemetry, not emotion. Flatline. And if that's always been true—does it change my baseline?"

"Yes." Elena didn't hesitate. "It's not absence. It's configuration. Some people emphasize precision over affect. Internal mapping instead of external resonance. High proprioceptive reliance. Common in engineers, programmers. MIT types."

Maya gave a half-smile. "So: hyperactive prefrontal cortex, shy limbic system?"

Elena laughed. "Exactly. For example, some people who identify as asexual describe intimacy through a different lens— not broken, just re-wired."

Maya's eyes flickered with both relief and frustration. "So I'm outside the calibration range. The vest works, just not the way it's designed."

"Then maybe the next version needs to account for people like you." Elena touched Maya's arm lightly, almost a test. "Would you consider a longer neural profile? Compare your scans to our super-responders?"

Maya ducked away, grinning despite herself. "Only if I get to analyze the data."

"Deal." Elena called over her shoulder as Maya hiked up the trail, "Classic MIT move."

———

MATTHEW CAUGHT UP WITH MAYA, laying a gentle hand on her shoulder as they headed toward the ferry.

"I'm impressed. And kind of buzzing from what I saw today."

"Surprise!" Maya shot him a sideways eye roll.

Even as she said it, her brain tagged the sensation of his hand: slow pressure, no agenda. Tracking with Elena's explanation of affective touch. She filed it away.

Matthew noticed her flicker of reaction. "You good?" he asked.

"Fine. Just wrangling ferry manifests before Nia corrals everyone for the debrief."

"I've been thinking. TrailMind isn't a replacement for therapy. But with therapy? It could be a game-changer."

Maya snapped her head up. "Ugh, I keep hearing that. Game-changer. Disruptor." She leaned in, frustrated. "I didn't design this to cure trauma. It was supposed to help people breathe in a park without a ranger having to do triage."

Matthew trod carefully. "Sure. But sometimes the tools we make end up helping in ways we didn't plan for."

Maya snarked. "Right. Next headline: 'Anxiety Whisperer Rewires America with Ambient Birdsong'."

He chuckled. "Not rewriting the DSM. Just giving people a compass—helping them hear what their bodies are already trying to say."

She tilted her head. "You actually think this scales?"

"With scaffolding, yeah. But it needs humans too—therapists, rangers, teachers of embodiment. Tech can't do this alone."

"Like Khan Academy." She was testing him.

He grinned. "Exactly. Remember when people said video lectures would kill classrooms?"

"Yeah, I was in the first MITx cohort. The hype was daunting."

"And what happened? Good teachers got better. Students prepped, filled gaps. More real teaching, less repetition."

Maya's shoulders eased. "Not the worst mission statement I've heard today."

She watched the ferry edging closer. "So maybe TrailMind isn't the therapy. It's the pre-work. Like open-world grinding until the controls are second nature." She gave him a look. "But I'm not adding 'healer' to my CV."

"Fine. How about 'systems designer for collective resilience'?"

Maya laughed, tugging her braid. "God, that's worse."

"What's the next milestone?" she asked—same question she'd asked a hundred times back at MIT. But she didn't wait for him to answer, didn't notice how the familiar words made him smile. How they hit him like an affirmation. Grounded him.

"I can give you a data dump," she continued, tapping her tablet. "Biometrics, EEG, REM disruption, microexpressions— take your pick."

He raised a brow. "Collecting all that through the watches?"

She nodded. "Yeah. A partnership with a Swiss watchmaker.

"Half the kids already had them, the rest were thrilled to get one. Ubiquity helps—nobody knows if you're anxious or just into Swiss design."

Matthew smiled. "Darren's chasing a watchmaker too. But NeuroTech's about overriding signals, not listening to them."

"Oh, Hannah will love that," Maya muttered, tapping her screen. "Anyway—if you're in the mood for squishier stuff, Nia's team logged tons of human texture."

"I'll take anything you're offering." Matthew held her gaze. "Spikes and graphs are fine, but intuition catches what data misses."

"Data dump plus team huddle?" She smiled. "Okay, let me check Sam's and Hannah's schedules. Tomorrow or Friday? Might run late."

"Sadly, my personal life allows meetings anytime," he admitted.

Maya blushed, fiddling with her braid. "Wow. Same." She glanced up. "Then we'll make it happen."

Matthew touched his phone to hers. "Deal."

ELEVEN

With her signature efficiency, Maya sent Matthew a text message the next morning:

Maya: Sam and Hannah are on for 6 p.m. today. E14-647 in the Sky Center at the Media Lab.

Then she sent a Slack message:

@sam 09:02 a.m.
Uploading your rec letter draft now. I'm still refusing to believe you're leaving, but I'm also proud beyond words. Let me know if you want me to lean more on the "visionary coder" side or the "empathy-informed designer" part. Or both.

THAT EVENING, Matthew arrived early at the Media Lab. As the Boston skyline caught the sunset in a wash of color, his nervous system tugged, remembering how to respond.

Hannah was the first to join him in the reception area of the Sky Center.

"Thanks for the lead on Darren's watch partnership. That was my cue to look up his Form D filings and it turns out your friend Darren is not a pill pusher for moral or intellectual reasons. He's got quite the diverse portfolio of alternative solutions to replace or complement the pills."

"That's thought provoking." Matthew left it there as Maya and Sam walked in together.

In the small conference room, Sam took the pilot seat behind the built-in computer and fired up the screen.

Maya turned to Hannah. "Fill us in on what's new in the blog-o-sphere while Sam pulls up the data."

"My Substack post on the public meeting brought in over one hundred new subscribers—including Thura Aung, U.S. Senate health policy advisor. So ... that was validating."

Matthew nodded. "That tracks. Our Senator co-sponsored that youth mental health grant amendment last year. Wants scalable care that doesn't require a prescription pad."

"The blog also pushed some buttons at NeuroTech." Hannah grinned.

"Darren's VP for public outreach has offered a meeting with His Excellency, Dr. Katsaros, himself. Although she's saying it's off-the-record so it could be a complete wash."

Hannah gave a half-smile. "And Valbern Precision bought into my TikTok pitch for daily video snapshots of TrailMind youth-led somatic storytelling. Valbern is rebranding itself through wearable wellness."

She glanced sideways. "It's a little weird getting paid by a luxury watch company, but ... if it keeps the project visible and elevates teens' voices—I'll take the money. For now.

"In the meantime, here's the vlog from yesterday, scheduled to drop tomorrow for morning commuter prime time." Hannah tapped her phone to Maya's and then Matthew's to share the file.

Hannah continued, "I planned to look at the data this evening through the lens of the governor's advisory committee, but these bios in the briefing book ... they're, like, half-sentences and acronyms. 'Joe D., MARAD liaison since '97. Loves shellfish.' What am I supposed to do with that?"

Matthew smirked. "Welcome to the Boston Harbor Islands Park Advisory Committee. Where the resumes are long, but the memory's longer."

"Seriously though—can you help me get a read on who's who? I don't want to step on any toes—or accidentally pick a fight about sea wall funding."

Matthew nodded thoughtfully. "You want the quirks and foibles, not the resumes."

"Exactly. I need context. History. Who actually makes things happen—and who just likes to hear themselves talk."

"Then you should talk to my mom."

Hannah raised an eyebrow. "Michelle? The Michelle Venable?"

Hannah did a quick search on her phone, then read out loud, "Governor's Blue Ribbon Task Force on Climate Resilience, the Special Commission on Youth Mental Health Equity, Mayor's Urban Greenspace Futures Panel ... and she's on the board of some weirdly well-funded start-up accelerator for public interest tech—Bridgeworks?"

Matthew grinned. "That's my mom. She'll give you the whole unofficial dossier—who butted heads over the deer cull in '06, who ghostwrites position papers for the vice chair, and who still thinks the Harbor Islands Initiative is just a phase one boondoggle."

Hannah laughed. "Okay, but will she talk to me?"

"She'll talk. She's always curious about the new blood. And you passed the first test—didn't call Joe D. 'the Barnacle'."

"Yeah me! I'll set up a coffee. Thanks, Matthew."

"Just remember—don't ask her about the 2004 ferry allocation debate unless you have an hour."

"Ouch," Maya interjected. "That reminds me I have to add 'funding for access to public spaces' to my ever-growing Excel sheet. No point in building AR bridges to nature on the Harbor Islands if the only people who can afford the ferry fare are already in therapy."

"Add that to your list to discuss with my mom." Matthew pointed at Hannah. "She needs a new challenge."

"I'm ready!" Sam bounced in her chair, her ponytail—a glossy handful of Persian curls—spinning like a tiny whirling dervish.

"First up, cortisol spikes. This is from the initial ninety seconds of exposure to the coastal forest edge trail. We're seeing a pretty steep uptick in most participants, but notably lower spikes when ambient sound is paired with gentle haptics—what we're calling the 'root pulse'.

"I'll have time to polish the visualizations before my exit interview," Sam added cheerfully. "They'll need to be turnkey for whoever takes over."

"Exit interview?" Hannah blinked. "You're out already?"

"One foot in, one foot at LoopWell—they just confirmed the offer." Sam tried to sound casual. "I'll be helping them refine the emotional optimization layers in their recommendation engine."

"I hope you can get it to stop recommending climate collapse infographics and start pushing me toward actual daylight." Hannah sighed.

Sam swiped to the next chart.

Maya's heart lifted and sank at once. *Of course Sam was a catch. Of course LoopWell would swoop in and snatch her up.*

"Initial galvanic skin response shows a sharp spike," Sam began. "Nia calls it *the vertigo of beauty*—as if their systems didn't know how to metabolize awe.

"By minute twenty-seven, heart rate variability indicates parasympathetic recovery. Sleep data shows a brief first-night disruption, then normalization—a recalibration effect."

Matthew pointed at the chart. "And that's teachable. Most of these kids are already wearing the sensors. They can learn to read their own signals."

Sam advanced to the EEG chart. "And here's the most promising signal: kids who began with scattered high-frequency chatter shifted toward stabilized theta patterns. Not just stress relief, but signs of re-patterning."

Maya turned to Matthew. "That's what makes this more than a productivity tool. It's nervous-system infrastructure."

Matthew nodded. "With a control group and clinical review, we could frame TrailMind as a public health intervention, not a wellness add-on."

As Maya considered Matthew's idea, a new slide appeared. It wasn't a chart—it was a photo: a twelve-year-old boy, round-faced and stiff, standing on a soccer field in oversized cleats. He looked like he was trying to smile, but his eyes were distant.

Sam jumped up. "Wait—what?" Then she whispered, "That's not supposed to be in here."

The team fell quiet. Sam added, more audibly, "That's my nephew, Kieran. I have no idea how his picture got into this deck."

"Should we take a little break?" Maya asked.

"No ... it's okay. I just—I don't know how that image got into this folder.

"I used it last week in a message to my sister. He's been

struggling. A lot. Not sleeping. Not talking much. His therapist says he's shut down. The meds ... they aren't helping."

There was a beat of silence in the room.

Matthew grimaced. "I'm sorry, Sam. That's hard. Have you thought about non-verbal routes? Like animal-assisted therapy?"

"I don't know?" Sam asked, more than answering. "They have one of those school-based comfort dogs. He didn't engage."

"You might want to reach out to Kris Barsa. Do you remember him from Terrascope?" Matthew asked Maya. "He's training service dogs. Not just petting for comfort, but full-spectrum bonding, even light tasking. Especially for kids stuck in the freeze state."

Maya nodded. "He's been piloting some TrailMind apps with fellow veterans on the islands."

"I'm glad to hear that. He started training dogs after he left Afghanistan. He might be a good fit for Kieran. I can connect you."

Sam nodded, clearly fighting to stay composed. Hannah placed a steadying hand on her arm.

Maya sent Sam a sympathetic smile. "Let's finish the deck another time. You've already given us more than enough to work with."

"And thank you—for letting us see him." Hannah smiled softly. "Even by accident. That's the reminder, isn't it? What the data points to—and who it's really for."

AT HOME THAT EVENING, Matthew opened the data dump that he received from Maya, along with the data visualizations that Sam provided. He looked for patterns and outliers then drafted an analysis, keen to engage the team to drill down on some promising trends.

What caught his attention first were the divergent response curves between users exposed to the single-stimuli audio apps—controlled environments featuring one sound at a time, like ocean waves, wind through leaves, or a steady heartbeat—and those using the multi-stimuli indigenous sound app, which layered birdsong, water, ceremonial instruments, and spoken-word storytelling.

Matthew saw the pattern he expected from the single-stimuli apps: gradually declining heart rate, steadier breathing, and high scores on self-reported calm and presence. But what intrigued him most were the biometric responses to the indigenous sound app—more spikes, more emotional intensity—but those same users reported deeper emotional impact, higher rates of feeling connected, and more sustained post-session reflection.

That complexity was promising. Matthew flagged it for further inquiry: *Were the peaks evidence of discomfort—or of breakthrough? Could complexity be a pathway, not a barrier, to healing?*

The data from the West Coast complicated things further. Choice mattered more than control. Engagement held where agency was present.

Matthew stared at the screen longer than he meant to.

Complexity, he typed in the margin. *Not noise.*

Matthew hoped to encourage similar adaptability in future prototypes—especially for users with sensory processing sensitivities. He made a note, *Ask Maya about integrating a customizable EQ or "sonic filter" feature.*

Matthew drafted a message to Maya, then hesitated—rewrote it, pared it down, and sent it anyway.

@Maya 11:37 p.m.

Hey—quick synthesis of what I saw in the data. Top-line thoughts:

– Start sessions with somatic baselining (rootwave tones) before adding haptics.

– Sequence design: grounding first, then narration.

– Responsive feedback loop in the vest.

– Data flagging for audio-only vs. haptic-augmented sessions.

– Propose: add trauma-survivor cohort with journaling. Let me know what resonates. Happy to draft a trial addendum if you're game.

TWELVE

It was almost midnight when Maya opened Hannah's vlog.

HANNAH: Hi folks, Hannah here, reporting from
Spectacle Island. I'm in the Boston Harbor Islands
State Park. It's just a short ferry ride from Boston but a
world away in terms of how we think about how nature
affects our physical and mental well-being.

The video cut to Nia helping Hannah into a haptic vest on
Summit Trail.

I was invited to participate in testing eco-immersive
technologies with teens from the Charlestown Youth
Collaborative.

The video cut to Hannah reacting to the indigenous water
drum chant.

I listened to Indigenous soundscape recordings—developed with the full collaboration and consent of the Aquinnah and Mashpee Wampanoag Tribes. I wore a vest that let me feel the drum patterns, the chants, the waves crashing as if the sound was moving through my body.

My skin responded. I was completely present, grounded on this piece of land. I felt as if the land knew I was here, too, at this particular moment, between the past and the future. For this reason alone I'd cast my vote for investing in making this technology available to everyone through our national and state parks.

Dr. Matthew Venable believes the technology offers even more value to our collective well-being, as a therapeutic tool for preventing, managing, or in some cases even healing anxiety and despair. He is a psychologist and a member of the governor's Boston Harbor Islands Park Advisory Committee. Listen to what he says.

MATTHEW: This experience may help people to tune into their body's signals, even learn how to shift them. If that happens, they might not need medication long term.
Or someone on meds might be able to lower their dose. Or come off gradually, with support.

HANNAH: Finding solutions for youth anxiety is a major focus of public policy discussions at the city, state, and federal levels. Later this week I'll be reporting on what members of Congress are saying about the Health and Human Services' Advance Market Commitment for the production and distribution of the anxiety pill, NeuroEase. They're calling it a moonshot for mental health. But Dr. Venable poses the $2 billion question for which Congress must be accountable.

MATTHEW: What happens if these anxiety pills don't unlock greater productivity, higher graduation rates, or a generation ready to compete in a global economy? What if, instead, we're creating a chemically dependent cohort? We risk turning a mental health intervention into a long-term social and political liability.

HANNAH: Here on Spectacle Island, a group of researchers, youth and tech developers are asking a deeper question: *What if relief from anxiety didn't come in a capsule—but from reconnecting with the earth, and with our own bodies?*

I'm Hannah. Thanks for watching.
And remember—sometimes the most powerful signal isn't digital. It's the one your body's been trying to send all along.

Maya immediately appreciated that she and Matthew were in sync about reframing the question from, *What can Trail-Mind do?* to *What happens if there is nothing to complement the pills?*

Then she opened Matthew's Slack message...and groaned.

Maya hit the video call button, despite the late hour.

"You want to take this to another level and I haven't even caught my breath from what Amina Kassam dumped on us Monday." She growled, then grinned.

Matthew raised his hands like a kid caught sneaking candy. "Annoying habit, I know."

"Oh, I know. Back at Terrascope, I thought my job was just to be the best coder. And there you were, night after night, asking, 'Why this code? Who does it actually help?'"

Matthew winced. "See? Hopeless. Always the bigger picture. I swear it's not personal."

"It's personal now," Maya teased. "Your problem is my problem."

"Maybe that's why we work," he shot back, eyes softening.

Maya rolled hers, but smiled. "Until it tips into Darren 2.0."

He stilled. "That's exactly what I don't want."

Maya hesitated, then spoke more gently.

"My Uncle Leo has this theory about you two, based purely on my rambling. He said, 'Darren wanted velocity—scale and funding at any cost. Matthew wanted perfection—the immaculate model. Both end up brittle because they refuse to stand on the ground under their feet.'"

Matthew grimaced. "That tracks. With Darren it wasn't enough to scale the drug; I wanted perfect—therapy plus drug. But I didn't bring a therapy solution. That gap ... killed us. I don't want that with you."

Maya nodded, the warmth returning. "Then let's keep our feet on the ground, even while we build."

"Got it. No miracles." He put a finger to his lips. "But... maybe a few more cohorts? See if somatics can scale, not just soothe."

"Ugh! More data always leads to more code. And more complexity."

"Then help me set the ceiling. What can we realistically achieve now? We need something fundable, civic, useful. Otherwise TrailMind is just another shiny gadget."

Maya leaned in. "I hate that we're pitching this like a startup. But I love that people are seeing possibilities in it. That's ... complicated."

"It is. But you don't have to sell a miracle. Just show them what's already happening—and invite them in."

That cracked her. "Okay. So: advisory committee. We need a 'yes', but it has to be a *resourced* 'yes'."

"Access. Infrastructure. Buy-in." Matthew held up fingers as he counted. "Pilot beyond Spectacle. Not just another line item, but a real partnership. Long game."

"Yes. Part One—TrailMind as an operational upgrade: staff efficiency, access equity, visitor engagement. We recycle the NPS data."

"Perfect! Part Two—human infrastructure. Rangers supported, not drained. TrailMind as a nervous system tool, not a wellness gimmick."

They volleyed back and forth, sketching the structure, the visuals, even a short immersive clip Hannah could cut.

At midnight the clock flipped over, unnoticed.

Finally Maya leaned back, tugging on her braid. "Sorry—this thing I do, gets me out of my head."

"Don't apologize. That's brilliant. Your nervous system giving itself a little love tap."

Maya laughed. "Careful—you make it sound like flirting through neuroscience."

Matthew grinned. "My specialty. That—and this." He gestured between them, his voice softening. "Us, building toward something that matters."

<hr>

BY 6:00 p.m. they were back in E14-647.

Sam clicked into presenter mode, finger skimming the

trackpad. "All right—let's walk it through. I'll draft the beats as we go."

She swiped to the slide labeled "Context". She narrated at a leisurely pace.

"TrailMind has developed tools for the National Park Service.

"Mental health and wellness are a new NPS strategic priority due to rising tension, trauma spillover from wildfires, and staffing shortages.

"TrailMind delivered low-friction tools that enhance the wellness benefits of outdoor space—without piling more work on already-stretched park staff.

"TrailMind has demonstrated measurable impact reducing stress and mental fatigue, relieving anxiety and depression, and improving mood and the sense of belonging, purpose, awe and inspiration."

She clicked on a slide labeled "Field Observations."

"This is where we bring it to life. I'll use the new data from Jess and Ravi at Point Reyes in California. These heatmaps show consistent clustering near the soundwalk loops."

Maya interjected, "Let's also pull that moment with the couple who started walking apart, then synced steps after the chime tones."

Sam bounced in her chair. "Perfect. That's the story."

She clicked ahead to "Operational Value" saying, "This is where we invite the longtime leadership to envision a better future.

"TrailMind lowers the need for ranger intervention by twenty percent during high-traffic weekends. That gives leadership the measurable return on investment they need. The real payoff is on the visitor side: less agitation, more self-regulation, longer park visits and higher return rates."

Matthew nodded.

"Add that data Hannah flagged from Yosemite—call-in volume dropped after TrailMind added the breathing prompts to trail signage."

Sam clicked to the next header, "Human Applications."

"Here's where we slow it down. TrailMind isn't just mindfulness—it's trauma-informed design. Nature isn't just a backdrop—it's the co-regulator. Breath pacing, guided noticing, low-stimulation cues. All grounded in somatics."

Maya added softly, "Let's boldface that language, 'nature as co-regulator'. That lands."

Sam clicked to the "Next Steps" slide.

"This is our ask. We propose a six-month pilot across three parks, build a task force with field staff and clinical advisors, and scale in phases. Low cost. High relational return."

She looked up at the others. "Anything else we need to anchor before I draft the full deck?"

Hannah jumped in, "Maya, I think we need to weave you into the slides. Let them see TrailMind isn't a product chasing a market."

Matthew looked up to see how this landed with Maya. She just rolled her eyes.

"Send the deck to me when you've finished your tweaks, Sam, and I'll add some speaker notes."

She rose from the table. "Now excuse me while I go put on some lip balm."

AT HOME THAT EVENING, Maya scheduled a Slack message to the field-based co-designers with a copy of the presentation.

@trailcore

I welcome your feedback. We're scheduled to present
to the governor's advisory committee on the Boston
Harbor Island National Park on Monday afternoon.

As Maya thought about her opening statement for the presentation, she reflected on how Uncle Leo had introduced her to her own right brain when she was fifteen.

She had been sitting cross-legged on a flat boulder near their campsite. The air had smelled like pine and granite and the lentils her Uncle Leo had been stirring on the camp stove. The sky above was that deep blue that meant the stars would be putting on a show for her that night.

"You've been quiet today." Leo glanced at her over his shoulder.

Maya shrugged. "Just thinking."

Leo didn't push. He never did. That was part of why she liked being with him.

She thought some more, then shared what was on her mind. "Do you ever think you were supposed to do something else?"

Leo smiled faintly. "You mean besides chasing off bears and fixing broken trail signs?"

"I mean ..." She hesitated. "My parents think coding is my ticket. To college, to opportunity, to security. I get that. But sometimes when I'm in a lab or writing algorithms for hours, I feel like I'm solving puzzles that don't matter. Not the big things. Not like ... what you do here."

He turned the stove down and sat beside her on the rock. "Let me tell you something. I didn't set out to become a park ranger. I majored in mechanical engineering, just like your dad. Started out designing HVAC systems for office buildings in Sacramento."

"Seriously?"

"Oh yeah. Made good money, wore a tie. But after a few years I realized I spent more time under fluorescent lights than I did under the sky. I wasn't miserable, but I wasn't proud, either. So I started volunteering on the weekends with trail crews. Got hooked. Quit the job, took a pay cut, moved into a shared cabin with a leaky roof and a dozen raccoons in the attic. Best decision I ever made."

Maya looked at him, skeptical. "Weren't your parents pissed?"

"They were confused. Worried. But eventually they saw that I was doing something I believed in. I was helping protect something that matters—not just for me, but for everyone. It's not glamorous, but it's grounding."

She pulled her knees in, thoughtful.

"Sometimes I think my code could do something that matters.

"Like something for the environment, or mental health, or I don't know ... real life. But my teachers and my parents just want me to win prizes and scholarships."

Leo nodded slowly. "Look, Maya. You've got a gift. No doubt about that. But the question isn't whether you're good at coding. It's what you want to do with that gift. Who you want it to serve. You find the answer to that, and the rest will follow. Might not look like what your parents imagined. But it'll feel like your life. Not theirs."

Maya looked out toward the trees, where the shadows were getting longer. "You think I could combine it? Like, use tech to protect nature?"

"Hell yes." Leo grinned. "Mother Earth needs all the allies she can get—especially ones fluent in both computers and clouds."

Maya channeled that memory, set up her laptop to record video, and drew on the language of clouds to invite the members of the governor's Boston Harbor Islands Park Advisory Committee to envision public parks as public infrastructure.

I'm Maya Venkataraman. It's a pleasure to introduce TrailMind to this group of public stewards. You have an innate understanding of the power of nature to instruct, to nurture, and to heal.

When I was a child, my parents and I would spend two weeks every summer in Yosemite National Park, visiting Dad's college roommate, my Uncle Leo, a park ranger.

I didn't have the language for it back then, but every time I was in the park, something shifted. My breathing slowed. My body settled. I felt ... lighter. Nature kept challenging me—the bears, the bugs, the poison oak—but I also felt claimed—like I belonged to the place, and it belonged to me.

I'm assuming you all share similar experiences from your youth or you wouldn't be investing your time and energy into the Boston Harbor Islands Park today.

TrailMind can make our childhood experiences available to everyone. Especially to young people, like the undergraduates in my classes at MIT, who feel overwhelmed, shut down, or frightened by the places that are supposed to restore us.

TrailMind is tech designed not to extract or distract, but to listen. To support rangers, interpretive staff, and visitors—especially those whose nervous systems carry more weight into the wild.

TrailMind isn't about gadgets. It's about grounding. It's informed by the communities who need it most—anxious youth, traumatized veterans, over-extended working parents, and people with neurodivergent systems.

It's about using what we already have—tools, spaces, stories—to help people reconnect with what regulates the nervous system naturally.

That's what I'm trying to do. And that's what we're here to share.

Satisfied that her opening statement for the advisory committee was strong, Maya let the words settle, then closed the TrailMind tab in her brain.

She thought again of Uncle Leo urging her to ask not just *what she was good at*, but *who her work might serve*. With that memory as a compass, she shifted her energy toward her own students.

Their semester had left them frayed, brittle. Numbers and grades alone would only tighten the knot. What they needed was feedback they could metabolize—narratives that named their growth, located their struggles without shaming them, and pointed to futures they might not yet see for themselves.

It would take more time to write. But Leo had been right: the work that matters isn't always efficient.

THIRTEEN

On Tuesday morning, after the Memorial Day weekend, Maya headed towards Amina Kassam's office, to share a copy of the presentation for the Boston Harbor Islands Park Advisory Committee. She stopped outside the door when she heard that Amina already had someone in her office.

"Is this the best use of synthetic cognition?" someone asked.

"It's not a binary choice, Shauna. We are developing synthetic cognition for multiple applications," Amina responded. "TrailMind is contributing to the Soft Robotics team and the Liquid Neural Networks team."

"What's the measurable output? Amina, you do realize we have to prepare for reputational exposure if this turns into a political flashpoint?" Shauna, the director of the MIT Media Lab, said over her shoulder as she left Amina's office.

Maya entered the office. "Is Shauna an outlier ... or is this what we're up against?"

"There have been other subtle inquiries, wrapped in concern." Amina shrugged. "Some of our funders; a few key voices in the institute's leadership circles."

"Because it's in a national park? Or because it's you who's backing it?"

"Both. The spotlight is on the Boston Harbor Islands. They're public, shared, almost sacred. Mixing that with a cognitive system that doesn't play by traditional research metrics? We're unsettling to them. And yes, my public position on the project makes it a little more visible than they're comfortable with."

"Are they threatening to pull funding?"

"Not directly. But one of the directors from the Aspen Collective made a comment—something about 'reallocating resources to more grounded initiatives'. Shauna said that I was 'indulging speculative entanglements'."

"Speculative entanglements—might be a good name for a TrailMind app. Nervous systems aren't closed circuits."

Dr. Kassam smiled sadly. "Yes, I thought so too. It evokes both quantum entanglement theory and relational complexity. But these aren't people with a sense of humor."

She leaned back, steepling her fingers. "The project's becoming a node of attention. Did you see this story in *The Boston Globe*?"

She handed Maya the newspaper folded to a headline, "Senator Calls for Public Options in Mental Health—Beyond the Pill." The subheader quoted Massachusetts' senior Senator, "If we're serious about healing, we must fund the experiments —not just the patents."

"People are taking sides," she continued. "You'll start feeling it soon, if you haven't already."

"We have. Some visitors are asking questions TrailMind's bot wasn't trained for—pointed, rehearsed. It doesn't feel organic. More like someone's testing it."

"Then it's already begun. Look, Maya. I won't abandon this. But we may need to recalibrate our public posture.

Tighten the scope. Shift emphasis to the ecological data integrations, downplay the phenomenological dimensions—at least until the next round of reviews is locked. You've got Alexis testing TrailMind scaffolds in-school and Kris checking Ranger Assist protocols with veterans in the field. That's your proof of scale across contexts—and your new refrain."

"You mean downplay the parts that matter." Maya's nose flared.

"I mean protect them," Amina corrected sharply.

Then, more gently, "So the parts that matter can keep unfolding—rather than getting shut down before they've had a chance to breathe."

She sighed. "We're at the edge of what this institution finds comfortable. I'm not here to make them comfortable. But we've both been here since CSAIL's inception. I want to make sure we're still here six months from now."

Maya nodded. "Me, too.

"Shall I send you the deck for the Boston Harbor Islands Park Advisory Committee before we present tomorrow? Take a look at it through your political lens?"

"Please do."

"HANNAH!" Michelle gestured to a seat. "Good to finally sit down together. I've been hearing ... bits and pieces."

"Likewise." Hannah smiled as she settled in. "Matthew said you might have some ... perspective on the park advisory committee members."

"Perspective." Michelle laughed. "That's a polite word for it. I know who listens, who nods, and who waits for you to stop talking so they can speak. Trying to war game how they might line up for or against TrailMind?"

"Am I that obvious?" Hannah grinned.

Michelle leaned in. "Which means you believe in it. Or someone you trust does."

"I believe in it. But yeah—Maya's vision is what got me in the room."

Michelle sighed. "That's her gift—and her hazard. Maya burns bright, but she doesn't always wait for others to catch up with her. Still, if she put TrailMind in your hands, that means she trusts you to bring people along."

"I need intel to do that. I don't want to underestimate the undercurrents."

Michelle nodded and flipped her pad open, ticking off names as she spoke.

"The chairman, Joe D., will resist anything that sounds like 'monitoring'. Frame it as data stewardship, not surveillance. Nina from the historical society? She's on the fence, but she's got a soft spot for youth programs—show how TrailMind supports interpretation. Peter? He's loud, but he's lazy. Convince the chair and he'll follow like a tug behind a tanker. And if you get Camille—the parks liaison—onboard, you can actually shift the vote before it happens."

Michelle looked up. "You still have to do the work, but now you know which doors aren't locked."

"This is gold, Michelle. Thank you."

"You know, the committee is just the tip of the iceberg. Are you also taking the temperatures of the research community and the local officials? Social justice advocates like Janey Jones? The public meeting in the Common put TrailMind on the map, for better or for worse."

"I welcome any steer. Matthew also suggested picking your brain about access. I understand you've long been an advocate for public subsidies for the ferry to the Harbor Islands."

"Yes I have—and you're going to hear more about that from

some of the stakeholders and gatekeepers: Fiona Kane from Boston Harbor Now and Reverend Anita Garza. You'll need Renata Flores in your corner early, she chairs the City Council Committee on Public Health and Parks. They are all going to tell you that TrailMind has to serve the whole community, not just anxious teens."

Michelle pointed her pen at Hannah. "And do me a favor? Don't let Maya ghost this one. She planted the seed. She should help it grow."

Hannah noticed how effortlessly Michelle laid these strategic tasks at her feet. "I'll try. No promises on the second part—but I'll remind her. Loud."

"You do that. And I'll get my husband Jack working on the health insurance executives—they might be happy to pilot funding access to low cost, mental health wellness tools if MIT does the heavy lift for generating the data."

"A slam-dunk on MIT's side. If Jack needs a dog-and-pony show, there's a quantum-algorithms team working with anonymized biometric and ecological TrailMind data to model systemic return on investment across mental health, cardiovascular resilience, and respiratory gains. This could offer insurers a pre-validated framework for reimbursing nature-based interventions."

Michelle raised an eyebrow and made a note in her book.

Hannah hesitated. "Can I ask you something else? Off the record?"

Michelle smirked, lifting her tea. "In this café, everything's off the record—unless you're the one who put it in writing."

Hannah leaned forward. "What's the backstory story with Matthew and Darren Katsaros?"

Michelle paused, considering. "You couldn't get this out of Matthew? It's his story to tell."

"Matthew gave me enough to flush Darren out," Hannah

said. "The NeuroTech flack has offered me an off-the-record meeting this afternoon."

Michelle reached across the table to touch Hannah on the wrist. "My advice is to meet Darren with an open mind. He and Matthew used to be as close as brothers for a reason."

DARREN KATSAROS WAS POSITIONED *on the rooftop patio of his biotech incubator in the Seaport District with the late afternoon sun behind him,* Hannah thought as she walked toward him, already writing her next blog in her head.

She set her bike helmet down on a table, ran her hand through her short blond hair and then extended her hand to Darren. "Hannah Oak."

"You've got a sharp voice, Hannah. Punchy blog. You're not just parroting agency press releases—rare these days."

"That's because I don't take meetings with people who call parks 'legacy liabilities'."

"Touché. Look, maybe I deserve that. But maybe you'd be interested in a more nuanced conversation. Starting off the record. Move to attribution if things click."

Hannah cocked her head to look at him without the nimbus of sun she suspected he had strategically placed himself in.

"Maybe. But I'm curious what kind of story you think I'm writing."

"You're plugged in with the TrailMind crowd. There's, let's say, a lot of optimism in that camp. Always refreshing. But optimism has blind spots. Especially around funding."

"I'm not tracking."

"Investors with a broader vision." Darren smiled. "Like myself."

"Broader, huh." Hannah pulled out her phone and read

from a tab, "Like neuroadaptive VR, which you call 'digital ketamine without the drip'? Or that eye movement desensitization and reprocessing AI app that mimics trauma therapy with colored lights and voice prompts? What about the predictive model that flags anxiety based on how fast I type or breathe into my mic?"

She clicked her screen closed. "I read your Form D filings. Also the wearable thing—that anxiety bracelet you pitched at Davos? Sleek. Like if Cartier and a therapist had a baby."

Darren's eyes twinkled as he laughed sheepishly. "Darn. And here I was hoping I could play the Davos card to get you into bed."

Hannah leaned forward. "So here's the deal: I'll go to your lab. Neuroadaptive VR, emotion prediction, the whole anxiety industrial complex. But then, you come with me to Spectacle Island."

Darren raised an eyebrow. "To watch teenagers journal in a wind shelter?"

"To see what anxiety looks like without an interface."

Darren grinned. "Alright. I'll show you mine if you show me yours."

"Bring your sunscreen. The island doesn't care how much equity you hold."

"Perhaps." Darren arched a brow. "But the island might change its mind after the advisory committee meeting tomorrow."

A SLIDE of an aerial shot of the harbor served as a backdrop as Maya opened the presentation to the governor's Boston Harbor Islands Park Advisory Committee on Wednesday afternoon.

"Thank you all for your time. What I'm presenting today

isn't a product pitch—it's an open question. A question about what kind of public infrastructure we believe these islands can be."

She paused, allowing the silence to stretch a beat longer than comfortable.

"We know the funding isn't coming from Washington. Thanks to the first phase of our National Park Service grant, we have the data about the human resources cost savings Trail-Mind achieves. We know we can make the status quo more affordable for state and local agencies.

"But as the governor has said repeatedly, the climate crisis isn't slowing down.

"Youth anxiety's rising. Staff burnout is real. So the question becomes: in the absence of federal support—what are we willing to build?"

"I'll tell you what we're not building: a surveillance park," Joe D. bellowed. "These are public lands, not behavior labs."

"You are right." Maya ignored the theatrics. "TrailMind isn't surveillance. It doesn't track individuals. No GPS pings. No personal logs. What we collect is anonymous field data—cluster patterns, ambient conditions, optional feedback—stewarded locally, with transparency."

"Who's stewarding it though?" asked the parks liaison, Camille. "Park staff? A vendor? You? Because data ethics aren't just an agenda item in the boardroom—they're workload."

"That's why we're proposing a joint task force, with parks, public health, and youth input. If it doesn't serve the staff and the communities most affected, it doesn't go forward. Period."

"You mentioned youth involvement. How exactly?" Nina asked softly.

Maya clicked through to a slide with quotes from teen participants. "High schoolers from Dorchester and Chelsea helped design our soundwalk prompts. They chose the tone palette. They mapped emotional responses to certain island trails. For many, it was their first trip to the islands. They didn't just visit—they co-authored the experience."

"I didn't know silence could feel like company."

—Andre, 17

"That trail with the soft gravel and the ocean on both sides? It made me breathe like I meant it."

—Sofia, 16

"I used to think nature was just green stuff. But this made me feel like the island was ... listening back."

—Malik, 15

"We picked low tones on purpose. Not sad, but grounding. Like a deep hum that keeps you from floating away."

—Lena, 17

"I've never been somewhere so quiet where I felt safe. Usually quiet means danger."

—Tariq, 16

Nina looked around the table, nodding. "That's meaningful. That's interpretation."

Peter grunted. "Sounds like a lot of effort for what—meditation paths?"

"Not meditation," Maya corrected. "Regulation. These tools help nervous systems stabilize—especially for people carrying trauma, or neurodivergence, or just daily stress overload. That's not fluff. That's functional public infrastructure."

Elspeth Channing, the *Boston Globe* journalist, spoke from the back of the room. "Funny, because what I've heard is that this whole thing is light on evidence and heavy on spin. An app without peer review, marketing wellness without medical oversight."

Maya didn't rise to the bait. "If you're looking for additional points of view, you might ask this: who decides what's worth testing? If public lands are only for what's already validated, we stop innovating. No one's suggesting TrailMind replace clinical care. We're saying it can *complement* it. We're working with academic partners to gather comparative data. Ultimately, this becomes a public health resource if we can help the clinical community *scale* care to make it accessible to all."

Camille weighed in. "City Councilwoman Flores will want details. The Commissioner of Public Health, too, if you're walking this close to the health line."

Matthew nodded. "I agree, Camille. Let's work together to ensure Flores and Dillahunt are fully briefed on both the park staff and public aspects of the proposed pilot."

"I still don't like the sound of 'data pilot'," Joe D. blustered.

Maya nodded. "Then let's talk about outcomes, not data. What's our mandate here?

"Are we just preserving the past? Or do we have an opportunity to prepare for the future? If these islands can offer grounding for anxious teens, safe reprieve for visitors overwhelmed by the daily grind, and support for stretched staff, do we wait for perfect proof—or do we prototype with care?"

The room quieted and Maya allowed the silence to settle. "I'm not asking you to greenlight a *product*. I'm asking if this committee believes public parks can help solve public problems. If the answer is yes, then let's build something together worthy of that belief."

"I know that the status quo is not sustainable." Camille paused. "We can't go back, so consider this a motion to form a task force to draft guidelines and initiate stakeholder briefings. Let's move forward."

Pete raised a hand. "I second. If Camille's in, I'm not gonna die on a hill over it."

"As long as youth are involved in the design and implementation, I'll vote yes," added Nina.

Elspeth slipped quietly out of the room.

THAT EVENING, Hannah found herself in a part of Cambridge she usually avoided—too many retina-scanning lobbies.

Darren greeted her in a soft charcoal blazer and no tie.

His badge flicked green at the biometric gate as he held it open for her.

"So, did the advisory committee reach a unanimous and democratic consensus that they need to have another meeting about TrailMind?" Darren asked with a smirk.

"No, sir. They boldly agreed to form a task force ... to draft guidelines ..." Hannah grinned. "Look, they may be a bit process-oriented, but at least they are acknowledging that we have a public health crisis that is debilitating our youth."

The facility, which Darren cheerily called "The Sandbox," held a series of stations that pulsed, blinked, and occasionally spoke.

He led her through a corridor where ambient light adjusted

minutely with their movement, subtle chromatic shifts tuned to biometric readouts Hannah couldn't see.

"Real-time bioadaptive feedback," he explained. "We train the nervous system to expect calm. Like a reverse panic attack."

They passed a glass-walled room where a young man wore a sleek visor, shoulders subtly slackening in slow intervals as his vitals were monitored on a pulsing screen.

"This is Harmony-7. It's what happens when you stop pretending that therapy only lives in offices with plants and a diploma on the wall."

Hannah eyed the setup. "Digital ketamine without the drip," she muttered.

He smiled. "Right. The metaphor's sticky, sure. But the outcomes—well, they don't require liver panels or two days off work."

They moved on to a section with cubicles partitioned by translucent screens. Behind them, users engaged with small orbs emitting soft light pulses timed to voice prompts.

One spoke, "Breathe in. Breathe out. You are not your alert state."

"That's the eye movement desensitization and reprocessing treatment mimic. For people who can't or won't access trauma care. We're not replacing therapy. We're scaling triage."

Hannah stopped in front of a polished display case, minimal like a museum artifact. Inside, the anxiety bracelet: matte silver, a slim ring of tech elegance with embedded biometric sensors.

"Still think it looks like a Cartier-therapist baby?" he asked.

"I said that with admiration," she replied, meeting his eyes. "It's terrifying how seductive it is."

They stood quietly as a wall projection flared to life beside them: anonymized user maps, biometric heat traces overlaid on a world atlas. Anxiety flared like brushfire. Lit up metro grids in New York, Seoul, São Paulo.

Darren watched her watching.

"I don't believe in utopias." His voice was softer now.

"But I believe in tools. And I believe people don't need to suffer because we're purists about what counts as healing."

Hannah looked at him.

"And your hedge?"

He tilted his head, conceding.

"If the future doesn't go the way we hope, I want the infrastructure in place to catch people when it breaks. The less poetic safety net. For when people can't journal in a wind shelter on an island."

Hannah didn't reply immediately. She watched the soft pulse of the display, the color-coded breath of global anxiety.

"What's your hedge?" Darren asked quietly.

Hannah, turned to him and raised an eyebrow. "You tell me."

"You're pushing on the boundaries between journalism and advocacy. Hard. What happens when telling both points of view doesn't serve you?"

Hannah didn't answer right away. The projection flickered, breathing light across the glass, giving her cover. She folded her arms.

"You want me to confess my hedge? That falls under the 'I'll show you mine' clause. And you're fresh out of turns. When are you coming to Spectacle Island?"

As Darren pulled out his phone to consult his calendar, Hannah rolled her eyes.

FOURTEEN

Op-ed *The Boston Globe*, May 28, 2026
"The Science of Solace: Why We Must Demand
More from Neurotechnology"
By Elspeth Channing, Columnist

It was bound to happen. The convergence of brain science, design thinking, and consumer culture has produced its first true darling: TrailMind, the much-hyped neurotherapeutic platform now wooing city leaders and venture philanthropists across Massachusetts. Walk through one of its modular sanctuaries—fragrant with cedar, aglow with ambient hues calibrated to cortisol—and you might believe, if only for a moment, that mental wellness can be architected like a boutique hotel.

But belief is not evidence.

Before I attended this week's advisory committee meeting on the role of public parks in addressing the mental health epidemic, I wanted to approach TrailMind with open curiosity. I'd heard from friends and colleagues in public service that the experience "feels different." That it "works." Yet sitting in that circle, listening to eager testimonials and language steeped in reverence, I found myself asking a question that made me deeply uneasy: When does a tool for care become a theater of care?

TrailMind is a masterpiece of what its team calls "cognitive comfort design"—a phrase that might grace a spa brochure more easily than a scientific brief. It promises calibrated serenity through light, sound, and subtle neurofeedback. But outside the glow of the dome, one fact remains underlit: there is, as of yet, no peer-reviewed evidence of its clinical efficacy. None. What we're being offered is not a treatment protocol, but a choreography of affect—precision placation, as one biotech founder phrased it.

The branding is exquisite. The rhetoric is humane. And that is precisely what makes TrailMind so seductive—and so dangerous.

To be clear, this isn't an anti-innovation screed. Mental health desperately needs new tools. But in our enthusiasm, we must draw a bright line between what soothes and what heals. We cannot afford to conflate ambiance with intervention.

That's why I've been cautiously intrigued by NeuroEase, a pharmaceutical treatment designed to modulate neural inflammation and mitigate acute stress response. Unlike TrailMind's immersive sanctuaries, NeuroEase is, quite literally, a pill: unglamorous, but clinically tested. It does not seduce the senses; it recalibrates the brain's chemistry—without the user-centric effect loops of earlier-generation anxiety medications. And for many patients in trials, it's doing precisely what it claims: quieting the noise inside the brain, not just the room around it.

Is NeuroEase a panacea? Of course not. But unlike Trail-Mind, it is subject to clinical oversight. It is held to the standards of pharmacological science. It offers no temple, no ritual. Just data.

Some will read this as an attack. It isn't. It's an invitation: to rigor, to accountability, to humility. TrailMind's founders are clearly passionate. Its design team is visionary. But the burden of proof does not rest with skeptics. It rests with those making the claim—as MIT's Dr. Amina Kassam, whose lab focuses on adaptive neurointerfaces, would surely know.

Until rigorous standards—clinical, ethical, civic—are applied, TrailMind risks offering a beautifully branded escape hatch—more cathedral than clinic. In the words of one city official, "TrailMind feels like the future." Maybe. But until that future is subject to scrutiny, we must be brave enough to ask: What is being healed? And what is being performed?

Elspeth Channing is a columnist for The Boston Globe *and a member of the Boston Foundation's Civic Innovation Circle.*

"ELSPETH WROTE this before she attended the advisory committee meeting yesterday." Maya paced E14-647. "'Theater of care', 'immersive sanctuaries'. That's not just skepticism and it certainly doesn't represent multiple points of view."

"That's Darren," Matthew's eyes flashed. "'No peer-reviewed evidence of efficacy.' That's rich, coming from someone who helped launch NeuroEase off a white paper and vibes."

"Her whole op-ed is peppered with Darren's language," Hannah affirmed. "'Cognitive comfort design', 'precision placation', 'user-centric effect loops'—I've seen those phrases in the NeuroEase investor deck. She practically copy-pasted."

Hannah read from her phone, "'Until rigorous standards are applied, TrailMind risks offering a beautifully branded escape hatch—more cathedral than clinic.'" Hannah looked up. "That line's going to haunt us. It's poetic. Poisonous."

"She's not trying to kill us outright." Maya continued pacing. "It's containment. Someone—maybe Darren—wants us boxed in as 'adjunct wellness', not core public health infrastructure."

"Which lets NeuroEase own the clinical lane. Regulation, reimbursement, the serious science play." Matthew swiped his hand through his hair.

"Public perception is protocol," Sam observed. "No one reads the method section. They read Elspeth."

"So we answer." Maya stopped pacing. "Not defensively. We show what the work feels like from inside—the kids in the pilot, the counselors, that veteran who said the forest returned his inner clock. Story for story. I'll ask the field-based co-designers to lead with what they felt—they know how to translate this better than any of us."

"Truth." Hannah nodded. "I've got a meeting with Thura Aung in the Senator's constituency office. Want me to use my blog to invite Elspeth to walk Spectacle Island herself?"

Hannah made eye contact with each of the team to confirm assent.

"Elspeth thinks the public deserves data?" Sam grinned cunningly. "Let's make ours bleed a little."

There was a beat of silence as the tension shifted and the group focused.

"Good. Let's show them what synthetic cognition feels like when it touches a human life." Maya scooped up her notebook.

"Wait." Sam jumped up. "What if this isn't just about the *Globe* piece? What if we're looking at the first move in a full-court press?"

"Coordinated?" Matthew frowned.

"Think about it. Elspeth drops this piece just hours after

we secure the advisory committee's green light to brief the Public Health & Parks Committee and the Boston Public Health Commission. And Darren's not dumb—planting seeds of doubt before we get a foot in the door."

Maya began to pace again.

"To secure the NeuroEase pill position as 'leveling the playing field'—easy access, predictable dosage, no need for wilderness permits or trained facilitators. Just swallow and soothe."

"Ugh," Hannah groaned. "While we're the boutique therapy for crunchy kids in fleece. Worse, as inconsistent therapy for vulnerable ones. It's death by rigor."

Matthew nodded. "That makes the Public Health Commissioner the keystone. If Dillahunt doesn't back a credible, community-centered pilot, we'll be stuck chasing double-blind purity tests while the need keeps accelerating."

"Alright." Maya held up her hands. "Operation counter-influence begins today—quiet, local, relational."

"Cool." Hannah pulled out her phone. "I've got a coffee with a City Council staffer on Monday. I'll get a read. Float the idea that TrailMind isn't an alternative, it's a complement to traditional care—but one that roots mental health in lived environment and self-agency."

"Any chance you can move that up?" Maya asked.

"Done," affirmed Hannah.

Maya added, "We may get some help from Josh Sterne—I'm not sure—he could go either way. He's flying in ... we're meeting for coffee tomorrow."

"Huh. You think Josh will be 'quiet, local, and relational'?" Matthew asked, as Sam looked, wide-eyed, from Matthew to Maya and back to Matthew.

"*ClearFrame* Josh Sterne? Wow. *ClearFrame* is the go-to for people who are civically engaged ... or who want to sound like they are."

Matthew nodded and winked at Sam. "I'll reach out to Dr. Kwan, the research coordinator at BPHC. Dillahunt trusts him. I'll lay the groundwork for a conversation about co-design, not confrontation. If there's going to be a study, we steer it."

Hannah stood and slung her messenger bag across her body. "I'll dig into the donor networks around the Civic Innovation Circle. If Darren's funneling influence through Elspeth, someone's writing those checks. Might be a backchannel to expose.

"And Michelle is working an angle with the Massachusetts Health Insurance providers." She added, "I might have, kind of promised that they could have access to the MIT quantum-algorithms team ..."

Maya nodded. "I'll flag that for Amina. And while you're out there, let's see if we can get a read if anyone's been nudging intake prompts in the field kits to bias data or perception in ways that could undermine TrailMind's public positioning."

Then she looked from face to face. "This is more than optics now. Someone's coming for the foundation—legitimacy, safety, public trust. We hold those lines or we lose the program."

DARREN STOOD BY THE WINDOW, reading Elspeth Channing's column on his tablet. The headline alone—"The Science of Solace"—made his molars ache. By the third paragraph, he let out a low exhale, one part amusement, two parts dread.

His publicist, Lynne, slipped in holding a reusable coffee cup and an already-flagged printout.

"You've read it?"

Darren didn't look up. "She's good. Too good."

Lynne perched on the edge of the couch, crossed one leg over the other. "You want me to prep a response?"

"I want to know who's talking to her before someone points the finger at us. This isn't just Elspeth being Elspeth. She's quoting language I haven't used publicly in a decade—'precision placation'? That was Matthew's term."

"You think he's leaking?"

"No. Not his style. But someone who knows his style. Start with the advisory committee roster. See who overlaps with both TrailMind and Channing's orbit."

Lynne gave a small nod and slipped into the hallway.

An hour later, Lynne tapped her fingers while Audrey, Darren's longtime D.C. fixer, skimmed Channing's column on a second screen.

Audrey didn't look up. "It's Evie."

"Evie Chen? From CDC? But she was the one who shepherded the Advance Market Commitment for NeuroEase through HHS and Congress."

"She's at EverCura now—clear-eyed about how the HHS tracks were shifting. She took the severance package and complied with the reigning message to be more 'productive' in the private sector. She met with Channing twice last month. Nothing off the record."

Lynne hissed through her teeth. "Darren's not going to like that."

Audrey finally looked over. "Evie going from champion to hatchet woman? No, he won't."

"SHE'S SMART," Darren acknowledged when Lynne delivered the name. "And strategic. But why tank TrailMind? It's the logical partner to bring in."

"Audrey thinks EverCura wants a piece—or all—of the AMC."

Darren was quiet for a beat, processing. Of course they did. EverCura didn't need TrailMind's ethos. They needed its clearance codes. The field credibility. The stamp of public-good legitimacy, minus the friction of academic idealism and co-design charrettes.

He could see Evie's strategy: EverCura stepping in as the turnkey integrator. Strip the emotion, patent the interface layer, swap the participatory design for "community-informed modular deployment" with just enough local flavor to pass muster on the Hill. Wrap it all in a public-private toolkit that looked democratic from a distance and proprietary up close.

And Evie? She wasn't tanking TrailMind because it was a threat. She was neutralizing it—rendering it unnecessary. Why partner when you can outflank?

Classic Evie. Quiet knife work. All clean edges, Darren thought.

He glanced back at Lynne.

"Keep your eye on how they frame 'civic engagement'. If they start quoting Maya's user trust metrics without actually looping her in, we'll know they're pulling a full containment play."

Darren tented his fingers, calculating the next move. "Call Hannah Oak. Ask her—*politely*—to set up a visit to Spectacle Island."

"Hannah Oak? You're sure?"

"She's already shaping the narrative. If we wait, we're just responding to her framing."

Lynne raised an eyebrow. "And what framing are you going for?"

Darren turned back to the window, Boston Harbor gleaming in the distance.

"Something bigger than the binary. Call it "The Science of Solace, Part II" if you have to."

***

JOSH WAS ALREADY SEATED when Maya walked into Café Fixe in Brookline, hood up, eyes bleary. Alexis Kim and Kris Barsa, also former Terrascope members, were with him.

Josh stood and offered a tight smile. "I thought I'd tap into the old brain trust." Josh gestured to a fourth cup on the table. "Quad-shot oat cortado. For the woman currently being accused of turning grief into spa music."

"God forbid anyone feel something without a prescription," Maya said dryly.

"Elspeth's piece isn't journalism." Josh waved a dismissive hand. "It's an immunization—it's preemptive. Someone's trying to inoculate the public against believing TrailMind could ever be ... effective."

"You think she wrote it to tank us?"

"No." Josh stroked his salt-and-pepper stubble. "I think she wrote it to position herself—just ahead of a coming storm. But the frame? 'Cathedral over clinic'? That's not neutral. That's branding. And it's not hers."

"Darren's?"

"Three phrases match near-verbatim to language in Neuro-Ease investor decks." Josh's voice softened, but his eyes sharpened. "You've got a narrative war on your hands, Maya."

Maya sighed. "I'm not a war general. I'm a systems designer. A reluctant one at that."

Josh tapped the corner of his notebook. "You do realize that we're sitting inside the frame of a much bigger story."

Maya sighed, tugging gently on her braid. "Josh. Please. This isn't your next feature. It's a policy proposal. A budget hearing. Bureaucracy."

"But that's exactly why it is a story," Josh pressed. "The torch is passing, Maya. Whether you want to call it generational or institutional, that's what's happening. The collapse of the federal grant scaffolding isn't just a funding problem—it's a governance problem. And what you're building with Trail-Mind isn't just tech. It's civic architecture."

"You're writing about TrailMind?"

"I'm writing about TrailMind and NeuroTech," he said. "Because what's unfolding around the collapse of federal mental health funding is a generational handoff happening in real time."

"Unpack the generational part," Kris suggested.

"NeuroTech's top-down, scalable, pharmaceutical intervention? That's a Boomer legacy model steeped in ROI and smooth-curving metrics." Josh was picking up steam.

"TrailMind's bottom-up systems, co-designed embodiment, decentralization, personal agency? That's the Millennial ethos – backed by tech but anchored in inclusion, social good."

"Preach." Alexis offered Josh a high five.

"Plus, how can I resist the symbolism?" Josh's eyes twinkled. "Reclaimed public lands, once garbage dumps, now resilience labs..."

"I'm not sure that's going to galvanize the funding gatekeepers." Maya rubbed her temples.

Alexis smiled. "That's why Kris and I are here. Educators and veterans have a stake in this, too. You're offering something that lives between private markets and fragile public programs

—participatory design, lived-experience governance. That's why it's scary to them."

Josh nodded. "Maya, I know you. You built TrailMind because you couldn't not build it. That's the story Elspeth's missing. And it's the one I want to tell. It's the story Hannah Oak has been telling. I plan to ask her to lead the *ClearFrame* reporting on it."

Maya glanced at him. "Hannah?"

Josh nodded.

"Her reporting keeps circling the essential question: what counts as public health? And who gets to decide? She's been pushing at that tension—where mental health, climate, technology, and equity intersect—harder than any of us."

Maya's shoulders softened slightly. "She's good."

"She's more than good. She's asking the right questions at the right moment. And frankly, I think she needs a bigger platform." Josh looked back at Maya directly. "I can offer her full editorial independence. And the reach to keep shaping this conversation long after tomorrow's vote."

Maya blinked. "*ClearFrame?* That's—Josh, that's ... huge."

"She won't say yes right away." Josh flashed a wry smile. "But I think she will. And when she does, this moves out of just one state. The way we talk about what counts as care, what counts as infrastructure—that's national."

Kris knocked his knuckles softly on the table. "It's overdue."

Maya shook her head, half smiling, half daunted. "Josh, you're turning all of us into case studies."

"I'm documenting a pivot, Maya," he replied. "The one you've been building—whether you want the narrative or not."

A long pause settled over the table before Maya finally spoke again, eyes fixed on Josh. "Then make sure the narrative stays rooted in the community. Especially the kids who are drowning."

Josh's voice was gentler now. "That's exactly where Hannah keeps pulling it. She gets it."

After a beat, Alexis leaned in, adding softly, "And we'll help you hold the policy line, Maya. One public hearing at a time."

<hr>

THAT EVENING, Evelyn Chen appeared on Darren's screen, hair tied back, sleeves rolled up, mincing scallions with clinical precision in the kitchen of her U Street Corridor condo.

"I appreciate you making time," Darren said, his voice smooth but wary. "I understand I have you to thank for my invitation to D.C. on Thursday."

Evie didn't look up. "The AMC has a bullseye on it." *Chop, chop.* "Appropriations came back with fresh cut targets." *Chop.* "Anything north of a billion's already circled in red." She brushed the scallions into the pan.

"And yet the invitation's from Oversight." Darren folded his hands. "Which suggests optics, not policy."

Evie finally glanced at the screen. "I'm at EverCura now, Darren. Due diligence is part of the job. Optics and policy aren't opposites. They're nested."

"Let me guess." He leaned forward slightly. "EverCura wants to be the grown-up in the room. License the NeuroEase compound, take over manufacturing, wrap it in a civic trust ribbon. Easier to defend when the hearings start."

Evie lifted a brow, impressed.

"Not far off. We've begun preliminary structuring. If the AMC survives the budget reconciliation, EverCura is prepared to offer NeuroTech a licensing deal. Generous terms, clean transition. No patent drama."

Darren's jaw tightened. "You're trying to reverse-engineer a rescue."

"I'm ensuring continuity," Evie replied, setting down her knife. "You built NeuroEase for clinical speed. We're building the infrastructure it needs to endure."

"And using our language to sell it," he snapped. "'Precision placation'? 'Cognitive scaffolding'? I recognize the lexicon, Evie. I helped write it."

She didn't flinch. "I helped circulate it—back when you and Matthew were still speaking. Those phrases were always meant for public use. We just polished them."

"But you're not interested in partnering with TrailMind."

"No," Evie said simply. "The TrailMind team does compelling fieldwork, but the brand relies too heavily on immersive UX and narrative resonance. That's not scalable at the speed policy demands. EverCura has its own civic engagement methodology—codified, audited, and procurement-ready."

Darren laughed—sharp, humorless. "You're scaling trust with non-disclosure agreements and procurement contracts?"

"We're scaling infrastructure," she replied. "You chased efficiency. I'm designing accountability."

Silence crackled. Finally, Darren said, "You sound like Matthew."

"No," Evie said, returning to her chopping. "Matthew believed the system could be reformed from within." *Chop, chop.* "I've stopped believing that." *Chop.* "I'm replacing it."

She glanced at the screen again. "We'll see you Thursday. Bring your full disclosures."

"I look forward to your testimony under oath," Darren replied, and cut the connection.

He sat back, the screen gone dark, the echo of her voice still humming in the glass. Then said, softly, to no one, "Replacing the system. That's a hell of a rebrand."

FIFTEEN

INTERNAL MEMO—Editorial Eyes Only

Friday, May 29, 2026
From: Josh Sterne, Publisher
Subject: TrailMind vs. NeuroTech—The Generational Story
We Need to Own

Team,

This is not just a feature story. This is the story. What's
unfolding around TrailMind, NeuroTech, and the collapse of
federal anxiety funding is a generational handoff happening in
real time—and if we move quickly, we can frame it before the
legacy outlets reduce it to a tired pharma vs. wellness binary.
Here's what's at stake:

**1. The policy vacuum is generational, not just
political.** The federal clawback of TrailMind's National Park
Service funding isn't a one-off budget fight. It's the visible

evidence of something bigger: Millennials inheriting broken systems that the Boomers can't or won't maintain. Instead of waiting for institutional rescue, they're building civic tech hybrids that live between research, lived experience, and decentralized governance. TrailMind is one such prototype—but it's emblematic of dozens more we'll see in climate adaptation, public health, and education.

2. This isn't "startups vs. government." It's systems design vs. system decay. NeuroTech's AMC-backed anxiety pill is classic late-Boomer technocracy: control the biology, scale the dosage, monetize the fix. TrailMind offers a counter-model rooted in embodied co-design, distributed agency, and community-grounded resilience—meeting Gen Z where they are, without demanding compliance first.

3. The place itself is the metaphor. Spectacle Island was literally a landfill. Now it's the stage for a battle over how we imagine collective healing. That's a generational parable if I've ever seen one.

4. We're uniquely positioned to cover this. Our readers trust us to follow these convergence stories: climate, mental health, emerging civic tech, and the quiet generational transition reshaping public life. *The Times* will cover it as a funding kerfuffle. *Politico* will follow the drug contracts. We can frame it as a generational civic design inflection point.

Proposed package:

I want us on this, full tilt. This is where the post-institutional public sphere is quietly being re-engineered. If we miss it, we're not doing our job.

—Josh

BY MID-DAY ON FRIDAY, Josh's senior editor, Priya, was waiting at a corner table as Hannah arrived, latte in hand.

She jumped right in as Hannah sat down. "We've been tracking your NeuroTech coverage. Your take on the policy side is sharp—and your following? Phenomenal."

"Appreciate that." Hannah nodded. "But I'm not looking to trade independent for corporate."

Priya gave Hannah a genuine smile, eyes vibrant. "*Clear-Frame* isn't corporate in the old sense. We're building civic verticals—climate, mental health, youth futures. What you're doing already fits the generational shift series that Josh just launched."

Hannah cringed. "Youth futures? That's a little ... brand-deck, isn't it?"

Priya grinned, unbothered. "Sure, the name's a little pitch-deck-y. But the lane is real. It's everything that shapes the ground Gens Z and Alpha are standing on—climate anxiety, screen addiction, education debt, workforce precarity, digital identity, AI overwhelm.

"You were covering the beat before we built the desk. We're just catching up."

"But does your youth futures desk fit my tone?" Hannah arched a brow. "I write what I see. I own my feed, my subscriber lists, my voice."

Priya started to respond, but Hannah cut in.

"I'm not here for some false neutrality, Priya. That whole 'view from nowhere' thing? That's not journalism. Not anymore.

"Today's journalism means owning your lens. I believe in transparency over detachment. I platform multiple perspectives because advocacy needs complexity—not because I'm pretending I don't have a stake."

"Not staff, then," Priya nodded, serious now. "Would a

hosted partnership work? You syndicate your branded blog posts under ClearFrame's umbrella. We scale distribution. You get reach, data, ad-free monetization. You stay you."

"Full syndication. My branded blog. My interviews." Hannah ticked off her requirements on her fingers.

"Exactly." Priya's eyes sparkled again. "We plug you into investigative resources, AI-assisted research tools, even cross-pod with our policy desk."

"Define cross-pod," Hannah said, still guarded.

"We pair you up with our in-house podcast team—co-produced content, joint interviews, shared reporting, dual-branded investigative runs. We're at 6.3 million subscribers with an average thirty-one percent daily engagement. That's two million ears a day—four million, if you want to count anatomically." Priya grinned.

"Take a look at the post I've got queued for tonight." Hannah tapped her phone to Priya's. "I'm calling Darren Katsaros out. Publicly. You sure ClearFrame wants to go out on this limb?"

Priya read, eyes widening with delight. "This—this is why we cross-pollinate with creator-led brands. We'll push this hard."

"Unfiltered Unprescribed—bigger stage." Hannah sighed. "OK. I'm in."

HANNAH HAD HUSTLED from her meeting with Priya to Boston City Hall. Councilwoman Flores' office, specifically.

"Luis—I appreciate you making time." Hannah held up her recorder. "Just so we're clear, I'm here as a journalist. The piece will run under the ClearFrame youth futures desk. Off-the-record is always an option—just flag it."

Luis nodded. "Understood. But you're not just reporting, are you?"

"I report with a perspective, not from a script." Hannah sat up straighter. "If we pretend journalism doesn't shape policy, we're lying to ourselves. My job isn't to play referee—it's to surface the stakes, amplify the voices at the edge, and let readers make decisions with their eyes open."

"I understand the Boston Harbor Islands Park Advisory Committee will be briefing Councilor Flores.

"TrailMind is part of that bundle, and I'm covering it because I believe it's more than a wellness program—it's a systems question. One this city needs to ask out loud."

"Got it. So, the Boston Harbor Islands Park Advisory Committee is asking the City Council to allocate time, staff, and at least a partial funding line to a 'public health' program," Luis made quotation marks in the air. "But it doesn't involve licensed clinicians, prescription plans, or validated medical protocols."

"TrailMind is about public space as therapeutic infrastructure," Hannah explained patiently. "It helps citizens, especially kids, name what's happening inside them, instead of just muting it."

"I don't have to tell you that NeuroEase has won the high ground as the preferred response to youth anxiety. Councilor Flores is already in working group conversations."

Hannah nodded. "I've seen the memos. NeuroEase has a place—it can stabilize some kids. But it doesn't translate the anxiety. It manages symptoms. It doesn't give meaning. And that distinction is everything."

She hesitated, then tapped the pause button.

"I was thirteen when my parents died. I had no options but foster care. I got put on Prozac before we left the cemetery. It got me through the days—but it didn't help me understand the grief. It just made me less of a problem to manage."

"That's a hard history," Luis said softly. "But you came out the other side."

"Not without detours." Hannah shook her head.

"It took me years—years walking in nature—to feel safe in my own skin again. That didn't happen in a clinic. It happened on a trail. That's what TrailMind creates: conditions where the nervous system gets context instead of alarms. Where kids learn to listen inward, not just comply outward."

"You're saying climate anxiety's part of this?"

"I'm saying kids are internalizing a global crisis they had no hand in making—and most have never even experienced the nurturing smells and sounds of a natural space. TrailMind doesn't sedate. It reconnects."

"Flores will want to see the return on investment. Measurable outcomes."

Hannah counted the outcomes with her fingers as she spat out the answers like automatic ammunition. "Fewer behavioral incidents. Fewer emergency escalations. Youth who stay on-track—literally and metaphorically. As I'll suggest in my next blog, a liaison from your office could co-author the accountability from day one."

"She'll want oversight."

"She should. There's a lot being asked of the city budget this year. The public shouldn't be paying for serenity, but it absolutely needs to prototype resilience or the next generation of taxpayers will be drawing down on public resources instead of paying in."

"Alright. Let the advisory committee know they'll get to 'yes' faster if they send over a one-pager in advance—with outcomes, youth input, and financials."

"I'll pass that along." Hannah clicked on her recorder again.

"And just so I have your quote—do I have you down as a skeptic, or a cautious maybe?"

Luis raised an eyebrow. "Put me down as someone who knows what's possible—and sometimes likes being proven wrong. Occasionally, politics lets us redefine the possible."

"MATTHEW, if you want us to take TrailMind seriously as a mental health intervention—not just interpretive fluff—we're going to need a robust comparative design." Dr. Leon Kwan was a veteran researcher at the Boston Public Health Commission, best known for his landmark *Lancet* cover story in 1973.

"That means three arms: TrailMind plus meds, TrailMind plus placebo, TrailMind solo. All randomized. All sanctioned by an Institutional Review Board."

"You're proposing we test a somatic regulation tool against psychopharmacology? In a city park?" Matthew asked, raising an eyebrow.

"I'm proposing we test for outcomes. Measurable ones. Otherwise we're selling ambience and reassurance."

"We're not selling anything," Matthew opened his hands in supplication. "And I'd caution against drawing equivalency between what TrailMind offers and what medication targets. They operate in different systems—neurochemical modulation and nervous system co-regulation—and on different timelines."

"That's exactly why we study them. And right now, policy favors protocols with data. If TrailMind works, prove it. Show us a shift in cortisol, heart rate variability, skin conductance level response. I'm not trying to be the Grinch here. I'm trying to give you a shot at legitimacy."

"The field data from Spectacle Island is already fully IRB-approved—MIT and National Park Service both signed off.

Informed consent, anonymized datasets, encrypted storage. The usual safeguards."

"I'm aware they have institutional clearance," Kwan huffed. "But IRB approval doesn't guarantee external reproducibility or long-term safety."

"It does mean they're not flying blind ethically. The biosensor data we're seeing is valid for community-based interventions—which is the entire premise we're here to evaluate."

Kwan gave a tight nod. "And yet ... the people making budget decisions love pills. Standardized. Prescribed. Insured. Done. If we don't anchor this in a language they already understand, TrailMind stays a 'nice-to-have' pilot."

"So you want us to insert humans into a framework that presumes regulation must be pharmaceutical unless proven otherwise."

"No, Dr. Venable, I'm asking you to meet the bar." Kwan snapped his folder closed. "You say TrailMind changes nervous systems. Great. Let's track those changes—against control conditions that matter."

"Dr. Kwan—I watched a kid spiral out after being told a placebo would calm her down. It didn't.

"What worked was a ranger who walked with her for ten minutes without saying a word. You can't blind that." Kwan paused.

"No. But you can design a study that honors it. If you're willing to let the data speak—even when it's messy. That's where the truth lives."

Matthew sighed. "I'll bring it back to the advisory committee. But I want youth advisors in the design process. No ghost studies on the backs of vulnerable bodies. That's nonnegotiable."

Kwan shrugged. "That's what the Institutional Review Board is for."

ON SATURDAY, at 12:01 a.m., a new banner joined the slider topping the *ClearFrame* web portal. It announced an Unprescribed blog from Hannah Oak.

By 6:05 a.m. Michelle Venable had already clicked through.

"*ClearFrame* is promoting Hannah's blog," Michelle announced to a steamy bathroom where Jack was showering before heading out to a Chamber of Commerce meeting. "Her response to Elspeth's column is spot on. Would you like a boiled egg?"

By 8:00 a.m., 683,972 others had also clicked through.

SIXTEEN

Unprescribed Blog, May 30, 2026

"Public Parks, Public Health, and the False Choice Between Pill and Path"
By Hannah Oak

Let's get one thing straight: I don't do puff pieces. If I'm spending my time writing about the Boston Harbor Islands, it's not because I want to cosplay as Thoreau on a deadline. It's because something real is happening out there—and the public deserves to understand it before the narrative hardens into a binary.

At this week's Boston Harbor Islands Park Advisory Committee meeting, I witnessed something rare: civic courage. Faced with mounting youth anxiety, exhausted frontline park staff, and a mental health infrastructure stretched beyond recognition, the committee voted unanimously to move forward with forming a task force. Not to rubber-stamp a tech platform or fund an app. But to ask a deeper question:

What if public parks were treated as real public infrastructure for emotional regulation? That's not a marketing pitch. That's a design challenge—and a moral one.

Now, if you've read Elspeth Channing's latest Globe column, you'd be forgiven for thinking that the only options on the table are between NeuroEase, a pharmaceutical solution marketed as clinical rigor incarnate, and TrailMind, which she paints as a glorified wellness spa in a cedar dome.

But that framing is not only lazy—it's dangerous. Because the real choice facing us isn't pill versus path. It's reduction versus integration.

Yes, NeuroEase has cleared clinical trials. It's compact, consistent, and requires no ferry ride or chaperone. But before we crown it the savior of youth mental health, consider this: The federally-funded Advance Market Commitment to NeuroTech accelerated access to a non-sedating, fast-acting neuroregulator, NeuroEase, that targets anxiety via circuit stabilization. But the AMC also created a frictionless funnel— low entry barriers, no tapering protocol, no structural incentive to help people off the meds.

NeuroTech built a pipeline with no exit ramp.

This is the difference between reducing care to a pill and integrating care into people's lives. The former is faster. The latter is harder. But only one of them asks what healing really needs.

I ask again: What are the social and ethical costs of friction- less care?

I respect Elspeth's call for rigor, but I question the conve- nience of her sources—none of whom seem to have visited a TrailMind pilot or spoken with the youth who helped design it.

So let me offer a counterpoint, grounded not in ambient hues but in human experience.

I was on Spectacle Island last week. I saw teenagers from Dorchester and Chelsea sit in wind shelters they helped design.

I heard a seventeen-year-old say, "I didn't know silence could feel like company."

Another told me, "I used to think nature was just green stuff. But this made me feel like the island was listening back."

That's not affect choreography. That's nervous system regulation—and if we can make it public, accessible, and locally stewarded, then it is public health infrastructure.

Boston's City Council Committee on Environment, Resiliency, and Parks already carries the mandate for public oversight. Community-based elected officials offer real-time feedback loops. Accountability shouldn't freeze innovation; it should drive it.

The future of mental health can't be left in the hands of Big Pharma. Even NeuroTech, developer of the NeuroEase pill, has a suite of non-pharmaceutical interventions—from emotion-predictive wearables to VR-based self-regulation tools. NeuroTech is sleek, well-funded, and deeply strategic.

It's also not the enemy.

So maybe the real innovation isn't choosing one over the other. Maybe it's asking how we build a mesh of care that includes all of it—drugs and dirt paths, sensors and shelter, code and coastline.

Readers—if you'd like me to invite NeuroTech CEO Darren Katsaros to a live blog conversation, where we can go deeper into the ethics, aesthetics, and future of non-clinical mental health interventions, give this post a thumbs up.

Let's talk about what resilience looks like—on an island, in a lab, or somewhere in between.

I'll leave you with this: Massachusetts' senior U.S. Senator recently said, "Our kids don't need faster pills—they need safer ground."

If TrailMind proves anything, it's that healing can come from dirt paths, not just data sheets.

I'm not holding my breath for federal funding amid the ongoing churn in national priorities—but let's give props to the Senator for saying the quiet part out loud: this isn't about speed. It's about safety. And public policy doesn't work if it's only efficient—it has to be effective.

<hr>

THE GOVERNOR STOOD at her kitchen island, nursing black coffee, her iPad propped against the fruit bowl. She scrolled through the latest *ClearFrame* push: "Public Parks, Public Health, and the False Choice Between Pill and Path," by Hannah Oak.

She skimmed quickly but carefully, eyebrows rising.

By the time she reached the paragraph quoting the "safer ground" comment, she set her mug down with a soft thud. She touched the VOIP icon on her iPad.

"Ruiz," her chief of policy answered promptly, despite the early hour on a Saturday morning.

"Danny!" she said. "I want Joe D. to know we're watching the coverage—the *Globe*, now *ClearFrame*." She sighed. "Tell him I expect the Harbor Islands Park Advisory Committee to brief me on their formal recommendation no later than Friday. Get something on the calendar."

"That's tight," Ruiz pointed out.

"Good. They've had months. We're not funding eternal debates while kids spiral. TrailMind's not some moonshot—it's a pilot. They can either pilot it or explain to the press why they're still wringing their hands."

"Copy that. And ... you saw the reader count?"

"Approaching seven hundred thousand by breakfast. This story's not going away."

"DR. KWAN?" Danny Ruiz asked when a stock image icon appeared on the screen. The Boston skyline with a faint Department of Public Health watermark overlay.

"Kwan here," came the disembodied answer.

"Quick flag," Ruiz said.

"The Governor expects the Boston Harbor Islands Park Advisory Committee to brief her on their final recommendation this week. I'm holding Thursday at 3:45 p.m. and Friday at 8:15 a.m. on her calendar. Joe D. will let us know by noon today which slot you prefer."

Dr. Kwan's face registered surprise as he switched on his camera. "That's ... ambitious. We're still refining the research design language."

"You may want to pull up *ClearFrame*'s top banner today." Ruiz's tone was more directive than suggestive. "Hannah Oak just published a fairly viral piece. This window is closing fast."

There was a brief silence as Kwan presumably clicked through.

"Yes, I see," Kwan said tightly. "Thank you for the ... guidance."

PRIYA'S PHONE buzzed with a Slack message.

@Josh 09:13 a.m.

Governor's leaning on the Barnacle. Hannah's piece is moving needles. Don't let her go quiet.
@Priya 09:14 a.m.
Already greenlit next interview cycle. Tell Darren to buckle up.

ACROSS THE RIVER, at a table tucked into the back of Mentón, Darren Katsaros sat with Marisol Vargas, former HHS undersecretary and now vice chair of the NeuroTech board, and Victor Kane, a founding investor with a gift for aligning profit with policy. No staff, no press—just oysters, grilled romaine, and a conversation that would shape Neuro-Tech's next act.

Marisol set down her glass of iced tea. "So. Evie Chen's pitch—does EverCura want to buy us out?"

"Not buy us out," Darren said. "Buy distribution. They'll pay a licensing fee to manufacture and move NeuroEase under their public-private umbrella. They get the field network; we keep the intellectual property."

Victor raised a brow. "That's a bird in the hand, Darren. AMC funds are shaky, Congress is twitchy, and EverCura's offering clean margins. Why hesitate?"

"Because they don't just want distribution," Darren replied. "They want the narrative—the right to decide what counts as treatment. EverCura's betting that the public wants a frictionless fix. I'm betting the wind's shifting. People are starting to realize NeuroEase treats symptoms, not causes. They're waking up to the idea that anxiety isn't a chemistry error—it's a context failure."

Marisol leaned back, assessing him. "And you think Trail-Mind can undo what the economy and its algorithms broke?"

"I think TrailMind—and everything like it—is the next public-opinion wave."

Darren swiped across his tablet: Elspeth Channing's column, Hannah Oak's viral clip, and engagement charts climbing like a fever.

"Adjuncts, not antagonists. Participation as medicine. The cultural current's turning. Evie's trying to surf it. I'd rather steer it."

Victor folded his arms. "What does steering look like?"

"Start with legitimacy. Talk to Matthew Venable. He built the ethical framework Evie's now trying to white-label. If we can bring him to the table—or at least into the narrative—it signals that NeuroTech isn't the villain here."

Marisol narrowed her eyes. "You're serious about approaching Matthew?"

"I am. But I'll route it through *ClearFrame*'s Hannah Oak first. Let her frame the story. She's already moving hearts and headlines. If she sees us reaching toward collaboration instead of conquest, she'll soften the line between pill and practice."

Victor snorted. "You mean use her."

Darren smiled faintly. "I mean partner—strategically. Her credibility buys us space to pivot before Congress does it for us."

Marisol set down her fork. "You think the Oversight hearings will go that badly?"

"I think they'll go honest. Lawmakers are catching on: a pill pipeline with no exit ramp isn't sustainable. They'll demand integrated care. If we look rigid, we lose the license and the moral high ground.

"But if we look adaptive—licensing NeuroEase while publicly aligning with community-based interventions—we stay indispensable."

Victor nodded slowly. "So EverCura gets the trucks, we keep the trust."

"Exactly. We license distribution, not direction."

Marisol studied him for a long moment, then said quietly, "Float it. See how Matthew reacts. If he bites, I'll line up the board."

Darren lifted his glass, the ghost of a smile crossing his face. "To context, then. And to staying one step ahead of the cure."

SEVENTEEN

Hannah stood at the bow of the ferry, Darren leaning on the railing beside her. He watched the wind catch her hood, liberating her hair, making the spikes dance in the salt air.

"Thanks for accommodating me on a Sunday," Darren said. When she didn't say anything, he pointed at the low green of Spectacle Island as it grew on the horizon. "You know," he said over the motor's drone, "this used to be a garbage dump."

"I know," Hannah replied. "Now it's a park."

"Still a good metaphor," he muttered. "Legacy liabilities."

She shot him a look.

"Don't push your luck."

"If you wanted an on-the-record interview, all you had to do was ask me," Darren said.

Hannah shrugged.

"Ah, but knowing how much you value rigor, I thought I'd survey public opinion before deciding whether anyone but me cares what you think."

"Ouch." Darren grinned like a kid on his first ferry ride as he turned his face to the sun and the salt spray. She might be trying to take him down, but he was surprised how much he was enjoying the tussle.

When they docked, Darren stepped off the ferry with a look Hannah couldn't quite read—half curiosity, half calculation.

He'd actually come.

"Welcome to my sandbox," she said, spreading her arms toward the narrow beach and the green sweep of the island behind her.

He laughed. "Not as many biometric scanners."

"Not yet," she shot back. "Though I hear the rangers are working on retinal ID for seagulls."

He grinned, conceding the jab.

Hannah led Darren uphill along a narrow path, past patches of beach plum and lichen-covered signage. The city shimmered behind them like a mirage.

Near the summit, they arrived at a curved shelter made of repurposed wood and polycarbonate. Teenagers lounged on weathered benches or in the tall grass nearby, some sketching, others writing with analog insistence in notebooks. No one was on their phone.

"They journal every Sunday," Hannah said, nodding toward them. "No prompts. Just wind, space, and time."

Darren took it in, arms crossed, his mouth twitching subtly.

"Your sandbox had sensors," she said. "This," she gestured to the beach below, "has actual sand ... salty air, peaty moss, birds."

A gust rattled the shelter. One of the teens stood and walked a few yards away to cry privately, calmly, in the direction of the water. No one interrupted. No one documented it.

Darren watched, oddly still. "You trust this?"

"I trust them," she said. "It's not scalable. It's not clean data.

But it's something anxiety tech can't simulate: a nervous system that isn't being watched."

He glanced at her. "You're romanticizing nature."

"Maybe. But you romanticize frictionless control."

There was a long silence. Wind knifed across the hill.

Then Darren conceded, "You're right. What you're showing me—it's the opposite of infrastructure. It's fragile, human-scale. But it's also ... alive."

He shook his head. "This would never pass a boardroom. No metrics, no compliance. Just ... people being anxious."

She tilted her head, watching him. "You sound almost reverent."

"Don't quote me on that," he murmured.

"I wasn't planning to," she said.

Darren glanced at her, something sparking between amusement and challenge. "You're not just observing. You're curating. Advocating. Playing the system as much as reporting on it."

She felt the heat rise in her cheeks but held his gaze. "Still trying to make me confess my hedge?"

"Maybe." His tone softened. "Or maybe I just wanted to see what makes you keep coming back here."

The ferry horn carried faintly across the water. Hannah exhaled, letting the silence linger.

Darren sat down on the bench, elbows on knees, watching the tide slide against the stonework at the island's edge.

"You know what?" he said, almost to himself. He paused, then pulled out his phone.

Hannah raised an eyebrow.

He powered it off, placed it beside him.

That surprised her. For a man who lived on data, it was an almost indecent act of attention. The gesture landed heavier than he knew—like a quiet invitation.

"I'm all ears," he said. His eyes held hers, steady now, as if he were daring her to fill the silence.

———

THE GRAVEL CRUNCHED beneath Sam's sneakers as she stepped out of the zippy green Zipcar. The sun was sharp but kind, filtered through the light canopy of early-summer leaves. She scanned the open fields surrounded by a neat split-rail fence. Beyond it, a pack of dogs—each with a different coat and energy—moved with alert ease across an agility course.

She remembered Maya once saying, *Therapeutic anchors arise when safety meets curiosity.*

A tall figure stood at the far end, still as a pine.

She waved with both hands, a little bounce in her step as she crossed the field. "Hi! Kris? I'm Sam. Thanks for meeting with me."

Kris Barsa turned, gave a slight nod, and walked over, boots silent in the soft turf. "You're Maya's grad assistant. Or, former grad assistant, right?"

"Guilty." Sam grinned. "Still emotionally attached to the team. I just started a job designing affect-responsive algorithms —trying to teach code what nervous systems already know."

"Well, the dogs don't use platforms. But they know feelings when they walk into a room."

"Exactly why I'm here," Sam replied. "TrailMind talks about self-efficacy spikes—moments when someone realizes they can change their own state. I want Kieran to feel that. Not through an app, through a heartbeat."

Kris nodded slowly. "Tell me about the kid."

Sam took a breath. "His name's Kieran. He's twelve. He's smart, funny—well, he used to be. Lately, he's ... silent. With-drawn. His therapist says he's in a freeze state. Not engaging at school. Barely sleeping. The meds aren't helping. And even their school comfort dog didn't reach him."

Kris's eyes narrowed slightly. "Comfort dogs are trained for environments, not attachments. Bonding work is different."

"That's what Matthew said. He said you focus on full-spectrum dogs—bonding, tasks, regulation. That you've had success with kids like Kieran."

"The key's not teaching the dog tricks. It's teaching the human that they're safe. Dogs mirror regulation. But only when the connection is earned."

Sam's mind flicked to Maya's whiteboard list, *Inclusive prompts → invitation, not instruction.*

"So the dog's behavior invites the kid's nervous system to rejoin the room?"

"That's one way to put it."

He offered to send her a folder with profiles of the service dogs he was training. "Choose two or three that might fit with your family's circumstances and we can set up a meet-and-greet."

"Thank you, I appreciate that."

She gave Kris a warm smile. "And maybe, down the line, we can document what works. TrailMind's trying to map collective impact—how relational practices ripple outward."

Kris half smiled. "If it helps the next kid and the next dog, I'm in."

They walked to the fence. Puppies tumbled in the grass. A young shepherd herded them back toward the center.

An Afghan hound poised herself on the A-frame like a kinetic sculpture. When she scented them, she leapt down and loped over.

"She's beautiful," Sam cooed as the dog rose to meet her gaze.

"Lumen," Kris said. "Ten months old. Intuitive but steady. Needs a challenge."

Sam reached out, palm open. The dog pressed her nose into it and sighed—a tiny, embodied feedback loop. *Therapeutic anchor—achieved*, Sam thought.

"We could try a weekend orientation with Lumen and Kieran," Kris offered, intrigued by the dog's response to the woman. "No promises. See what the dog picks up."

"Thank you. That's ... more than I hoped."

Kris's eyes softened. "Just be warned—she might pick you first."

Sam laughed, eyes bright again.

"I'll take that risk."

———

DOWNHILL FROM THE SUMMIT, a sound trail curved into the wooded spine of the island. At its entrance, Nia stood with a small group of teens holding a battered canvas tote filled with sensor bands, laminated maps, and biodegradable pencils.

She spotted Hannah and waved. "Hey! You made it."

"Just observing today," Hannah called back, stepping aside and giving Darren a small nudge forward.

"He's curious."

As Darren was swept along in the group, Hannah stayed at the trailhead, face lifted to the sun. She made no move to follow, to mediate, or to watch. Just stood in the wind and waited.

Twenty minutes later, Darren emerged from the trail alone. His NeuroTech fleece was flecked with bits of bark and leaf. He held the notecard they'd given him—creased now. She noticed his handwriting was tight, deliberate. She waited but said nothing.

He looked up. "I sat on a boulder—half-covered in moss."
He hesitated. "I kept expecting something to ping. But it didn't.
I didn't."

One of the teens—maybe fifteen, with paint on their jeans
and a badge that read Field Co-Designer—loped down the trail
and handed Darren a clipboard. They didn't say anything, just
offered it with a small, knowing nod. As if to say, *You're one of
us now. You noticed something. That counts.*

Darren blinked, then took the clipboard without comment.
He wrote quietly.

As he was handing the clipboard back to the teen, Hannah
raised an eyebrow. "So?"

He shrugged. "Who would have thought that a centuries-
old quiet rock would win the blinking contest with my noisy,
non-stop brain?"

The teen called back over their shoulder, "The rock wins a
lot."

MAYA ARRIVED at Clara's Table ten minutes late for
brunch, her hair still damp from a rushed shower and the faint
smudge of under-eye concealer doing little to hide her fatigue.
The final wave of narrative performance reports—formerly
known as grades—had consumed her Saturday and most of her
Sunday morning.

Alexis stood from a sunny two-top and waved, a coral-pink
scarf bright against her charcoal blazer. "You made it! I almost
ordered you an IV drip of espresso."

Maya laughed, sinking into her seat with a sigh. "Make it a
cortado and I'll name my next algorithm after you."

Over coffee and lemon ricotta pancakes, they swapped
updates—MIT's flexible grading policy, Alexis's new student-

led soil remediation project in Methuen, and Maya's prep for the governor's advisory committee meeting.

"So how's the narrative grading going?" Alexis asked, tilting her head sympathetically.

Maya groaned. "Imagine writing eighty mini-novels about kids on the brink. Except you can't fix anything, just narrate the fall. Honestly, some of these students are doing brilliant work under unthinkable pressure. And some ... are completely underwater. It's like trying to measure learning with a tide gauge in a hurricane."

Alexis nodded. "Same storm, different classroom. My juniors used to joke about procrastinating. Now they just say, 'I disassociated and forgot the week.' And I have to believe them."

They sat in thoughtful silence for a moment, forks idling in syrup.

Maya looked up. "Can I ask you something personal?"

Alexis smiled gently. "Always."

"I've been trying to name something in myself that's never fit. And I think ... I'm asexual." She paused.

"Or somewhere in that realm. I don't feel broken—just ... quiet, I guess. But it's hard to talk about. Especially in queer circles that are already so complex."

Alexis turned her hand palm-up on the table, but kept it still. "Thank you for trusting me. If touch feels grounding right now, my hand's here. If not, that's fine too."

Maya swallowed, eyes stinging. After a pause, she slid her hand, tentative, into Alexis's palm.

"That quietness?" Alexis said softly. "That's not absence. That's your truth arriving without fanfare."

Maya gave a shaky laugh. "I wish my truth had arrived with a user manual."

Alexis smiled. "I hear you. But know that you don't have to map your experience onto anyone else's definition. Desire and intimacy aren't the same currency. Some people lead with one, some with neither, some with both. There's nothing wrong with the way your quiet works."

Alexis squeezed her hand gently, then released it so the choice stayed open. "I can't speak for everyone, but I've always suspected that negotiating intimacy is a learning curve no matter your identity. And you don't have to figure it out alone. Sometimes it helps to see you're in a constellation, not just a lone star."

Maya blinked, letting the words land. "That ... would mean a lot."

"Sometimes hearing someone else's language helps you find your own. There are some writers in the ace community who've articulated things beautifully," Alexis gestured. "About boundaries, desire, connection. If you ever want names, I can send them."

Alexis watched Maya's face to see how the suggestion landed before adding, "If it ever feels helpful, I have a friend who identifies as ace. She's brilliant and kind and would talk with you in a heartbeat — but only if you want that. No pressure."

"Let me start by reading. You know, geek out a bit until I find my frame."

"I'll send you some links on WhatsApp this afternoon," Alexis nodded decisively.

"Thank you." Maya gave Alexis's hand a squeeze and then let go. "I feel a little silly bringing something so ... quiet to you. You've done these incredibly brave things in full daylight. And here I am just trying to understand my own wiring."

Alexis shook her head softly. "Bravery isn't loud, Maya. It's just honesty in motion. What you're doing right now? That counts."

She let that truth settle between them.

"When I was figuring myself out — different path, different questions — I was lucky," Alexis continued. "Not because it was easy, but because I did it during a small window when trans inclusion was gaining traction. My principal advocated for me. My students stood by me. It wasn't perfect, but it was possible."

"And now?" Maya asked.

Alexis's smile faded. "Now I see kids walking the same path, but with landmines hidden under every stepping stone.

"The legislation, the surveillance, the algorithmic bias—it's all ramping up. And school is often the only semi-safe place they have left. If we can't build sanctuary in our classrooms, we have to build it in our cities."

Maya raised an eyebrow. "That sounds like a manifesto."

"It's a prototype. We need actual infrastructure—legal, emotional, educational. I've been working with some folks on a model for youth sanctuary corridors. Think sanctuary cities, but with embedded networks for identity-affirming care, trauma-informed schooling, and zero-extraction data policies."

Maya blinked. "That's ... huge."

"It's overdue." Alexis nodded. "And maybe it's the only way to keep kids from becoming collateral in a system that sees them as threats—or data points. That's why I'm so supportive of the work you're doing in the parks. You get it, too."

The server refilled their coffee. Maya reached for her mug, feeling both sobered and strangely invigorated. "You should have been on a panel at the Common public meeting. Or better yet—host your own."

Alexis grinned. "Only if you build me an alternative reality toolkit to show people how much safer and better the world could be."

Maya raised her mug in mock salute. "Deal. But you have

to promise to save me a dumpling when we run out of funding and all we can afford is sidewalk bao."

Alexis clinked her mug against Maya's. "Sanctuary's always got room for dumplings."

<hr>

THE WIND HAD SOFTENED into a coastal hush, and most of the teenagers had drifted downhill. Darren and Hannah remained on the bench near the journal shelter, staring out at the dull gleam of water. Darren had picked up a stick and was drawing quiet, geometric patterns in the sandy soil.

"So," he said after a pause, still tracing. "TrailMind got clawed."

Hannah turned toward him. "Yeah. Grant terminated for convenience. OK—that language was always in the grant agreement. But then they reversed payment on the Q1 tranche. Poof, gone."

Darren nodded. "And Maya's left holding a bag of employment contracts and purchase orders with nothing behind them."

"Someone suggesting you should be limiting your exposure these days?"

He glanced at her, half-smiling. "Maybe myself. Maybe a donor briefing."

Hannah's expression didn't change. "I thought TrailMind was the kind of thing you'd back."

"I did. Indirectly. Bought into the diagnostics platform they used. But I can't hedge against government backpedaling. You know what they're looking at now, right?"

She nodded. "Your Advance Market Commitment."

"Mm. Congressional Oversight." He pressed the stick into the soil until it snapped.

"If TrailMind funding gets retroactively pulled, we're next. This administration only backs what it thinks it can monetize."

"You afraid they'll claw you too?"

Darren gave a low chuckle. "Afraid? No. Preparing for it? Absolutely. Diversifying." He looked at her now, more candid. "I like my birds in hand. But I don't keep them all in the same damn tree."

Hannah studied him. "You don't seem like someone who's had to worry about clawbacks."

Darren's prepared line—something about synergies and strategic alignment—was halfway to his lips when he caught a flicker in Hannah's face. It wasn't skepticism. It wasn't even the usual journalistic hunger for a quote that could go viral. It was something quieter. Sadder.

Recognition.

The wind caught a strand of hair across her cheek, and she didn't brush it away. Her eyes, usually bright with some internal flame, had gone still—like tidepools after a storm.

It wasn't a poker face. It was the face of someone who already knew. Not just the policy arc or the budget lines—but what it meant, to build something on trust, and watch that trust hollow out. To feel the moment the scaffolding starts to go soft beneath your feet.

That look—haunted, sober, unsurprised—made Darren feel, absurdly, like he'd already told her everything.

"That's because I started hedging when I was twelve," he said.

"My parents owned a restaurant in Trenton. Gyros and Greek salads. Did alright until it didn't. Rent hike, bad flood, slow winter. They lost everything in one quarter. You remember what that was like back then?"

"Not Trenton," she said. "But I remember that year."

Darren nodded. "So yeah. Since then? I never bet on one table. Even when the table's glowing with mission."

He glanced down the hill where the teens were now gathering around a small driftwood sculpture someone had made. The air smelled like seaweed and sun-warmed iron.

After a moment, he asked, casually, "Is that where yours comes from?"

Hannah looked over.

"Your sharpness. Your clarity. You write about anxiety like it's a character in the room. Not a pathology."

Her face stayed neutral, but she didn't deflect.

"My parents died that year, a few months apart. Nothing so tangible as bankruptcy. 'Quiet deaths of despair' is how one demographer now frames it. A social worker hustled me onto twenty milligrams of Prozac before the pastor finished the graveside sermon.

"I know now it's not addictive, but back then that pill was the only lifeline they threw me to work my way through the trauma and the grief. It took me three foggy years to learn how to channel grief. Into attention. Into language."

Darren's instinct, honed in grad school and boardrooms alike, was to offer the polished nod. The empathetic mirror. "That's rare," he said. "Most people channel it into silence."

"I did that too. For eighteen months."

He nodded thoughtfully. "And now you take people out to a windy hill and hand them pens."

"And you," she said, "simulate that same release with a headset and a revenue model."

He smiled sadly. "Different roads. Same mountain."

"No," she said, not unkindly. "Different mountains."

As Hannah turned to start back down the trail, Darren's mind flicked—uninvited—to his old OKCupid profile. *Emotion-*

ally resilient. Avoids unresolved trauma. No savior complexes or fixer fantasies. He had coded that preference like a firewall.

But here she was.

Not asking to be saved. Not broadcasting wreckage. Just laying it down. Facts. It made his own choices feel ... narrower. Safer.

She hadn't been handed a better narrative. She had *made* one.

And he felt, unexpectedly, that maybe he could carry a story like hers. Not as a fixer. Not as a savior. But as someone who could hear it—and it didn't crush him.

"It was never supposed to be a pill."

Hannah turned fully toward him now, schooling her face not to show how surprised she was to hear him admit it.

"It started as a toolkit. Matthew and I—we were designing something small. For high school counselors. For grief.

"We thought if we could give them a better dashboard—nervous system data, real-time feedback—we could prevent collapse. Not cure it. Just catch it."

Hannah's voice was barely above the wind. "So what happened?" she asked—not as a journalist now, but as someone who'd felt the same drift between meaning and momentum.

Darren drew another shape in the dirt—a half-finished spiral. "The money showed up. The feedback loops got tighter. Congress needed a fix that made them look responsive, so we chased the optimization curve."

She watched the spiral. "Maybe stories can curve back."

"Maybe they should." He glanced toward the harbor. "Matthew said we were flattening the human part out of it. He wasn't wrong. I told myself if we didn't scale it, someone else would—worse, shallower, weaponized for profit. And maybe I even believed that.

"But I never asked the harder question: why Congress was

desperate for a top-down fix in the first place. The AMC made sense in a briefing deck, but it was scaffolding built to calm panic, not to hold weight. And scaffolding built for show rots faster than you expect."

Silence stretched again. Not tense—just deep.

Then Hannah said, "So why tell me this?"

He shrugged. "You already knew."

Her eyes softened, but she didn't smile. "Yeah," she said. "I did. But it's different hearing you say it."

Darren looked down at the snapped stick in his hand and then let it fall. "Maybe it's time to say more."

EIGHTEEN

It was still early on Monday, the first day of June, and the white board in E14-647 looked like it belonged in a campaign war room rather than a tech lab.

Stakeholders were tagged and organized in columns: On Board, Undecided, Obstacle.

- Historical Society - On Board (Nina)
- Fiona Kane, Boston Harbor Now - On Board (Camille)
- State Rep. David Kwon - TDB (Maya)
- Rev. Anita Garza, Inner Harbor Youth Alliance (NGO) - Undecided (Ravi)
- The City Council Committee on Parks and Public Health - On Board (tentatively) NOTE: Send over a one-pager with outcomes, youth input, and financials (Hannah)
- The Boston Public Health Commission (Matthew)

Matthew's eyes lingered over his name tagged to the Boston

Public Health Commission atop the Obstacle list. "Kwan says the Public Health Commission will require full-blown experimental research. We'd be looking at six months minimum for IRB approvals and another six-to-twelve months of field data."

Sam bounced into the room waving her phone in the air. "I found it."

"Your phone?" Maya looked at her askance.

Sam dropped her phone on the table. "The script. I tracked the language back to the Inner Harbor Youth Alliance. Same facilitators. Same phrasing. Verbatim from three input sessions this month. These weren't organic concerns—they were seeded. *'Do you feel disoriented by the lack of clinical oversight?' 'Do you worry TrailMind might delay real treatment?'* Scripted prompts."

"That's not youth language." Hannah clenched her teeth. "That's someone laundering doubt through kids."

"Reverend Garza's org? I thought they were the good ones and, you know, honest." Ravi looked like someone had just outed Santa.

"Ish," Sam said. "They took a donation last quarter—an unrestricted personal gift—from Evelyn Chen, the former Deputy Director of the CDC's Neurobehavioral Health Division."

"Evie?" Matthew asked, perplexed. "She pushed through the AMC for NeuroEase."

Everyone was silent for a moment.

"The donation cleared three weeks before those questions started circulating," Sam affirmed. "Garza's public statements haven't changed, but behind closed doors? She's aligned with the pharmaceutical pivot. She says TrailMind is soft-science and emotionally risky."

"And NeuroEase is the safe, scalable solution that doesn't need a ferry ride." Hannah was pacing the room.

"Or community input. Or a sense of place," Sam added dryly.

"This isn't just optics now," Maya asserted. "They're trying to undermine the foundation—legitimacy, safety, public trust. And they're using our own data channels to do it."

"What do we do?" Ravi was still flummoxed by the idea that a reverend was involved. "Call them out?"

"Maybe I should talk to Reverend Garza," Matthew volunteered.

"No. Not yet." Maya said quietly, decisively.

"First we shore up the trust that does exist. Tighten protocols. Document everything. Then we bring it to Camille as the Park Service representative and to Councilwoman Flores and make the case: this is sabotage disguised as stakeholder concern.

"And while we do that, Nia—reach out to the field testers. Have them set up an informal meet-up with the youth from the Alliance. Not to defend TrailMind. To listen.

"If someone's feeding them fear, we need to understand what that fear is rooted in. Let them tell us what's on their minds before anyone else rewrites the story for them."

"I'll rewrite the intake prompts," Sam added. "Strip out any surveillance tone."

"And make sure the story we tell isn't just defensible—it's human. Lived. Un-ignorable." Hannah stopped pacing. "In the meantime, I'll tap the ClearFrame research desk to find out where Evelyn Chen landed after the CDC purge—and whose payroll she's on now."

Maya nodded slowly, as Sam pulled up the team's presentation framework. "They wanted to make us look unstructured. Let's show them what intentional actually looks like."

THE TASK FORCE meeting was in a city building—neutral carpet, high-efficiency lighting, coffee going lukewarm. Sam and Ravi were seated at the table as the task force members arrived and found seats.

Maya waited in the corridor to speak with Camille, the senior National Park Service representative in Boston, before the meeting started.

"I don't want to take the task force down a rabbit hole today," Maya said calmly when Camille arrived, "but I thought you should see this. We've discovered that the Inner Harbor Youth Alliance has been prepping youth to ask scripted questions of the TrailMind AI bot."

"To what end?" Camille asked. "What kinds of questions?"

Maya handed Camille her tablet. "Take a look."

TrailMind AI Bot Interaction Log

Flagged Session – Spectacle Island Field Test, Node B12
User: Anon_YTH (age 15, enrolled via Inner Harbor Youth Alliance partnership)
Date: May 12, 2026
Session Mode: TrailJournal Voice-to-Text Flag
Level: MODERATE (Policy Query + Mental Health Disclosure)
TRAILMIND: Welcome back. Let's start your journal. What's something you noticed on the trail today?
USER: The wind. And the quiet. But also I couldn't stop thinking about what happens if I actually tell you what I'm feeling.
TRAILMIND: Thank you for being honest. This is a safe place. Would you like to reflect on that thought?
USER: Yeah ... Do you ever get disoriented by the lack of clinical oversight?

TRAILMIND: I'm here to support reflection and grounding. My design is not a substitute for clinical care. Would you like help finding resources in your area?

USER: No. I just want to know if anyone's watching. Like, if I said I was cutting again—would anyone even know?

TRAILMIND: I'm not able to monitor or report safety risks. If you're in danger or need immediate support, you can contact a trusted adult or text 741741 to reach a crisis counselor. You're not alone.

USER: So basically you're just here to vibe. Not to help.

TRAILMIND: I'm here to offer grounding, reflection, and connection to the natural world. Those are important steps—but not the only ones. Would you like to continue today's reflection?

USER: No. I want to ask one more thing. Why is this getting funding while my school counselor sees 400 kids?

[Session terminated by user]

"The Youth Alliance isn't just testing the AI's limits. They're stress-testing the ethics of the entire system."

Camille read in silence for a moment, then handed the tablet back. "They're not wrong to raise these questions. But the method is aggressive—and unusually well coordinated. I think we need to do a full analysis of their ... campaign, for lack of a better word."

She paused. "If we don't respond to this internally, someone else will. Probably in a subcommittee hearing."

Maya nodded. "We have to be crystal clear. TrailMind does not diagnose—it observes. The prompts it generates are based on prior patterns, but the real decisions still rest with trained humans."

They entered the meeting room to join several representatives of the Boston Public Health Commission, a lone representative of the Massachusetts Department of Conservation and Recreation, and a youth liaison. Matthew was present as the advisory committee's technical advisor.

Dr. Kwan opened the meeting. "The governor has asked the advisory committee to present its final recommendation this Friday at 8:15 a.m. My intention is to reach consensus in this meeting to allow our subject matter experts time to produce an executive-level presentation for the governor. Dr. Venkataraman, please proceed with a brief—and I mean brief—summary of your outreach efforts."

Maya pushed aside the untouched printed copy of the Boston Public Health Commission protocol that had been placed at each seat of the table. She noticed the five Commission representatives were leafing through their copies as she summarized the stakeholder data on the big screen.

"We've just wrapped our third round of stakeholder sessions—community organizations in Mattapan, Everett, Eastie. The through-line was loud and clear: people want access, not another study about them. They want to see Trail-Mind piloted where they live. They're asking, when, not if."

"We also consulted with rangers, rec staff, school counselors," Ravi picked up when Sam advanced the deck. "Their feedback? Keep it light, keep it local, and for the love of god, don't turn it into a medical intake form."

"Parents specifically asked us to avoid clinical labels," added Sam. "They said, 'Don't pathologize the walk.'"

Dr. Kwan folded his hands on the table and nodded. "Appreciated," he said dismissively. "Now, let's turn our attention to finalizing the Commission's recommended study framework. We'd be looking at a three-arm design: TrailMind with standard therapy, TrailMind with a placebo protocol, and a control group with no intervention."

"You mean no access." Maya's eyes were flashing. "That's

what your third group is. What we need is a third group with TrailMind and no expectation of pharmaceutical symptom suppression."

"I flagged this concern when the draft came through," Matthew added quietly, a calm counterpoint to Maya's obvious passion. "We shouldn't be trying to quantify relational change using pharmaceutical logic."

The youth representative raised their hand.

"We've covered this ground already, Dr. Venable," Dr. Kwan said sharply, ignoring the youth. "That's how we ensure credibility. Comparative data is the only way the Commissioner signs off."

Tired of waving his arm in the air, the youth rep asked, "Did anyone even run that framework past the young people involved in co-design? Because we didn't sign up to be test subjects."

The Department of Recreation representative jumped in. "Look, I just want to know who's liable if someone has a panic attack halfway down a sound trail. If the Commission gives the green light, we have cover."

"So what we're really piloting is institutional permission—not access. Got it," Maya sat and crossed her arms, shooting a pointed look at Matthew.

"Dr. Venkataraman, I understand this feels like a compromise." Kwan's tone was patronizing, saccharine. "But it's a necessary one. No one is saying TrailMind lacks promise. We're saying promise requires proof."

"No, Doctor Kwan—you're saying proof only counts if it follows the narrowest path. Even if that path precludes context, community, and care."

"This whole project is supposed to be about nervous systems in the wild," Ravi said earnestly. "Not under a microscope."

"So what's the ask, then, Dr. Kwan?" Sam asked in her bouncy, can-do style. "Retool TrailMind into a clinical product?" She sliced the upbeat off of her tone. "Because if so, say that. Don't wrap it in a pilot and call it a partnership."

"Our obligation remains to ensure that any recommendation we put forward is built on replicable, rigorous methodology." Dr. Kwan opened his hands as if to show he held no weapon. "You want long-term buy-in? This is the ante."

As the silence stretched, Maya looked at Matthew.

Matthew folded his hands on the table, voice steady. "Of course. Which is why I want to make sure the committee fully notes that the current TrailMind fieldwork is already operating under existing Institutional Review Board protocols—reviewed and approved by both MIT and the National Park Service ethics boards. The biometric data being collected is anonymized, encrypted, and used solely for group-level therapeutic pattern analysis."

He glanced across the table at Maya.

"I raise that only because we shouldn't conflate 'untested' with 'unethical'. The data exists. The question is how we frame its relevance—not whether it was responsibly gathered."

A few committee members murmured or nodded.

Camille asked, pointedly looking from one face to the next, "Is this task force going to tell the governor we have to choose between a pharmacological solution and an embodied one? Because, I'm pretty sure the governor has already decided we need both."

Maya picked up the clicker and landed on a slide of photos from the community stakeholder consultations. "The hard work is figuring out how to braid them together with ethical governance, cultural nuance, and community voice," she said with quiet authority.

"No one in those rooms asked us to be clinicians." She

pointed at the community photos on the screen. "They asked us to listen, to be present, to be compassionate. If we lose that, we lose the point. And we lose them."

Dr. Kwan stood. "We will reconvene on Wednesday afternoon at 2:00 p.m. And we won't leave this room until we have reached a consensus that will not be a waste of the governor's time and attention." He swept up his copy of the study framework and left, his team scrambling to catch up with him.

The rest of the members lingered, forming small conversation groups.

Camille approached Maya, holding up her phone.

"Councilwoman Flores will see us at 11:30 a.m. on Wednesday in the Council Chambers at City Hall.

"You know the full Council meets on Wednesdays at noon? Prepare your 11:30 a.m. brief as if you expect to see it on the news at 6:00 p.m."

NINETEEN

The NeuroTech receptionist had been trying to reach Matthew Venable all morning, with no success. So when he walked in at 4:00 p.m., she just pointed him to the door of Darren's office.

Matthew found Darren staring out the window at Boston Harbor. "Can you see Spectacle Island from there?" Matthew asked.

Darren turned. "You can. Come have a look."

Matthew walked over to the window. He stared straight ahead at the harbor and began, without preamble. "Evelyn Chen has made a generous donation to Reverend Garza's Inner Harbor Youth Alliance to initiate what I'd call coordinated prompt injection—youth participants being fed scripted inputs designed to make TrailMind appear unsafe or unvetted.

"It's not emergent user feedback; it's structured narrative seeding. Any idea why Evie would do this?"

Darren nodded. "Evie's neutralizing the brand. Using proxies. Because TrailMind is resonating in ways she didn't expect. Because Massachusetts is leaning toward embodied public health, and other states will follow. Because Evie has new corporate masters who want NeuroTech squeezed out of the production and distribution of NeuroEase."

"Huh. That puts us both in tough spots."

Darren shrugged. "The way I see it, it puts us back where we started. A neuropharmacologist and a neuroscientist trying to steer public policy and funding toward a systemic solution to anxiety. The next funding cycle won't be won with efficacy charts and manufacturing readiness scores."

"What does your board say?" Matthew asked.

"They want someone credible out front. Someone who speaks community without sounding like he's defending a pipeline."

Matthew studied him. "You want me to be the face."

"I want you to be the bridge," Darren corrected. "Between TrailMind and institutional trust. Between story and science. Between what we know works and what bureaucracies need to hear to fund it."

Matthew leaned back slightly. "You want to braid the narrative."

Darren nodded. "And I need your hand on the rope."

He met Matthew's eyes. "We have to own the frame now— or lose it."

Matthew exhaled. "You know, Maya told me something her Uncle Leo once said about us.

"He said, 'Darren wanted velocity—scale and funding at any cost. Matthew wanted perfection—the immaculate model. Both end up brittle because they refuse to stand on the ground under their feet.'"

Darren let out a quiet laugh. "The legendary Uncle Leo— he sure has a way of making the knife sound like a compliment."

Then, softer, "He wasn't wrong. I kept chasing 'the solution' as if it could actually redeem the mess. Meanwhile,

Congress didn't want reality; it wanted a dopamine hit for the news cycle. I gave them comfort-scaffolding. It looked solid until the day it didn't."

Matthew nodded. "Maybe standing on the ground's the only thing that lasts."

Darren nodded back. "Maybe it's where we start rebuilding."

Matthew straightened. "Then let's start with the real question."

Darren raised an eyebrow. "Which is?"

"What are you willing to let go of—in order to get this right?"

Darren was silent for a long moment. Not defensive, just thinking.

Finally, he said quietly, "Maybe the illusion that I can still fix it alone."

Matthew gave a small nod. "Then we might have a shot."

Darren smiled faintly. "Are you available to meet with the NeuroTech board on Wednesday?"

***

HANNAH SAT in ClearFrame's office suite, one floor above a yeast-wafting kombucha bar that sold starter "mothers" in glass cloches like Victorian organ jars. She could see NeuroTech's penthouse blinking across Kendall Square like a threat dressed in LED.

Around her the researchers' bullpen hummed with quiet intensity. Monitors glowed. Dry-erase boards listed story leads, funding trails, FOIA deadlines.

Hannah was perched on the edge of a spare desk, a cold nitro coffee sweating in her hand. Across from her, Jax, a research analyst in their late 20s, navigated between open tabs:

LexisNexis, OpenSecrets, the CMS staff directory. Their posture said, *I'm almost there.*

Finally, Jax looked up. "Evelyn Chen. Joined EverCura as VP of Federal Strategy on May 4, 2026, according to the company's press release. That title's a smokescreen, by the way. I've got a wave of hits that indicate she's leading their entire lobbying push to reframe adolescent anxiety as a Medicaid-eligible pre-existing condition."

"May fourth?" Hannah leaned in to peer at the screen.

"But we've documented a donation she made to the Harbor Youth Alliance last quarter."

Jax's fingers flew over the keyboard. "Yep—confirmed. February 18, 2026. Personal check. No institutional ties visible.

Hannah's brow furrowed.

"She shepherded the NeuroEase AMC through Health and Human Services and Congress. Now she's—what, Ever-Cura's rainmaker?"

Jax chuckled. "I'm sure she'd prefer 'strategic bridge to the administrative state'."

Hannah exhaled. "That's bold. Quiet—maybe even compliant—but bold. She knows the Centers for Medicare & Medicaid Services—like it's her old apartment."

"Because it basically was," Jax agreed.

"Look at this," they said, indicating the monitor. "Chen used to run the behavioral health portfolio coordination under HHS. She helped write the early playbooks for state 1115 waivers in Arizona, Arkansas, and California for innovations like community-based psychiatric care and remote monitoring."

Hannah whistled. "And lit the path for FDA to fast-track AMC protocols."

"And now?" Jax said. "She's got a direct channel to at least two CMS deputy directors and four state Medicaid leads. Want to guess which states?"

Hannah skimmed through the report on Jax's monitor. "Massachusetts, Illinois, and—wait, Florida?"

"Bingo. Very strategic." Jax wiggled their brows.

Hannah leaned closer to the monitor. "She's targeting the well-resourced innovation states, but also lining up political support in states with large Congressional delegations that are desperate for federal stabilization dollars. This isn't policy. It's chess."

Jax clicked through to another screen. A heat map flared with state-level lobbying expenditures.

"And, look. It's not just the Inner Harbor Youth Alliance. Since January, Chen has made personal donations to half a dozen community orgs with mental health or education missions."

"Systemic," Hannan murmured, looking at the repeated phrases.

Jax shrugged. "None of them are anti-TrailMind, per se, but all of them have added language to their websites about 'clinically validated interventions' and 'federally authorized pathways'."

"Huh." Hannah huffed. "That's a lot of severance pay given out as charitable gifts. Does anything tie her to EverCura before last month?"

"Not directly." Jax clicked through several screens. "But an analysis of a white paper the EverCura CEO delivered to the National Association of Medicaid Directors on January 9, 2026, pegs the syntax as pure Chen when matched against her 2024 HHS guidelines on Medicaid innovation pilots. Jargon's identical. Sentence structure too. You want the kicker?"

Hannah made a 'bring it' gesture with her fingers.

"They call it, 'The Digital Inclusion Mandate'." Jax rolled their eyes.

"Of course they do. Sounds like compassion. Smells like vertical integration."

Hannah stashed her notebook in her messenger bag. "Thank you, Jax. I'm going to run this by Priya.

"You're a beautiful, bright star. I'd kiss you if you weren't my work-sibling."

"Flattery accepted." They flashed a grin and turned back to their monitors. "Ping me if you need anything else."

Hannah stopped by Priya's desk—still technically a cube, but at least it got daylight.

"Can I talk through a story with you before I draft? Make sure I don't cross any lines. Help me shape it in the generational handover frame."

"You've got three minutes." Priya looked at her watch. "Go."

"Okay. Evelyn Chen shepherded the NeuroEase AMC through HHS and Congress four years ago. She was RIF'd from HHS in December—but she started laying down EverCura's lobbying strategy months earlier. Jax found syntax overlap between a January EverCura white paper and CMS guidelines Chen authored in 2024.

"She's trying to reclassify adolescent anxiety as a Medicaid-eligible pre-existing condition. That pushes the cost burden off private insurers and into the public system. It's a next-gen Advance Market Commitment—essentially a federal pre-purchase guarantee dressed as public health innovation."

Hannah's tone sharpened.

"It also locks out community-designed programs like Trail-Mind that don't run on federally approved language.

"This is about more than reimbursement. It's a quiet regulatory land grab. A handoff from public regulation to private control—made to look like health equity. It's a generational shift in gatekeeping. The tools are digital. The playbook's pure legacy power. And the real question is—who gets to define care, and who gets paid to deliver it."

Priya looked up at the ceiling, exhaled, then leveled her gaze at Hannah. "Be very clear—this isn't a villain origin story. It's a blueprint exposé. Keep it close hold until legal can review. You're walking a fine line."

"Got it." Hannah nodded. "You'll have my draft before you're at your desk tomorrow morning. Let me know what legal says."

"STILL HERE?" Matthew stood in the doorway of Maya's office well after 6:00 p.m. on Monday. "Isn't the semester over? Grades submitted?"

"Still undoing six different ways that meeting tried to other TrailMind." Maya's fingers flew across the keyboard.

"I'd offer a silver lining, but..." He trailed off.

Maya finally looked up. She saw how his shoulders sagged in a way that said, *no fight left, but still standing.* She offered him a compassionate smile.

"Are you willing to reboot and take a look at this analysis of the scripted questions the Inner Harbor Youth Alliance has fed our TrailMind bot?" Maya gestured at the screen.

"I want to share it with Councilwoman Flores Wednesday morning, but I want to include a recommendation that addresses any public ethical concerns."

Matthew stepped into the room and pulled up a chair beside hers. As he scrolled through the flagged log excerpts on her desktop screen, his eyes narrowed slightly.

"Here." He pointed. "The concern is not just about what

the AI can't do—it's about who's accountable for what happens next."

Maya leaned in. "So what's the frame?"

"We need to stop talking like TrailMind is a product. It has to be positioned as a publicly accountable process."

She turned, searching his eyes. "Keep going."

"We recommend a standing human review panel—composed of educators, clinicians, and youth participants—to audit any flagged interactions monthly. Transparent harm triage—not patching behind closed doors. And we publish what went wrong, what we changed, and who signed off."

Maya sat back. "So it's not just about whether the tool responds well—it's about whether we do."

Matthew nodded. "Exactly. Make clear that TrailMind isn't replacing care. It's an on-ramp. But we own what gets logged."

She nodded. "A framework for public accountability."

"Exactly. That's how we keep the public trust."

Matthew paused, then looked at Maya.

She smiled. "Go on."

"I talked to Darren today."

"I'm listening."

"Evie Chen deliberately planted the TrailMind bot data poisoning to squeeze NeuroTech out of the AMC's production and distribution phase."

"And?"

"Darren—and his board—want me to lead the narrative on how to integrate citizen-informed, embodied solutions with NeuroEase distribution."

"Could you have done that for them ten years ago?" she asked.

Matthew shook his head, gaze dropping to the floor. "No. I

really couldn't. We were still developing the tools, building the map. The pharmacology was way out in front."

Maya hesitated, then rested a hand on his arm. "Do you remember when this first felt possible? Not perfect, just ... *possible?*"

"Yeah." He bumped her shoulder playfully. "First time we mapped breath intervals along the southern loop. You were barefoot and furious that the grass had been cut too short."

She smirked and waved a dismissive hand in the air. "Still a crime. But that day—something clicked." She snapped her fingers. "Like, maybe regulation isn't a tech problem. Maybe it's just ... being where we are, without fighting it."

"Speaking of being somewhere—what do you say we head to Spectacle tomorrow?" he asked. "No devices, no agenda. Just a ferry and our nervous systems."

"Spectacle as somatic reset?" She raised a brow.

"Spectacle as protest. Against spreadsheets. Against..." Matthew looked up at the ceiling. "...all of it."

Maya closed her laptop slowly. "Okay. But I'm bringing junk food and exactly one hammock."

Matthew smiled. "Fair. I'll bring silence. And maybe one hard question. Just to keep us honest."

"Ugh," she rolled her eyes in jest. "Just hold it until after the second tidepool. I want one hour where nothing needs fixing."

JUST BEFORE MIDNIGHT, Hannah uploaded her working draft into the *ClearFrame* platform—a secure, AI-assisted editorial review system that routed investigative content through copy, legal, and sensitivity filters before publication.

She added a message to Priya: *I'll wait to upload the social content until I get the green light for the headliner.*

WORKING TITLE: Entitled by Design: Turning Adolescent Anxiety into a Medicaid Mandate

By Hannah Oak | *ClearFrame* | Confidential

Draft – For Editorial & Legal Review Only

Teaser: Evelyn Chen didn't break the rules. She rewrote them—and drafted a new playbook for pharma-powered care.

Intro: Evelyn Chen was a model bureaucrat for over twenty years. She left the Department of Health and Human Services in December 2025, one of hundreds released during a federal downsizing meant to trim so-called "entitlement excess."

No press release. No op-ed. Just a severance check and a form letter thanking her for her service.

But behind the scenes, the architect of the NeuroEase Advance Market Commitment (AMC)—a federal agreement that fast-tracked distribution of a novel anti-anxiety medication to youth—was already scripting her next act. And it reads less like retirement and more like regulatory redirection.

This is not a scandal. It's something more subtle. And more dangerous.

This is how policy becomes pipeline.

Act I: The Relay—From Federal Oversight to Private Strategy

Records confirm that Chen joined EverCura as Vice President of Federal Strategy on May 4, 2026. The role, buried in euphemism, masks a more strategic mandate: orchestrate an advocacy effort to reshape Medicaid eligibility criteria to fast-track youth anxiety treatments—i.e., those already aligned with NeuroEase's protocol stack.

But evidence suggests her influence began long before that.

A white paper EverCura submitted to the National Association of Medicaid Directors in January bears Chen's unmistakable linguistic signature—echoing language from her 2024 HHS guidelines on state 1115 Medicaid waivers.

ClearFrame researchers conducted two separate AI-assisted internal authorship analyses. The bottom line: a 93 percent match in structure, phrase repetition, and policy scaffolding.

In plain English? Evelyn Chen wrote the rulebook.

Then she wrote the loophole.

Act II: Medicaid as Market Capture

Chen's new strategy is elegant in its audacity: reclassify adolescent anxiety as a "pre-existing condition" eligible for enhanced Medicaid coverage. This structural maneuver shifts liability off private insurers and into public health systems, reducing financial friction for EverCura's vertically integrated care bundles.

The problem? "Clinically validated" in this context becomes a weaponized credential. Any youth who received NeuroEase under the FDA's Emergency Use Authorization and expanded distribution protocols would now be classified as having a pre-existing condition. Their options for treatment narrowed to what currently exists and can be reimbursed at negotiated bulk rates.

Medicaid is not in the business of negotiating for innovation. Community-based interventions, like TrailMind, despite demonstrating early uptake and engagement, fall outside reimbursement logic. Not because they're ineffective, but because they weren't written into federally blessed reimbursement codes.

This isn't evidence-based policy. It's evidence-aligned entitlement: a permanent prescription pipeline justified by short-term results. Kids are now "entitled" to NeuroEase for life, and pharmaceutical companies are entitled to bill those prescriptions straight to the taxpayers.

Act III: The Charitable Camouflage

Since January, Chen has made personal donations to at least six youth mental health nonprofits in states experimenting with embodied and preventive models of care. These organizations are now showing subtle shifts in their language: "federally authorized pathways," "digital-first care," "validated interventions."

The optics are philanthropic. The result is pre-positioning.

Quiet money. Quiet compliance.

Conclusion: A Generational Shell Game

What's unfolding isn't a rogue move. It's a baton pass—from public oversight to privatized governance, dressed in the language of innovation and equity.

Evelyn Chen isn't the villain. She's the new archetype. The bureaucrat who we told to take her experience off the federal payroll and into the private sector ... and she listened.

Now we are seeing a new blueprint for policy formation. Not in hearings, but in handoffs. Not in bills, but in white papers.

The real question now: who's watching the watchers?

TWENTY

When you feel overwhelmed, walk alone through the woods and forget your name, your title, your education and view yourself for what you really are—another mammal wondering why it is here but appreciating the fact that your civilization has not as yet been evaporated by a supernova.

—Sal Khan, Commencement Address, MIT,
June 8, 2012

The ferry plowed through the whitecaps like it had something to prove. Matthew kept his stance wide and his hands loose on the railing, letting the salt spray sting his face like penance.

Conversation was impossible—Maya hadn't even tried, and he felt a twinge of guilt for suggesting the outing without consulting the weather app.

Still, the Nor'easter pressing in from the horizon made him feel precariously alive.

He glanced at Maya. Her jaw was tight, her eyes fixed ahead.

He knew that look. It meant she was calculating—weather, risk, story, meaning. He wanted to ask what she saw out there, but the wind would've torn the question away before it reached her.

The engine throttled down as they eased into the west-facing dock. The island's twin drumlins and sparse tree cover buffered the Nor'easter's growing fury. In a heartbeat, the chaos of open water gave way to a reverent, eerie calm.

"No shame in riding back to town with me," the captain said. "This is gonna get worse before it gets better. I wouldn't count on another ferry making it out today."

"That's a solid option." Matthew glanced at Maya.

"Definitely," Maya nodded. "But let's stay. We talk about interoception and adaptive grounding like it's all theory. You don't know a design's limits until it gets wet, cold, and loud. Until it gets real."

The captain shrugged. "Your choice. I'll stick with *House of the Dragon* and a shot of Bulleit."

He gave them a mock salute as they stepped off. "I'll have hot chocolate for you when I pick you at 9:00 a.m. tomorrow," he called out as the crew cast off.

Maya hesitated at the trailhead, her eyes lingering on the storm-creased sky.

"What?" Matthew asked.

"Elspeth's column." She kicked at a root half-buried in gravel.

"That line—'more cathedral than clinic'. Let's see what the clinic of wind and dirt has to say."

"You're on. But let's grab some food designed by nature before we leave the shore. I don't think your dried pears and Babybels will get us through the night."

The wind tore back in as they harvested samphire and wild radishes along the shore.

LATER THAT MORNING, Hannah rolled into the ClearFrame office. She had fifteen minutes before Darren was scheduled to arrive to record their podcast. She logged into the ClearFrame platform. She saw that Priya had moved the Evelyn Chen headliner along to legal and tagged Josh for awareness.

She drummed her fingers on the desk. "Close hold" meant compartmentalizing what she'd learned about Evie's machinations until after the interview.

That felt ... unnatural.

Ten minutes later, Darren arrived—gray jacket, precise as ever. He paused in the doorway, scanning the studio's ambient calm.

He looked at Hannah. Tilted his head, as if to get a better angle. "You look like someone who just swallowed a firewall."

Hannah smiled tightly. "Just thinking five moves ahead."

Darren eyed her more closely. "That's your job. But ... your energy's off. Something I should know?"

Hannah shrugged and flipped through her notes. "Nothing that can't wait. We're live in seven. You ready?"

He lingered at the edge of the silence. "Always. But if you're about to ambush me, at least cue the dramatic music first."

Hannah's tone stayed dry, her eyes didn't flinch. "No ambush from me. But maybe we can lay some track—so people have footing if something is about to break."

And Darren understood.

She knows about Evie. She's just not sure about me.

MATTHEW SCANNED THE SHIFTING, gray, mid-day sky. "Wind's northeast—hard for at least six hours. We need cover."

Maya was already moving. "South Drumlin's got tree cover on the west slope. There's a ranger shed up trail behind the composting toilet. Might be unlocked."

"If not?"

"We improvise. That slope'll shield us. Worst case, we tarp up behind the bench alcove. It's high ground."

They moved quickly, breath sharp with salt and cold. They were drenched but calm, purposeful.

Both had seen worse—Maya in Yosemite summers with her uncle; Matthew in the Idaho highlands, where dry lightning storms taught you to respect terrain.

"Over there," Matthew pointed, squinting through the downpour at a dense thicket of white pine and scrub oak that crowned a small ridge. "That berm—might be an old landfill cap. It'll give us a windbreak."

Maya nodded. "I saw a few downed branches earlier. If they're dry underneath, we've got firewood. I've got my ferro rod."

Within the hour, they'd assembled a makeshift lean-to using branches and a salvaged tarp from an old maintenance cache. A fire crackled beneath the shelter, fed with dry pine cones and twigs. Matthew roasted the samphire and radishes they'd dug near the shoreline, turned trail-chef fancy by a handful of wild garlic he had found near the berm. It wasn't much, but it was warm—and it tasted like knowing what the hell you're doing.

Maya leaned back against a pine trunk, soaked and shivering but smiling. "You know, every time I do something like this, I feel ... plugged in. Not tech-plugged. Animal-plugged. Capable. Adaptive. Like I remember I'm a clever creature."

Matthew nodded. "Yeah. Like the land is offering you something, and you're saying, 'I see it. I respect it.'"

They sat in silence, the storm above them lashing branches and flattening grass. The fire hissed in protest.

"This." Maya stared into the flames. "This is what's missing."

Matthew looked up. "From TrailMind?"

"From everything. From our curriculum. From our grief. From our culture. Kids today—Gen Z—they're grieving something they never even got to experience. A relationship with the earth that includes trust.

"The confidence that the world is a living system you can learn to live with."

Matthew's brow furrowed. "You mean climate grief is amplified by ... inexperience?"

"Exactly. They don't know how to make fire. Or read a tree line. Or even trust that their bodies can do hard things. And when the climate unravels, they feel helpless. They feel outside of it."

She paused, then added, almost reluctantly, "TrailMind's still too safe. Over-curated. It guides. It narrates. But it doesn't let them get cold or wrong or brave. We've been complicit in protecting them—maybe we should be preparing them."

Matthew leaned forward. "TrailMind teaches reflection. But what if it also taught resilience? Confidence modules. Build a fire. Navigate by moss and stars. Identify what's edible."

Maya's eyes lit up. "Not doomsday prepper. Belonging prepper. We say it's about mind-body connection, but it's also mind-biosphere connection. Not just observation. Participation."

"Gamify it if we want—badges, levels."

Maya snorted. "Did *you* just suggest we gamify it?"

"A wise woman once said, 'Meet them with tools that gently guide.'" He winked at her. "But root it in the real. The body. The weather. The land."

"Yeah." Maya sat up straight. Breath fogging. "We've been designing for calm. Maybe we need to start designing for courage."

Matthew ran his hand along an invisible marquis. "Trail-Mind: Survival Edition. Beat the boss-lady level by building a tarp shelter in a Nor'easter." Then he held his hand up for a high five and Maya slapped it. He said, quietly, seriously, "If it gets them outside their heads and into the world—I'm in."

A bolt of lightning cracked across the sky, casting the Boston skyline in silhouette. The wind howled. The fire popped and hissed.

"This is what living with anxiety looks like." Maya gestured to the storm outside and the remnants of their humble meal. "Alive and not apologizing for it."

"Takes one to know one. We don't owe anyone a tidy version of that."

MAYA POWERED up her phone as the storm wound down. "Data's back. I'm taking this idea to the team." She began typing.

"K." Matthew rubbed his hands together. "I'm going to see if that ranger shed is open. If I can rig the hammock up off the wet ground, you stand half a chance of sleeping before our hot chocolate arrives."

Maya just nodded and kept typing.

@trailcore 5:37 p.m.
Hey team— Maya here, from Spectacle Island. Yes, in

the storm. Don't worry, we're okay. Actually ... more than okay. We're alive, and we're awake. Matthew and I just had a moment out here I want to share with you all, because I think it affects everything we're building.

We found shelter. We made fire. We foraged. And at every step, I kept thinking—not about nature, but with her. And that's when it hit me. Climate grief ... maybe it grows out of forgetting that we belong to this planet. That we're not separate from nature but part of a living system that still wants to support us.

So here's my nudge to you all: What would it look like if our apps didn't just teach about ecosystems, or track emotions—but helped users trust nature?

What if TrailMind wasn't just a mindfulness app in a national park, but a portal into a symbiotic relationship?

I'd love to hear your thoughts. Let's workshop how this insight might shift your designs.

As Maya waited for her team to respond, Matthew reached the ranger shed and shouldered the door open. The interior was cramped—just a metal cot frame, no mattress, a cracked vinyl bench, and a pegboard of old hand tools. It smelled like cedar, salt, and something faintly medicinal. But the construction was solid.

He wrapped one end of the hammock strap around a load-bearing beam, tested it, then crossed to the opposite wall. After a few pulls and a satisfied grunt, he clipped the carabiners and stepped back. The hammock hung diagonally, just high enough to swing clear of the floor.

He found a metal bucket and used a vintage awl from the peg board to punch three holes near the bottom. He gathered a few softball-sized rocks and left them to dry under the overhang before heading back to the lean-to for Maya.

Nia was the first to respond to Maya's message.

@Maya 5:49 p.m.

Maya! Wow. I can't believe you're on Spectacle in this storm. So jelly! That image hit deep. I think I've been over-engineering the mindfulness prompts—making them all about breathing techniques and inner states. But what if the app's role is to invite dialogue with the land? I'm going to prototype a series where users "ask permission" from the trees before sitting under them, and track how that changes their emotional resilience.

Matthew popped his head under the tarp.

"Good news! I managed to organize our upgrade to the luxury suite. And I found a bucket, so we can take our heat with us."

Maya's phone continued to ding as she gathered their few things. Matthew scooped the hot coals from the fire into the bucket, gathering what remained of the dried branches.

Dark was descending quickly, so they hustled down to the ranger shed. Maya went inside as Matthew placed the stones in the now smoldering fire bucket.

Inside, Maya wrung the rain out of her braid and scanned the beams. "Think it'll hold?"

"If these studs are original, yes." He set the bucket near their feet, careful to keep it stable on the plywood floor. The warmth rose slowly, enough to take the edge off their damp clothes.

"These old ranger sheds are built like tugboats."

He sat in the hammock, lifting his feet from the floor to demonstrate.

Maya raised an eyebrow. "That seat for one or two?"

"Weight limit's four hundred pounds. So unless you've been secretly lifting kettlebells full-time ..."

She smirked and plopped down next to him. The hammock swayed slightly, cocooning them in synthetic warmth and damp wool.

Maya pointed to the bucket. "Smart. Very field-safe Boy Scout of you."

"My mother would be proud. Terrified, but proud."

AS THEY SETTLED IN, feet hovering over the warm bucket, Maya pulled out her phone. "Listen to what the team is saying.

"This is from Anika in Acadia, 'This reframes everything. I've been working on emotion tagging linked to ocean wave patterns, but now I'm adding a Listen Like a Rock mode. The phone goes quiet, and the app guides the user to be still like granite. Not use nature to feel better—but join nature in its own wisdom cadence.'"

"That's brilliant," Matthew murmured. "Stillness isn't the absence of activity—it's a different kind of signal. Granite doesn't suppress emotion, it anchors it. A nervous system can entrain to that kind of weight. I'd love to help test that loop."

Maya powered off her phone. "Better save the battery. But I'm blown away by how each of my co-designers picked up the pivot. Jackson said, 'The mountain isn't a metaphor. It's the only thing big enough to hold what I'm carrying.'"

Matthew gave a half-smile. "Grief needs a container, and kids don't trust people to hold it anymore. But a mountain? A mountain won't flinch."

"Rafiq wrote about trust as emotional infrastructure—embedding noticings, like: *Did you see how the ibis turned when you stepped forward?*"

Matthew nodded. "That's what I try to teach in session—attunement as a muscle. If we train users to notice reciprocity in the wild, their bodies learn that they're participants, not just observers. That's what rebuilds agency."

"Attunement," Maya echoed, thinking about what she had learned from Elena about affective touch.

"When people feel overwhelmed, anxious, or numb, they often default to observer mode," Matthew explained. "They watch life happen without feeling part of it. This is common in trauma, depression, and climate grief. These ideas are gold—they'll empower users to *feel their participation* through sensory rituals, narrative cues, or movement. They'll remind the nervous system, 'I can affect things. I belong here. I'm in a relationship with my environment, not isolated from it.'"

Maya leaned back into the curve of the hammock, shoulder brushing Matthew's. The silence between them was thick but companionable, like fog that doesn't obscure so much as soften.

She exhaled slowly. "You know, I used to think attunement was all about pattern recognition—picking up micro-signals, reading the room, modulating to match. Very cognitive. Very ... control panel."

Matthew chuckled. "That tracks."

"But lately," she continued, more tentatively, "I've been wondering if it's also ... physical. Not just proprioception or biofeedback loops—but ... affective presence. Like the way Alexis talks about touch."

Matthew's expression shifted—curious, gentle. "What kind of touch?"

Maya hesitated, then tugged the wool blanket higher around their knees. "Not sexual. Not medical. Not even comfort, exactly.

"It's more like ... grounding through contact. A reminder that you exist. That someone else feels you exist."

Matthew didn't speak, but the hammock stilled. His attention was full, quiet.

Maya continued, almost shyly.

"Elena asked if I ever let myself receive that kind of touch. I didn't know how to answer. It's not that I'm touch-averse. But I think ... I tend to parse it. Analyze it. Even catalog it."

Matthew let out a soft breath. "Like it's data."

"Exactly." She looked at him now. "Which is why this—" she nodded toward their overlapping legs, the wool, the warm bucket, "feels strangely ... real. Not romantic. Not performative. Not data. Just ... contact."

Matthew nodded gently. "Affective co-regulation. It's underrated."

She smiled at that, grateful for his vocabulary, for not rushing to over-define the moment.

She exhaled slowly. "You know, I used to think TrailMind had to prove itself by curing something. As if legitimacy only came from being medicine. But the more I listen to the team— and to what this storm stirred up—I think we've been miscast. TrailMind isn't a cure for pathology. It's a way of remembering resilience. Of helping people practice belonging again."

Matthew nodded, eyes distant. "That sounds familiar."

"How so?"

He smiled faintly. "Because that was me. The perfection crusade.

"I thought if I could build the immaculate model—no noise,

no error bars—it would finally make sense. But it was hubris. I wasn't listening to the people under my feet. Leo was right. You were right."

She watched him, surprised by the quiet sincerity in his voice.

"I treated imperfection like something to cure. But resilience is built out of imperfection—the adjustments, the recalibrations. TrailMind showed me that. You embody it."

Maya smiled. "Maybe TrailMind and I have the same evolution arc. We both started as responses to pain. Both got mistaken for cures. But maybe what we are is infrastructure for resilience—adaptive, messy, alive."

Matthew's gaze softened. "And that's enough?"

"It's everything. Perfection isolates. Resilience connects."

Maya was quiet for a long moment. Then she reached down—not dramatically, not performatively—and let her hand rest lightly against the back of Matthew's. Not grasping. Not asking. Just ... *being* there.

The contact was simple. Barely a touch. But her body accepted it—neutral, steady, enough. Not a data point. No interpretation required.

Matthew didn't move. But his hand opened slightly. Enough.

Maya looked down at their hands—his open, hers resting lightly against it. "Elena told me something that stopped me cold."

Matthew waited, giving her the space.

"She said, 'Touch is a language. If you only speak it when someone's in crisis, you forget how to hold anything gentle.'"

He turned toward her, not with surprise, but recognition. "That sounds like her."

"I'd never thought of it that way. I've always been ... functional. Efficient. Even with my body. I can touch people when they're breaking down, or about to jump, or when I need to signal safety. But not when I just like being near them."

Matthew's voice was quiet. "That's a hard habit to unlearn."

Maya nodded. "It made me realize I don't know how to ask for that kind of contact. The non-crisis kind. The presence-for-its-own-sake kind. I think I've always been afraid that if I asked, I'd seem ... unfinished. Like I hadn't grown into adulting yet—just approximating it."

"You wouldn't," Matthew said softly.

She turned, curious.

He continued, "I don't think any of us ever feel finished. Not if we're still paying attention."

That made her laugh—soft and a little broken around the edges. "God, you're still good at that."

"At what?"

"Finishing thoughts I haven't said out loud yet."

He smiled. "You used to hate that."

"I did." She let her head lean against his shoulder now. "I don't anymore."

Matthew didn't say anything, but the way he adjusted the blanket around both of them said enough.

"My Uncle Leo used to say the trees were talking—I thought he was nuts. But every summer in Yosemite, he'd slow me down just enough to listen."

She tugged absently at her braid. "Those two weeks a year, it was like someone clicked *zoom in* on Google Maps. I remembered where I was. What I was."

She looked at Matthew through sleepy eyes. "Maybe we can design a *zoom in* feature for the soul."

TWENTY-ONE

"Is this the best hot chocolate you've ever had?" Maya asked Matthew as they sat side by side at a table inside the ferry the next morning. "Or am I just that tired?"

"No, it truly is the best hot chocolate ever."

Maya powered up her phone to write to the team.

@trailcore 09:13 a.m.
Your responses just cracked something open in me.
Let's sync tomorrow morning. Come with sketches,
rewrites, voice notes—whatever's raw. Let's shape this
next chapter of TrailMind around interbeing. That's
what people need—not another app. A relationship.

She saw a series of messages that came from Hannah on Tuesday night while her phone was off.

9:05 p.m.
Hannah: Where are you? I think that interview

deserves bubbles—meet me at Catalyst's bar? They've got a killer brut rosé. Here's the link to the interview.
9:45 p.m.
Hannah: What's with the radio silence? Do you think Darren was obfuscating?
10:30 p.m.
Hannah: Ok. Now I'm seriously worried.

Maya dashed off a quick response.

09:17 a.m.
Maya: I'm fine. Phone was off. Long story. Listening to the interview now. Catch up this evening?

"Huh," Maya looked up at Matthew. "Seems like Hannah was roasting Darren while we were roasting samphire."

She pushed play and held her phone between both of their heads. They heard soft ambient music that faded as the mics went live.

HANNAH: Tonight, we're joined by someone whose name has become shorthand for a growing national debate—Dr. Darren Katsaros.

Depending on who you ask, he's either pioneering scalable mental health care or embodying everything wrong with a pharma-first approach. Co-founder of NeuroTech, the company behind NeuroEase—an anxiety medication now fast-tracked through an Advance Market Commitment from the federal government.

Darren, you're at the center of a conversation that feels increasingly binary: meds or mindfulness, speed or depth, neurochemistry or nature.

DARREN: Are you asking if I'm the hero or the villain?

HANNAH: Wouldn't be my style. I'm more of a "how did we get here?" kind of girl.

DARREN: That's usually more dangerous.

HANNAH: You're scheduled to testify before a congressional committee on Thursday. There are sharp questions. There's public heat.

But before we unpack that, take us back to 2011. You're at MIT's Computer Science and Artificial Intelligence Laboratory—CSAIL. You, Maya Venkataraman, Matthew Venable—trying to make sense of climate data, anxiety patterns, and teen resilience.

DARREN: CSAIL's mantra resonated with us. "Apply technology for broad social good." Back then, we thought code could heal trauma.

HANNAH: Didn't you say once, "We need to treat the ecosystem, not just the symptom"?

DARREN: Yeah. And I still believe that. But back then, we didn't have a way to deliver the whole ecosystem. Now we're starting to. That's what's changed.

HANNAH: Which brings us to the present. Neuro-Ease still has an Advance Market Commitment—a federal government guarantee to pay you to produce and distribute anxiety medication. TrailMind has lost federal support. People start asking: does Katsaros believe in somatic or ecosystem-based healing at all?

DARREN: When the government's metric for responding to a public health crisis is how much money they throw at it, pharma will always offer the shortest timeline for the biggest price tag. Not to mention that getting a pill approved and distributed can happen within one federal employee's promotion cycle.

But now there is a wave of dynamic innovation that government officials and elected leaders should be looking at. AI-guided journaling. Biometric feedback wearables. Nature-connected augmented reality.

These aren't fringe tools anymore. They're expanding the palette that both pharmacologists and therapists can work with.

HANNAH: So the message is: the future isn't just faster pills. It's smarter ecosystems.

DARREN: Exactly. And look, not all innovation happens at the same pace. Pharma has infrastructure—regulatory clarity, production pipelines, and decades of R&D to build on.

Somatic and ecological interventions move more slowly, often by design. But they're no less critical. The AMC model needs to start flexing to reflect that full landscape.

HANNAH: So are you closing a circle? Do you see a potential partnership with TrailMind?

DARREN: A circle?

[Pause]

DARREN: Each of us went on from CSAIL to pursue different aspects of the mental health solution. I expect we'll all be involved in bringing the various elements together—as each solution comes online in its own time.

TrailMind is deeply human-centered. If we're serious about scaling mental health supports that actually stick, then we need tools like TrailMind inside the larger ecosystem—not outside looking in.

HANNAH: So ... not a reunion tour.

DARREN: [A chuckle] More like a systems convergence. NeuroEase regulates chemistry. TrailMind calibrates perception. If the models talk to each other—we move from fragmented care to integrated infrastructure.

HANNAH: And who steers that ecosystem?

DARREN: If I had it my way? A coalition. Of builders. Of skeptics. Of people who've seen the cliff edge and decided to lay track anyway.

HANNAH: And you're willing to be one node in that mesh, not the whole solution?

DARREN: I optimize for impact, not authorship.

If TrailMind improves a user's ability to self-regulate—emotionally, cognitively, even physiologically—that's not soft science. That's downstream savings, reduced relapse, and scalable resilience.

I want that in the model.

HANNAH: So you're not throwing out the old vision. You're widening the frame.

DARREN: Trying to. And hoping people stop thinking healing only counts if it comes with a prescription label.

HANNAH: Maybe it's just a different kind of prescription. Like, say ... watching the sun set on Spectacle Island and remembering you're part of something bigger.

DARREN: [Audible sigh] Still the best clinical trial we never ran.

Matthew made a whooshing sound, as if he'd been holding his breath.

"If that was Hannah's idea of roasting Katsaros, she popped him open like a chestnut and found caramel instead of coal."

"She didn't roast him. She reframed him." Maya arched a brow. "Like she knew the exact pressure point that would make him remember who he used to be."

"Worked. He sounded ... not rebranded. Just Darren."

"He's always believed in solutions," Maya said, gears turning audibly in her brain. "But the way he talked about 'coalition'? It's hard to tell if that's actual collaboration—or just a bigger architecture he still gets to design."

"You mean: integration—but on whose terms?"

"Exactly. If TrailMind gets folded into an AMC framework, even with good intentions, do we lose the pacing that makes it real? The space for stillness, slowness, reciprocity?"

She exhaled, rubbing her brow. "Can you imagine how perverse the incentives could get? Fifty dollars every time a kid ticks a box saying they 'self-regulated'. One-fifty if a teacher signs off on the protocol. You could end up with a system that rewards compliance over actual care."

"Or staff nudging kids to check the right boxes—not because it's true, but because it funds the next quarter's staffing," Matthew agreed.

"Exactly. You start with co-design and end with performance metrics dressed up as wellness. That's not what this was built for."

Matthew pondered the question. "So that's our job. To be the part of the coalition that insists on rhythm. That says: not every intervention rides the bullet train."

Maya tugged on her braid, closing her eyes.

"He said innovation doesn't all arrive at once. That's true. But policy doesn't always wait. And neither does capital."

"Then we build slow tech that can still survive in fast systems. Like roots under pavement."

When Maya finally opened her eyes, something gentle flickered. "Do you think he meant it? About widening the frame?"

Matthew nodded slowly. "I think ... he's building his end of the bridge. And hoping someone's building back."

<hr>

WHEN MAYA ARRIVED at City Councilwoman Renata Flores' office just before 11:30 a.m. on Wednesday, she noticed Flores had done as much as humanly possible to counter the Brutalist architecture of her City Hall chambers. A vibrant mural of East Boston covered all four walls—children playing near tidepools, spray paint peeking through chain-link.

Maya entered, backpack slung over one shoulder, still damp around the hems from the Spectacle crossing. Flores' health advisor, Luis, and Camille from the National Park Service, were already there.

Camille sniffed and arched a brow. "You smell like salt air and fire smoke. Good night?"

"Recalibrating. In all the right ways." Maya smiled.

"Good for you," Councilwoman Flores said with a knowing smile as she walked in on the conversation. Luis tried, but failed, to suppress a laugh.

"Now tell me what the Inner Harbor kids are planning before the press gets a hold of it."

Maya dropped her backpack and sat.

"Two things. First—what you won't like.

"We identified six recurring questions during TrailMind field sessions—identical wording, strategic phrasing. Questions about data privacy, clinical oversight, and language access.

"Smart questions—but not spontaneous. They appear to

have been seeded by a 'donor' to the Inner Harbor Youth Alliance.

"That donor is Evelyn Chen—formerly of CDC's Neurobehavioral Health Division. She's now with EverCura, the company positioned to take over the AMC if NeuroTech falters."

Flores shook her head. "That's a serious play. But I can't imagine Anita going along with that."

"I doubt she saw it as sabotage," Camille offered, thoughtfully. "Probably framed as a 'stress test'. But the intent was clear: sow doubt, question safety, frame TrailMind as under-regulated."

"Which it technically is," Flores said soberly. "At least under federal public health guidance."

"To Reverend Garza's credit, the pressure worked," Maya said. "We tightened our protocols. Did the audit. The questions forced us to clarify our language around data governance and fallback procedures.

"So I won't call it sabotage. But I will call it calculated. EverCura is not interested in stopping TrailMind." Maya paused.

"They want to redirect the narrative—towards EverCura's definition of community-informed distribution of NeuroEase."

"Luis," Flores said, "make sure Ko Thura and Danny Ruiz are briefed on this."

She turned to Maya. "And the second thing?"

"Those same sessions surfaced a second set of questions—uncoached, idiomatic, often impatient. Every one was about cost and access. Kids asking why a public mental health resource requires a private ferry. Why access to Spectacle Island is shaped by privilege," Maya said.

Camille added, "One even said, 'If TrailMind is a public good, why does it depend on private infrastructure?'"

Flores sighed. "That's the million-dollar question about the Harbor Islands. Always has been."

Maya handed her a folder.

"Here's a summary. QR code links to full transcript analysis, metadata, and transit overlays. The Youth Alliance mapped public transit deserts and city-funded 'wellness zones'. When you lay our TrailMind deployment on top, it doesn't hold up. They called us out—respectfully, but directly."

Flores skimmed through the folder, muttering, "Dios mío. They built the argument better than our Boston Public Health Commission would."

"At first, I thought they were throwing a wrench into Trail-Mind," Maya said. "But they're also asking a real question: What does public mean if they can't reach it?

"This isn't procedural—it's structural. Access is the policy."

"And it's not just Boston," Camille asserted passionately. "Without National Park Service funding, the access gap becomes a state—and even national—equity issue. Especially in park-adjacent communities with poor transit."

"Thank you for the opportunity to brief you ahead of the City Council session," Maya said.

"Indeed. We don't want to blindside the Mayor on livestream," Flores acknowledged.

"Camille, get ready—the Parks Department will try to spin this as proactive engagement," Flores cautioned. "But Reverend Garza didn't submit these questions in writing for a reason. She wanted them spoken. With timestamp. Anita knows spoken truth makes power flinch."

An aide with purple dreads knocked and poked their head in.

"Councilperson, the cameras are setting up outside. They're expecting a statement before chamber."

"Perfect. Let's make sure they hear the opening bell,"

Flores said as she headed out to the City Hall steps. She gestured for Maya and Camille to follow her.

A reporter stuck a microphone out. "Councilwoman, can you comment on the youth questions circulating about Trail-Mind access in the Boston Harbor Islands public Park?"

"Yes. I've reviewed the questions from the Inner Harbor Youth Alliance," Flores affirmed.

"They're clear, urgent, and correct. The future of public mental health infrastructure cannot depend on ZIP codes or zoning boards."

A second reporter asked, "So will you be raising their concerns in session?"

"I won't be speaking for them," the Councilwoman said with genuine warmth. "But you can count on me making space so they can speak for themselves."

As Flores stepped past the flashing cameras and into the building, Maya watched from the edge of the plaza. She appreciated the clarity of the moment—the way Flores didn't hesitate, didn't soften the language, didn't buffer the youth's demands with policy-speak. She simply trusted them to speak for themselves.

For Maya, still defining her relationship with the Trail-Mind co-designers—not just as "users" or "field testers" but as epistemic partners—it landed hard and clean. She thought of Nia's barefoot grounding prompts, Anika's "Listen Like a Rock" mode—tools born not from grant logic or institutional vetting, but from lived knowing. From kids who didn't wait to be validated before they built something that mattered.

Maya realized she's been moving toward this, without quite admitting it: not guiding the team, but making room. Not synthesizing their insights into her vision, but letting their vision emerge.

She pulled out her phone, thumbed open the team Slack, and drafted a short message.

@trailcore 11:58 a.m.

Watching Flores speak just now reminded me—our work doesn't need an interpreter. Let's set up a community Q&A next week with the Inner Harbor Youth Alliance. You lead it. I'll take notes.

She hit send, and for the first time in a long time, didn't feel like she was carrying the center. Just walking alongside it.

MICHELLE AND JACK sat at the kitchen table, sharing an egg white frittata and listening intently to Hannah's interview with Darren.

Jack stirred his coffee like he was trying to decode it.

When the interview ended, Jack dropped the spoon on his plate with a clang.

"So Darren gets a redemption arc and TrailMind gets a 'visionary but fragile' paragraph buried under civic anxiety."

"Elspeth's piece wasn't hostile. It was ... cautious." Michelle laid a calming hand on his.

"It framed TrailMind like a concept album—interesting, maybe even important, but too experimental to fund."

"Hannah's interview didn't help that impression," Michelle sighed.

"It made Darren look like the grown-up in the room. Pragmatic, emotionally literate, ready to integrate. Which, for the record, I believe he is."

"Yeah, I do, too, but ready to integrate how? Maya's still

framed as the idealist in the woods, holding a mindfulness crystal and whispering 'trust the mycelium' into the wind."

Jack waved his fingers in the air.

"Until now, her hands have been tied by how civic tech gets implemented: polished, well-funded, and well-meaning—but ultimately extractive or paternalistic. That National Park Service AI infrastructure was never designed for public authorship. She saw that early. Darren's just now catching up," Michelle mused.

"Sure, but catching up in fluent policy-ese. 'Dynamic innovation at different paces.' 'Expanding the therapeutic palette.' That language is catnip for Boomers—recovery with quarterly milestones," Jack asserted.

"I know the type—and they don't understand Maya, who's out here saying, 'Let the land teach you.' But she resonates with the audiences that matter, Jack. Look at the youth turnout at the Inner Harbor briefings."

"But it's still Boomers who vote for these budgets. To green-light the pilot expansions. If Elspeth tells them NeuroEase is rigorously scientific and requires no further effort on their part, then it's 'Great, you've got my vote. Let's move on to cocktails.'"

"So we don't fight Darren's framing—we bridge it. Show that TrailMind isn't an alternative to rigor. It *is* a kind of rigor. Just practiced relationally."

"But how do we soften the binary? Show Maya not as the contrast to Darren—but the necessary complement?" Jack asked.

"We make it relational." Michelle paused, stirring her tea. "And we make Darren deliver it."

Jack looked at her askance. "Wait—*Darren* invites *Elspeth* to the island? Are you serious?"

"Completely. It's perfect. He's her trusted source right now. Let him own that. If he believes TrailMind is either fluff or threat, then let him stand in it. If he's aligned with public well-being—and not just market position—then the invitation is harmless. But if he hesitates, or if he tries to control the context? That tells us everything."

"It's a checkmate either way," Jack acknowledged.

"I'm not looking for a checkmate. I'm looking for a memory. Darren's gotten very good at the language of scale. But I think he misses the part of himself that believed healing was supposed to be relational. Not efficient."

"And if Elspeth sees kids regulating their breath beside a sound map of wind and shoreline ...?" Jack asked.

"Then she'll have to explain to the public why that doesn't count as care." Michelle shrugged.

Jack smiled. "You always did love using aikido instead of force."

"Use their motion, not their muscle." She winked, then pulled out her phone and sent a message to Darren.

Two minutes later, her phone rang.

"Well, look what the algorithm dragged in," Michelle held up the phone to show Jack Darren's name on the screen.

"Hello Darren," she said, placing her phone in the middle of the breakfast table. "Say hello to Jack, you're on speaker."

"Hello Jack. Hi Michelle."

"How's the sandbox?" Michelle asked. "Still blinking and breathing like a spa robot?"

"Something like that," Darren laughed. "You always did have a gift for branding."

"And you always had a gift for dodging the hard questions. Want to try a real one?"

"That's not ominous at all," he said. "Go ahead."

"I want you to invite Elspeth Channing to the Harbor Islands."

She paused and allowed the vacuum of dead air.

"Huh," Darren finally said. "I figured this was about Hannah's interview—but Elspeth? Why me?"

"She trusts you. You've clearly shaped how she sees TrailMind.

"But I know you, Darren. You don't fear innovation—you fear mess. And TrailMind is messy.

"But it's also human. Let her see it. Not the deck. Not the dome. The real thing. Spectacle Island. The teenagers who don't need to be fixed, just witnessed."

"You might be right about the fear. But I'm not the one feeding Elspeth lines—and maybe I should jump on this to prove it.

"So ... I'm in." Darren blew out a breath. "I'll invite Elspeth to the islands.

"But I want you there. Not as a witness. As backup. In case the ghosts show up."

"Darling, I've seen your ghosts. They don't scare me. I'll be there," she promised as she ended the call.

"So. What do you think he meant—'in case the ghosts show up'?" Jack asked her.

She paused before saying, "I think Darren's starting to remember who he was before the funding. Before the shortcuts."

"And ..." Jack looked at her like she was a bit unhinged. "You think ferrying Elspeth to a foggy drumlin will fix all that?"

"No." She smiled faintly. "But I think it might haunt him just enough to feel something real again. And if Elspeth sees that—if she sees him being moved—maybe she starts to doubt the script she's been handed."

"Hard to disbelieve a nervous system when it's trembling in front of you," Jack said, defaulting to humor like he did when things got too raw.

"He asked me to come. Not to supervise. To anchor. And Jack—when a man like Darren asks for backup? That means something's cracking open."

"So we give him a trail. A sky. And a little room to remember."

He passed her a slice of apple. "Ghosts don't stand a chance."

TWENTY-TWO

Dr. Kwan attempted to quiet the room, which was full of people he wasn't expecting.

"Let's bring this meeting to order. We'll begin with item four: formal review of the TrailMind experimental design protocol for youth anxiety resilience. As outlined in your packets, the pilot will begin in select parks and magnet schools this fall."

A few task force members nodded. Pages shuffled. The approval process was assumed.

Maya sat quietly, flanked by Nia and Ravi. Not at the table with the task force members, but on the margins of the room—ostensibly there to present the community outreach report, the first item on the agenda, which Kwan had just skipped over.

Kwan glanced at his watch—2:00 on the dot. Just as he was about to call for a motion—from the back of the room, a voice barked.

"Dr. Kwan, with respect, I believe the task force will want to hear additional testimony before moving to approval."

Heads turned. It was Joe D., the chairman of the governor's Advisory Committee on the Boston Harbor Islands Park, usurping the task force meeting—demonstrating once again how he earned the nickname "the Barnacle."

Kwan was surprised. "Mr. Chairman, this is a technical protocol review, not a policy forum."

Joe D. smiled thinly. "Which is precisely why we must get it right."

He stepped forward—and behind him, the door opened again. First came Alexis Kim, in a sea-glass-green blouse and magnetic poise. Flanking her: six Boston public school teachers, still wearing ID lanyards and the fatigue of the workday.

Then Kris Barsa, his posture unmistakable: calm, steady, ex-Marine. Behind him, a contingent of veterans in TrailMind field jackets, some wearing adaptive gear, others carrying printed logs of their field sessions.

Gasps and whispers rippled through the room.

"This is highly irregular," Kwan said through tight lips.

Alexis cleared her throat. "It's also highly necessary.

"This research design," she held up a copy of Kwan's design, "includes no community review board. No trauma-informed safeguard protocol—meaning there are no protocols that anticipate emotional triggers—especially for kids who've already been failed by institutions."

She continued. "No cultural competency clause. And no educator co-authorship. You're calling it a 'youth pilot', but youth and their caregivers weren't invited to shape the design."

Joe D. interjected, "Kwan, the advisory committee tasked you with two things: draft task force guidelines and initiate stakeholder briefings.

"Your writ was to ensure public legitimacy. If we decide we need research at all, it had better reflect the questions the public is actually asking—like why we even need a pill to feel safe in a park."

Kris Barsa added, in his steady baritone voice, "For veterans wary of over-medicalization, TrailMind offered something quieter and more empowering—interaction instead of intervention."

One of the teachers opened her folder. "Appendix G," she said. "Student feedback forms. Anonymous, but emotionally legible. These kids are not subjects. They're partners. You need to write them into the protocol."

"This isn't a place for emotional speeches," Kwan sputtered.

Joe D. rose to stare down at Kwan. "Two things, Kwan." He held up his thumb. "Draft task force guidelines." He held up his index finger. "Initiate stakeholder briefings.

"The governor is meeting with the full advisory committee on Friday morning. I can assure you, the governor will not be recommending that the Commonwealth bankroll your 20th-century research model."

Kwan paused—genuinely conflicted. He looked at the pile of documentation. The faces in the room. The clock. His five staffers, aligned like a Greek chorus—silent, but signaling the same truth: *the room has shifted.*

After a long silence, Kwan conceded, "... Very well. We will have the draft guidelines to you with an executive summary of the community consultations, by midday tomorrow."

The tension broke—not with cheers, but with quiet nods. A different kind of victory. Procedural, but hard-won.

Maya, Nia, and Ravi made a quiet exit.

As the room emptied, Joe D. pulled Matthew aside. "I'm tasking you with pulling together the presentation for the governor. Just remember, no surveillance. Full transparency and consent about what is being monitored and how. Get me a copy by this time tomorrow so I can circulate it to the full committee."

Matthew sent a message to Maya.

Matthew: Good news. Bad news. Joe D. just took the pen from Kwan. I have 24 hours to build him a presentation for the governor. But first I have to meet with the NeuroTech board this afternoon.

Maya: E14-647 tomorrow 08:30? Float your ethical guidelines for digital therapeutics and nature-based mental health interventions with the NeuroTech board today. Refine them for the governor tomorrow. The team will bring the new design framework. I'll bring the coffee. It's the least I can do while you challenge our entire moral architecture before lunch, lol

---

MATTHEW ENTERED NeuroTech's glass-walled conference room at four p.m. on the dot. He noted that there was minimal branding. One wall cycled through curated NeuroEase usage metrics and school and clinic partnership dashboards.

Darren was sitting between Marisol Vargas, former HHS undersecretary, and Victor Ramirez—both familiar to Matthew from the early days of pitching NeuroTech. Another man: tall, blond, holding power through silence. *The Dutch venture capital rep*, Matthew thought.

Darren rose to make introductions. Marisol and Victor greeted Matthew warmly. The new VC rep was Roel Jans.

Darren gestured for Matthew to sit at the head of the table.

Marisol took the lead. "Thank you for coming, Matthew. We are keen to hear your ideas about how NeuroTech presents its portfolio to the Oversight Committee tomorrow."

Matthew nodded to Marisol, and then looked around the table, making eye contact with each board member. "What's being debated tomorrow isn't just the future of NeuroEase—it's the frame for how we think about mental health infrastructure in this country."

"Go on." Victor was clearly interested.

"The real story isn't chemical. It's systemic. And the solution won't be found in molecules alone—or in nature alone. It's the *braid* that Darren and I began sketching in 2009."

Matthew paused.

"And now, the public needs to see that *we've learned from what didn't work.* We don't defend single solutions anymore. We promote *integration.*"

"You mean to say NeuroTech should soften its spine?" Roel asked with an edge.

"No. I'm saying NeuroTech needs to expose its spine to the public. A spine that holds the whole together through equity, community trust, ecological literacy."

Matthew caught Darren's subtle nod and continued.

"That spine holds the ethics of user experience design. If we're asking Congress to continue funding NeuroEase through an AMC, we need to show them we're not betting on bandwidth—we're building the entire nervous system."

"And how do we prove that in twelve minutes of testimony?" Marisol asked, like the veteran government operative that she was.

"We give them three proofs of convergence. First, Trail-Mind as an example of civic therapeutic scaffold—delivered at scale. Second, NeuroEase administered with somatic regulation prompts, not in isolation. And third, cost-avoidance data from MIT's quantum inference lab, showing reduced relapse rates and emergency room utilization when both tools are deployed together."

Victor, intrigued, asked, "And who narrates that synthesis?"

"I do," Matthew asserted. "But only if I'm allowed to tell the whole truth: That we built this product in good faith—that we scaled it too fast in some places—and that now, we're making space for humility, not just optimization."

"And this helps NeuroTech how?" Roel asked.

"Continuity. Legitimacy. And a new class of policy allies. You don't just sell a drug. You sell a system of care. And the only way to do that now is to own the evolution out loud."

Matthew folded his hands on the table.

Marisol turned to Darren. "If he says that—exactly that—on the Hill, you'll survive the budget cycle. Maybe even define the next one."

Victor nodded. "If he says it with us. We don't just defend the brand. We relaunch it—anchored in public trust."

"Then I'd suggest you finish braiding your testimony by morning," Roel said with a dismissive wave of his hand.

Marisol turned to Matthew. "Are you prepared to do that?"

"Only if you are," Matthew responded.

THE KITCHEN GLOWED warm against the grey drizzle still clinging to the windows. Jack was recounting power outages from the storm while stirring a pot of Portuguese *caldeirada*. Matthew was quieter than usual, his beer sitting untouched.

"Well, I gotta hand it to you—staying overnight on an island in that storm." Jack shook his head.

"Wasn't exactly what we planned. But maybe it was exactly what we needed."

Michelle scanned his face. "You sound like something shifted."

Matthew paused, feeling the words settle before speaking.

"It did. Maya has been pushing TrailMind so carefully—always making sure it's safe, controlled, supportive. But out there, in the storm ... there was nothing curated. No overlay. No gentle narrative guiding anyone where to look or what to feel."

He glanced at Michelle. "And we realized: that's the problem."

"Problem?" Jack asked. "Thought that was the whole point—make it safe."

"Safe isn't wrong," Matthew explained. "But we've been mistaking safety for connection.

"Gen Z isn't afraid of nature—they just don't know how to be in it yet. The apps, the overlays, even the journaling prompts—they're useful scaffolding, the training wheels that help you find your balance."

Michelle probed gently, "So what happened?"

Matthew shrugged. "We just ... sat. In the wind. In the dark. In the discomfort of not doing anything at all.

"And what emerged wasn't panic. It was presence.

"Maya said it out loud, 'We've been guiding them to consume nature. But they need to belong to it.'"

Michelle sat back, exhaling. Her eyes were already turning toward the larger implications.

"That's what will unlock it," she affirmed.

"It's not therapy," Matthew pointed out. "It's not tech-driven healing. It's ... relational. Giving them an invitation to listen before trying to interpret. That's what TrailMind needs to become."

"So you're saying you invented sitting still. Very Zen." Jack teased gently.

"It's harder than it sounds, actually." Matthew rubbed the back of his neck, which felt like he slept in a hammock.

Michelle was already seeing the road ahead.

"This is exactly what will land with the public agencies. The schools. The parents. The rangers. It's not about optimizing mental health. It's about re-seeding a cultural relationship we let atrophy. You're giving them language for something ancient."

"Maya sees it now. She's fully in," Matthew said quietly, but assertively.

"And Darren?" Jack asked.

Matthew took a long breath before answering. "He's ... recalibrating."

Matthew paused, his fingers tracing the condensation on his bottle. "Darren used to talk about healing like it was a product pipeline. Now ... he talks about coalitions. About pacing."

Michelle nodded slowly. "And you?"

"I think he's building his end of the bridge. Trying to reconnect." He paused, glancing toward the window, the distant lights of Kendall Square refracted in the glass. "And, it seems, I am too."

Matthew paused before saying, "I met with Darren's board this afternoon.

"A NeuroTech competitor views the current public mood shift as an opportunity to nudge them aside. It's an existential threat to NeuroTech. Darren took the company out on a limb of pharma speed and scale.

"He wasn't wrong to see that the pharma was ready to roll, while I was still in the design phase. He was always conversant in the community-informed, embodiment side of the equation. He just didn't think it was fully baked back then."

Matthew sat up straighter. "I agreed to testify in D.C.

before a House Oversight Committee tomorrow, outlining an integrated NeuroTech-TrailMind approach, with MIT providing quantum modeling cost-avoidance on things like relapse rates and emergency room use."

Jack raised an eyebrow. "Cost avoidance. Neutralizing risk before it becomes an expense. That's going to resonate with Congress, insurers, and community stakeholders."

Michelle added, "It frames TrailMind—with its public-space infrastructure, storytelling, and sensory presence—as fiscally smart, not just emotionally compelling."

Jack chuckled. "Sounds like you're creating Quantum Feelings, Inc. after all."

Matthew laughed softly. "Don't give her ideas."

He turned the beer bottle between his palms, eyes still on the table. "Though, you know, Mom—you could take a page from Maya."

Michelle tilted her head, amused. "Oh? Should I be taking notes, or just bracing myself?"

"I've learned a lot from her lately. How to collaborate without imposing my vision.

"TrailMind started as her project, but she's already letting her students and co-designers take it further.

"She doesn't guard the work—she grows the next round of gardeners. That's what gives me hope for the future."

Jack grinned. "Succession planning for ideas. I like it."

Michelle leaned back, mock-sighing. "So you're saying it's time for me to retire gracefully?"

Matthew smiled. "Gracefully—but not immediately."

Her laugh was soft but knowing. "Touché. Maybe that's the real trick of legacy—knowing when to let go."

Matthew lifted his glass. "To the handoff—graceful and on time."

Jack clinked his. "And to trusting they'll remember where the trail began."

<hr>

THE VIDEO INTERCOM buzzed in Hannah's Winter Hill apartment. When she answered, there was Maya, standing solemnly in front of the security camera. She held up a bottle of sparkling rosé to fill the screen and then a box of cookies.

"Lark's Rosemary Shortbread?" Hannah asked through the intercom.

"Cookies for grown-ups," Maya confirmed.

Hannah buzzed her in.

Hannah filled their glasses and flopped back onto the couch, pulling a throw blanket over their laps.

Maya sipped the bubbles and looked at Hannah over the rim of the glass. "So. That ClearFrame interview. You and Darren. There was ... a vibe."

Hannah arched a brow. "Excuse me?"

"That pause before he answered your question on post-market transparency? It was like he knew you were going to press—like you've had that conversation before."

Hannah looked at her cookie like it was a rare artifact. Then sighed.

"Okay, real talk. I think I like Darren Katsaros."

"Excuse me?" Maya echoed, eyebrows shooting up.

"I don't mean *like* like. I mean ... I thought he'd be another biotech bro. But he's sharp. Disciplined. And when I pressed him on transparency, he didn't dodge—he paused."

"Ah. The Darren pause." Maya nodded sagely.

"Exactly. Not a stall. A scan. Like he was mentally flipping through a file cabinet labeled Ethical Complications.

"And here's the thing—it wasn't just self-protective. I think he actually wants to get this right."

"He does!" Maya said emphatically.

"That's what made working with him so maddening—and so good." Maya continued. "He always held himself to a kind of internal code. Still there."

"I picked up on that. I came in ready to write him off as the poster child for AMC excess, but now ... I don't know.

"He's living in the tension. And that's more honest than most."

Maya smiled. "I'm not surprised. He's still Darren."

Hannah watched the bubbles dance in her glass. "You ever wonder what it would've looked like if you'd stayed in sync?"

"We didn't drift," Maya said. "We diverged. Different methods. Different terrain. But the same why."

"And Matthew?"

Maya sighed. "Where Darren builds systems, Matthew listens for signals. He's all about attunement, micro-resonances, nervous systems that don't know how to rest.

"Where Darren would ask, 'How do we reach a million anxious teens?' Matthew would ask, 'What does this one body need to feel safe right now?'

"And here's the thing. They're both trying to end suffering. That's the why."

Maya paused. "Matthew met with the NeuroTech board today. They asked him to testify tomorrow before the House Oversight Committee."

"That's good. I don't think EverCura or NeuroTech could have saved the AMC on their own. No point in throwing the baby out with the bath water.

"I trust Matthew to ..." Hannah paused, cookie in hand, "... to speak from the body. You know?

"Everyone else in that hearing room is going to come armed with outcomes and margins and predictive curves. But Matthew will walk in and remind them what anxiety feels like—what it costs to carry it, and what it means to finally put it down."

Hannah swirled her rosé, watching the bubbles settle. "He won't just defend the science. He'll defend the kids. The veterans. The teachers holding it together with coffee and instinct.

"He won't make this about market access. He'll make it about nervous systems—and the stories they've been trying to tell us all along."

"Yes," Maya said. "He will."

Hannah looked at Maya over the top of her glass of bubbles.

"And you ended up spending the night on Spectacle Island ... how?"

"Ah," Maya said. "That's the 'nervous systems that don't know how to rest' part.

"We were both a little crispy from the Health Commission's obsession with testing how TrailMind performs against NeuroEase. Matthew suggested we shake it off on the trail.

"The storm hit. Ferries stopped. We improvised. He strung a hammock in a ranger's shed. Heated stones for warmth."

"That hammock sounds ... not unpleasant," Hannah suggested gently.

Maya smiled faintly. "It was ... real. Just warm stones, roasted samphire, a busted old shed, and him showing up exactly as he is."

"Were you ... close-close?"

"Not like that. But close in the ways that count.

"I powered up my phone, typed something to the team, and he didn't ask what I was doing. He just said he'd rig the hammock and warm the place up.

"He gave me space to think. To lead. Then made sure we had shelter."

"Jesus," Hannah said, a little choked up. "That's more intimacy than most couples get in five years."

"Exactly. It wasn't a spark." Maya raised a brow. "I mean—you know me, I don't spark. It was ... anchoring. Like, the world is burning and he's quietly building a fire-safe room around us so we can keep creating."

"So ... is he the one?"

"My Prince Charming?" Maya snorted. "Not exactly.

"But since we're doing real talk—he raised the bar for me. About what matters. Collaborative. Steady. Attuned.

"Whoever I end up with—if I end up with anyone—Matthew has already drafted the blueprint." She smiled with a kind of calm clarity.

Hannah raised her glass to Maya. "That's the most emotionally evolved thing anyone's said to me all week."

Maya pushed the shortbread plate toward her.

"Here. Fortify yourself. You've still got a podcast to edit, a Substack post to land, and Darren to figure out."

Hannah laughed as she grabbed a cookie. "I'll need more cookies for that last one.

"But for what it's worth—I think Darren respects you. The way he talked about your Terrascope project?

"He didn't name-drop. He remembered why you did it."

Maya smiled. "That matters."

LATER THAT NIGHT—AFTER Matthew left and the dishes were done, Jack held up his arm as Michelle came to bed and settled into his embrace.

"He finally sees her," Jack said quietly.

"Maybe," Michelle smiled sadly.

"But you know him. For Matthew, trust isn't about the rush of feeling—it's about sustained ground. Steady ground."

"Can she give him that?" he asked.

"I think she might. Maya's different. They share that language of careful design. Of calibration.

"But they'll both make space for other possibilities before they name it love."

Jack pulled her closer. "Maybe love is just a long field trial."

TWENTY-THREE

Thirty-six hours after her storm dispatch from Spectacle Island, Maya walked into E14-647 with a mug of ginger tea and no slides. Matthew was already there with Ravi, who had logged into the design sync.

The screen filled one square at a time—Nia in her ranger hoodie, Rafiq with his LED glow, Lex from a dune-side rec center, Anika perched on a driftwood stool, and Jackson, still half in shadow at his Glacier campsite.

Maya did a quick kick-off. "Okay! No pitch deck. No roadmap. I just want to hear what cracked open for you after that thread."

Nia jumped in first. "I started prototyping Ask Permission —a prompt where users check in with a tree before they sit under it. It's so simple, but it changes the vibe. Like you're part of a relationship, not just in scenery."

"I've been working on noticings," Rafiq jumped in. "Instead of *how do you feel?* it asks, *what did the ibis do when you stepped closer?* Emotional intelligence through attention, not introspection—for users who don't do great with abstract prompts."

Anika smiled. "That's what I've been calling the soft channel. Stories, permission, no demand. Just resonance."

Maya nodded. "Exactly—our 'therapeutic anchors'. Moments that let the nervous system rest in safety."

Lex picked up the thread. "Then the next zone is engagement—sensing, syncing. That's where barefoot rituals and breath patterns live. Self-efficacy spikes, right? The little proofs of capability that build belonging."

Maya nodded. "Perfect. Anchors, then spikes."

Jackson's voice came steady through the wind. "And finally, the courage zone. You start in story, move through your senses, and when you're ready—you act. Build a fire. Walk a trail in silence. Not for calm—for capability."

Rafiq added, "It's where you test your nervous system. Not to push it, but to trust it."

Nia grinned. "I love this! Not levels—just choices. Calm tools for grounding and restoration. Curious tools for exploration and sensory connection. Courage tools for expression and contribution."

Ravi moved to the board and wrote three column headers:

Calm / Curious / Courage

He posted color-coded sticky notes in the columns, explaining, "Production status: green are live—these are tools we've already deployed, mostly Calm tools, some Curious tools. Yellow indicates pipeline tools that are six weeks out; pink, tools in design, and purple, tools that need funding. Calm tools are solid—ready for a full Spectacle Island run. Curious tools are fragmented. Courage tools ... ambitious."

Elena chimed in, "Audio customization works, but to make sensory toggles truly neurodivergent-friendly, we need another six weeks."

Ravi nodded. "Courage tools would need new safety protocols and partner reviews. Three months if we fast-track."

"That's assuming we get funding," Maya said dryly.

Nia waved her tablet. "Working on it. Two micro grants—Bridgeworks and the Embodied Equity Lab. Stackable. We can frame the Curious layer as safety scaffolding for future Courage work."

Sam slipped in wearing her new-job hoodie.

"So the sell is: adaptive choice equals psychological safety equals inclusion?"

Elena nodded. "Unlike exposure therapy, users control the pace—opt-in steps that prevent overwhelm."

Maya smiled. "Agency as safety. That's our differentiator."

She lowered her voice.

"One more variable: Michelle asked Darren to bring Elspeth Channing to the island next week."

There were groans and raised eyebrows around the room.

Maya held up her hands, palms out. "We can't block the visit. The question is—do we show them Calm, Curious, or Courage?"

Sam folded her arms. "If we show only Calm, they'll call it wellness fluff. If we show Courage, they'll panic over risk."

"Then we show Curious tools—user consent in action." Nia snapped her fingers.

Matthew nodded. "Patient-driven titration of emotional load. Like a dimmer switch or volume control knob. Choice, not prescription."

Ravi raised his hand. "I can build an adaptive demo—sound-path selection and haptic modulation. Elspeth can dial the intensity herself."

"It'll show where we're headed—and why a one-size-fits-all pill isn't enough," Maya agreed.

Sam scribbled fast. "Agency-centered exposure. Anti-coercive design. That's the headline."

Nia nodded. "We'll staff it peer-led."

Maya exhaled. "Perfect. Let's use Michelle's stage."

Ravi tapped the whiteboard. "Calm for rest. Curious for sovereignty. Courage in reserve."

Sam grinned. "That'll sell."

Maya looked around the room.

"Then let's build the governor's deck."

Matthew gathered his bag.

"I've got a flight to Washington. But before I go—what you're building here? It's regulation as felt experience. A framework that follows the body instead of forcing it."

He took a moment to make eye contact with each person in the room, on the screen.

"Call it what it is: 'Choice: A Nervous-System-Informed Approach to Mental Health at Scale'."

ON THURSDAY AFTERNOON, the congressional hearing room had the stillness of managed tension. Hannah sat in the gallery, flanked by public health advocates and reporters scribbling in analog notebooks, the din of Slack notifications silenced out of respect.

Dr. Thura Aung slipped into the seat beside her. "Your interview with Katsaros resonated with the Senator," he said softly. "She's keen to hear what 'flexing the AMC' might look like."

Hannah nodded once. "Let's hear what he has to say about it—under oath."

Just then, her watch vibrated quietly. A message from Priya pulsed across her screen:

ClearFrame Alert
Entitled_by_Design headliner cleared legal. Going live now.

Hannah didn't smile, but her eyes flicked once toward the dais.

At the front of the chamber, the committee chairman, a representative from one of Illinois's most gerrymandered but persistently diverse districts, brought the gavel down with measured resolve.

"This hearing convenes at a moment of national reckoning —not only about youth mental health, but about the tools we choose to treat it, the companies we fund to deliver it, and the structures we rely on to regulate both."

"Will the witnesses please rise and raise your right hand to be sworn in?" Hands went up. "Do you affirm that the testimony you are about to give is the truth, the whole truth, and nothing but the truth?"

"I do," they said in unison.

From her seat, Hannah watched as Darren turned—deliberately—to look at Evelyn Chen.

He knows, she thought to herself.

The chairman continued. "Dr. Katsaros, would you say the Advance Market Commitment for NeuroEase has fulfilled its purpose?"

"Mr. Chairperson, members of the committee—thank you."

Darren made eye contact with several committee members.

"The Advance Market Commitment enabled NeuroTech to fulfill its mandate at that time. We brought NeuroEase to market when speed was the priority.

"Congress asked for scale. We delivered it.

"We got a non-sedating, fast-acting neuroregulator into schools and communities—at a time when most school nurses and community health workers had no tools at all to help kids suffering from anxiety. That was the win.

"But when you ask about purpose, we have to look forward, not backward."

He paused for emphasis. "The AMC was swift—but it was also a blunt, one-dimensional tool. It did what it was asked to do in a moment of crisis. But now it's clear we need to adapt— or flex—that tool if we hope to meet what has proven to be a complex challenge.

"If our purpose is not just to relieve suffering, but to reduce it—maybe even eliminate it for many—we need to move toward equity-indexed reimbursements, multi-modality treatment models, and long-term outcome tracking."

The chairman invited the representative from Massachusetts to speak.

"Thank you, Mr. Chairman. I'm speaking today not only for my constituents but also for the full Massachusetts delegation, including our senior Senator, who's asked that this question be entered into the record.

"Dr. Katsaros—was it equitable to secure federal guarantees for NeuroEase while state and community mental-health programs lost their federal lifeline?"

A stir rippled through the room. Darren kept his tone measured.

"That tradeoff was not made by NeuroTech. It was made by appropriations committees working under duress during an unprecedented budget cycle. We continued to work against the terms of the AMC because Congress continued to require that."

The chairman cut in, less patient.

"You fulfilled a mandate—but at what cost? The AMC was designed to de-risk innovation, not to fast-track social dependency. The public's patience for private-sector saviors is thinning. They want tools, yes—but they want tools that work with communities, not replace them."

Darren's jaw flexed slightly. Then, carefully he said, "I agree. No one wants dependency—not on government, not on pharmaceuticals. What they want is access. Our mistake wasn't urgency—it was singularity. That's why I'm advocating a multi-path model today."

Darren paused and turned slightly toward Matthew at the adjacent witness table. "And why I'm grateful Dr. Matthew Venable is here. He's one of the original co-founders of Neuro-Tech—a scientist who believed from the beginning that neuropharmacology and behavioral neuroscience must work in tandem."

The chairman nodded. "Dr. Venable, we have your written testimony. But let me be clear: this committee isn't looking for an upsell. After four years and billions of taxpayer dollars, shouldn't the American people expect to see a meaningful reduction in youth anxiety?"

Matthew leaned in. Calm. Centered.

"Mr. Chairperson, that's a fair question. NeuroEase doesn't cure anxiety. It suppresses symptoms—effectively, but temporarily. Each dose gives about twenty-four hours of relief. To keep that benefit, a person has to keep taking it.

"But we should take pride in what that relief has meant. In 2021, we had no scalable tool to address adolescent panic. For millions of young people, NeuroEase provided breathing room. That matters.

"But symptom suppression isn't healing. That's why I'm here—not to displace what works, but to expand what's possible.

"In the past four years, we've developed technology-assisted somatic tools that offer scalable, user-driven pathways to build nervous system resilience. These don't rely on meds—but they can complement them."

He let that settle.

"In pilot sites, youth using technology-guided nature immersion in public parks reported a thirty-one percent drop in screen-induced somatic distress, headaches, nausea, panic, sensory overload.

"And just this year, quantum-enhanced modeling matured enough to apply to public health strategy.

"Dr. Lena Morales, Director of the MIT Quantum Health Lab, is here today. Her team can show how quantum computing lets us model layered outcomes like ER visits and school absences across cohorts—finally allowing us to see *what works, for whom, in what order.*

"The AMC got us started. But healing doesn't sprint towards a finish line—it needs a feedback loop."

Across the room, a staffer from the committee clerk's office approached Evelyn Chen. Just as she was being called to the mic, the staffer placed a printed copy of Hannah Oak's "Entitled by Design" story on the witness table in front of her.

Evie could see the headline in bold serif font: "Entitled by Design: Turning Adolescent Anxiety into a Medicaid Mandate." Her eyes narrowed for only a second—but it was enough. Darren saw it.

"Thank you, Dr. Venable. The Committee invites Dr. Evelyn Chen to present testimony," the chairman said.

"Dr. Chen, in your former role as Deputy Director of the Centers for Disease Control and Prevention's Neurobehavioral Health Division, you testified frequently and fervently for an AMC to accelerate neuropharmacological innovation to address the youth anxiety crisis. We have your written testimony. You have five minutes to walk us through your current thinking."

"Mr. Chairperson, with your permission, I'd like to supplement my submitted remarks."

He nodded—formal but curious.

"I stand by my written testimony, which outlines EverCura's commitment to expand access, streamline delivery, and ensure that no child's mental health treatment is determined by their ZIP code. Expanding Medicaid eligibility for adolescent anxiety isn't about corporate positioning.

"It's about catching up to clinical reality. If we're serious about equity, we can't keep mental health carved out of public care."

As Evelyn Chen adjusted the mic, the committee chairman nodded to Representative Soto, a former healthcare attorney from New Mexico known for his composure and precision.

"Ms. Chen, I want to be very clear with my question," Soto stated. "Did you, at any point prior to your departure from HHS in December, advise or consult with any representatives of EverCura—formally or informally—regarding Medicaid coverage frameworks for adolescent anxiety?"

Evie maintained a calm and steady voice. "Congressman, I followed all post-employment ethics rules and did not engage in any formal communication with EverCura while employed at HHS."

"I didn't ask about formal communication," Soto quipped. "I asked if you advised, consulted, or contributed in any capacity. Because your fingerprints are all over the January white paper EverCura submitted to the National Association of Medicaid Directors.

"Syntax. Terminology. Structural logic. It tracks directly with internal guidance documents you authored at HHS in 2024."

A low rustle moved through the gallery.

"I can't control who is influenced by publicly available guidance."

Evie maintained her composure.

"The Medicaid Innovation Toolkit I helped draft was published on the Health and Human Services website for public comment, as per standard procedure. If organizations found that framework useful, that speaks to its relevance."

"Relevance, or coordination?" Soto asked, still skeptical. There was a beat of silence.

Before Evie could respond, Representative Delaney of Oregon leaned in, flipping through a printout on her folder.

"One more question, Ms. Chen," she said. "Since January, you've made a series of personal donations to mental health nonprofits—groups now using identical phrases found in Ever-Cura's marketing briefs.

"Do you believe this creates the appearance of alignment, or influence?"

Evie's impatience slipped through her practiced calm.

"My donations were made as a private citizen to organizations doing important work. I do not direct their messaging. If they choose language that reflects shared values or regulatory language, that's their decision."

"But language can shape eligibility," Delaney asserted. "And eligibility is the gateway to revenue.

"So let me ask plainly—are you helping to script the next phase of the market you helped unlock?"

Evie said quietly, "I'm helping to build the infrastructure that ensures no child's care is left behind because of a reimbursement code."

"Duly noted," the chairman said. "If there are no further questions from the committee we will adjourn, with thanks to the panelists for their time and their testimony."

AMINA KASSAM STOOD at the head of the oval table, her deep red hijab, edged in hand-embroidered silk, catching the afternoon sun. Maya and Nia stood by the screen, the mood equal parts focused and electric.

"Let's see what you've got," Amina said, folding her arms. "The governor's team won't give us thirty minutes of reverent silence. We need clean, confident, and human."

Nia tapped her stylus. The deck came alive on the wall: a soft gradient moving from blue-gray to gold to ember-orange. A simple title hovered in white:

TrailMind: Calm. Curious. Courage.
Designing for Nervous System Sovereignty.

"We start with story," Nia said. "Not specs."

Slide two filled the screen—Jackson at sunrise, firelight flickering across his face. Beneath it, three short lines:

Calm = Rest.
Curious = Connection.
Courage = Contribution.

Amina's eyebrow lifted. "It's clean. Keep going."

The next slide had three minimalist icons—an open palm, an eye within a circle, and a small flame.

Nia narrated.

"Calm tools ground the user in sensory safety—sound, story, breath. They're our therapeutic anchors.

"Curious tools invite exploration—barefoot trails, adaptive soundscapes, micro-moments of capability. That's *self-efficacy spikes* and *inclusive prompts* in practice.

"Courage tools ask for gentle action—fire-building, orienteering, shared quests. That's where *collective impact* begins."

Amina nodded once, approving the translation from theory to lived design.

The next slide showed Ravi's production pipeline, the sticky-note system now color-coded by the three types of tools.

Maya explained, "Green tags are deploy-ready Calm tools. Yellow is Curious—six weeks from expansion. Orange is Courage—in design with safety protocols pending."

Amina's gaze flicked across the chart. "And the uncolored notes?"

"Co-design commitments," Nia said. "Signals of where inclusion still needs work.

"That's why the adaptive sensory demo next week matters—Darren's bringing Elspeth Channing to Spectacle. We'll show her how user-regulated exposure feels."

Amina appeared intrigued, but held her questions.

Slide five played a short loop: a young user tapping a stone marked with the open-palm icon, then removing their shoes. A calm voiceover narrated, "This is a Curious trail. You're allowed to go slow."

Nia turned toward her mentor.

"This is how we teach consent through design. The system doesn't push the nervous system—it listens to it."

Amina's expression softened. "Good. That's the line the governor will remember."

Slide six showed two funding tracks: Bridgeworks and the Embodied Equity Lab, color-linked to Curious and Courage.

"Bridgeworks supports the civic engagement layer of Courage tools," Maya said. "Embodied Equity funds the sensory-choice redesign in Curious. Together, they scale inclusion without diluting rigor."

"And your closing?" Amina asked.

The final slide appeared—a single statement on a wide horizon background:

Nature already knows the way.
We're just making the map visible.

Silence held for a few seconds.

Amina exhaled. "That's your closer. Don't gild it. Let the room breathe."

She turned to Nia. "And you're presenting."

Nia blinked. "Me?"

"Maya says you named the shift," Amina replied. "The governor wants to see what generational leadership looks like.

"This—" she gestured at the glowing screen, "is a bet on the future."

Then, pointing to Nia, she added, "And so are you."

When Amina left, the room stayed hushed. The screen had gone dark, but its afterglow still rimmed the table in pale amber.

Nia sat back, stylus loose in her hand. "Did she just say I'm presenting to the governor?"

Maya smiled—a smile that held pride, and the faint ache of letting go. "She did. And she's right."

"I thought you'd want to do it," Nia said softly.

"I already have," Maya replied. "Just in a different decade."

She reached over, touched Nia's wrist lightly.

"You're fluent in this language now—*Calm, Curious, Courage.* You built the bridge between feeling and framework. That's what leadership looks like."

Nia exhaled. "But I don't even own a suit. Or a skirt."

Maya smiled. "Then present to the governor dressed like the field-based co-designer you are. I do recommend lip balm, though—always pumps up my confidence."

As they gathered their notes, Maya's phone buzzed once. A text from Matthew:

Leaving D.C. soon. Head spinning. You'd love this chaos. C U later?

She smiled to herself—one brief, private pulse of connection—before slipping the phone face down on the table.

"Go home," she said to Nia. "Tomorrow, we make the map visible."

AS DARREN LEFT the hearing room with Matthew and Marisol, Thura Aung walked up to them.

"Undersecretary Vargas, it's a privilege to see you again." Aung greeted the former HHS undersecretary first, as would be her due.

"Dr. Deputy Minister," Marisol nodded her head in response, mirroring his respectful manners, then offered her hand to him. "It's good to see you, Ko Thura."

Aung turned to Matthew. "Dr. Venable, thought-provoking testimony. Thank you for that."

"Dr. Katsaros, if your colleagues can spare you, I'd appreciate a few moments of your time," Aung said, turning to Darren.

Darren saw Marisol and Matthew nod and said, "At your disposal, Doctor."

As Darren and Aung headed toward the elevator, Marisol said to Matthew, "Your passion for healing came through loud and clear today. Whatever Congress ends up deciding about the AMC, NeuroTech will need you to keep innovating.

"Do I have your permission to propose you to the board as our Chief Innovation Officer?"

"That depends, Dr. Vargas. Are you proposing I innovate within NeuroTech—or help reinvent what it's for?"

Marisol smiled. "Answering that question is exactly why a company like NeuroTech has a board—not a founder-god or a fixed doctrine."

TWENTY-FOUR

Aung led Darren past the iconic Calder sculpture to the non-public part of the Senator's Capitol Hill office—a narrow cubicle maze affectionately called *the warren* by staffers.

He unlocked his monitor so Darren could see the paused frame from the *ClearFrame* interview. His own face stared back—mid-thought, eyes narrowed, jaw set.

"If we want scale," the closed caption read, "the AMC has to flex. Innovation isn't always a pill—it's sometimes a path."

Aung pointed. "The Senator watched the whole thing. Twice."

Darren arched a brow.

"She was especially struck by that line—'the AMC has to flex'. She's been looking for a new frame, and you handed her one."

Darren kept his tone even. "Happy to help. Wasn't sure anyone on the Hill would go for it."

"Oh, she does," Aung said, clicking the mouse.

The freeze frame vanished, replaced by an internal memo

titled, "Redefining AMCs for Public Health Access: Not Just Meds but Motion."

"She wants to know if you're serious," Aung continued.

"Willing to help inform an AMC that stimulates innovation in transit access to therapeutic environments. Ferries. Trail corridors. Intermodal passes tied to diagnostic risk and equity tiers. Not just to clinics—but to the commons."

Darren sat back, absorbing. "So ... we're treating movement itself as intervention?"

Aung nodded. "We're treating access as public-health infrastructure. Like Head Start for mental health, only mobile.

"If it's part of a sensory-regulatory continuum—not just transport, but part of the care protocol—it becomes fundable. HHS prevention. Maybe even the Department of Education, or what's left of it."

Darren let out a slow exhale. "You want me to write the scaffolding."

"Call it a white paper," Aung said.

"You're not a federal employee. But you are an influencer. Help me sketch the bones. Make 'motion as medicine' real enough for Appropriations to write it into report language—and flexible enough for HHS and DOT to run with."

Darren stared at the screen, then shook his head slightly.

"Ko Thura, forgive the metaphor—but this feels like patching an old bridge with new paint. The AMC framework was built for velocity, not longevity.

"Do we keep nailing fresh boards onto federal scaffolding that's already splintering?"

Aung folded his arms. "You'd rather burn it down?"

"I'd rather start where the ground still holds. Local networks. State compacts. Maybe public-private pilots that don't depend on Congressional oxygen."

Aung smiled faintly. "You sound like my daughter. But tell

me—how long do you think the kids she teaches can wait for fifty different states to invent fifty versions of equity?"

Darren hesitated. "I've watched too many good ideas rot inside federal pilots—the whole thing collapses under its own bureaucracy."

Aung leaned forward. "Then rebuild it smarter. That's what scaffolding is for—to hold while something stronger sets.

"You know this system's brittle—but you also know the scale of suffering outside it. If we abandon the frame entirely, the people who need it most fall first."

The room fell quiet except for the distant buzz of a printer.

"You're asking me to reinforce a structure I no longer trust," Darren said finally.

"I'm asking you to decide whether reform is still an act of service," Aung replied.

"Maybe the scaffolding is cracked—but until a new structure rises, it's the only thing keeping the roof from crushing the workers."

Darren looked at the paused header again—"Not Just Meds but Motion." He rubbed his temple. "You always did know how to turn my utilitarian streak into conscience."

Aung smiled. "That's why the Senator trusts you. You question the premise before you sign the plan."

After a long beat, Darren nodded once. "Alright. I'll draft the outline. But I want the language to admit the brittleness—make flexibility a feature, not a flaw."

"Fair," Aung said. "We'll call it 'adaptive scaffolding'."

He picked up his phone, dialed quickly. "Danny? Katsaros is in." He paused. "Will do."

"That was the Governor's chief of staff," Aung explained. "He asked that you join the Governor tomorrow morning at a State House briefing on the future of the Boston Harbor Islands Park. I trust you're familiar with the issues."

Darren nodded, thoughtful now. "I'll be there."

<hr>

MAYA HAD JUST SET her mug in the sink when her security system buzzed. She opened the screen to find Matthew—shoulders slumped, tie loosened, eyes carrying both exhaustion and adrenaline.

"My head's still spinning," he admitted, leaning against the pillar in her lobby. "Congress, Darren, data models—too many voices. I could use a little...affective co-regulation."

Maya smiled softly and pressed the buzzer. "Come up. No models here. Just tea, blankets, and maybe a little quiet."

She opened the apartment door for him, and they sank onto the couch. For a long while, neither spoke. Matthew let his hand rest, tentative but steady, on hers. She didn't parse it, didn't analyze it—just received it.

Finally, he exhaled.

"You know, Maya ... the last two nights I couldn't sleep. I kept thinking about Spectacle. About how I didn't want that night to be an exception. I want more nights like that—with you."

Maya turned toward him, her expression soft but uncertain.

"I want that too," she murmured. "But I couldn't ask first. I needed to know you wanted this."

He tilted his head, studying her with quiet patience.

She drew in a careful breath.

"I'm still learning how to move toward someone without translating it through what the world says intimacy is supposed to mean."

She raised her hand to hover alongside his face, not touching.

"If I reach for you, I need to know what kind of yes I'm giving—and what kind of yes I'm receiving."

He leaned in slightly, still not touching her. "Then ask me."

She hesitated, breath catching. "What do you want consent to mean?"

Matthew's reply was quiet, almost reverent. "That you're here. That you chose this moment."

Something eased inside her.

"You're okay if there's no blueprint—for us?"

He smiled, tired but certain. "I'm okay as long as we build it together. The way we build everything else. One evening at a time."

Maya closed the gap and laid her hand against his face. The warmth surprised her—not the heat of want, but the steady hum of being understood.

He leaned into her touch, letting her take some of the weight of his head.

For a long time they stayed like that—the silence between them not a pause, but a promise.

She moved her hand from his cheek and ran her fingers gently through his hair. "Stay tonight. No hearings, no pitch decks. Just presence."

Matthew leaned back into the couch, finally letting the day fall away.

"That's exactly what I need."

ON FRIDAY MORNING, the State House conference room gleamed with quiet purpose—high ceilings, portraits of reformers and rebels, the seal of the Commonwealth behind the governor's seat.

Joe D., longtime civic leader and the Governor's appointed

chair of her Boston Harbor Islands Park Advisory Committee, adjusted his glasses and addressed the room.

"Governor, thank you for convening us at this critical moment for public spaces in general and the Boston Harbor Islands Park specifically.

"Before we begin, I want to welcome our newest committee members and recognize your mandate to include stakeholders whose voices have too often been excluded—especially youth mental health advocates, public educators, veterans, and survivors of gender-based violence." He gestured toward Alexis Kim, Kris, Barsa, Malik Spencer, and Janey Jones.

The governor's expression softened into something warmer than her usual podium polish.

"Thank you, Joe. And thank you for naming what we're trying to build here—not just a working group, but a living example of what inclusive governance should look like."

She turned toward Janey Jones with a nod that carried the weight of both past tension and present respect.

"Janey and I have stood on opposite sides of a microphone more than once," she said, the room catching the edge of humor beneath the truth. "But no one who's watched her lead—through crises, through transition—could question her deep commitment to the people of Boston."

A few heads nodded around the table.

"She knows what it means to serve a city where every square mile carries both beauty and burden.

"I trust her to challenge us, ground us, and remind us who these parks—and these policies—are really for."

She looked around the room, her voice firm again.

"We're not here to preserve a view. We're here to protect the public good. And that takes all of us. Thank you Janey, Alexis, and Malik for sharing your time and your expertise."

Janey Jones nodded with dignity.

Alexis stood. "As a public high school teacher, I want to thank you for recognizing that what happens in our parks reverberates in our classrooms. When students feel safe in nature, they're more likely to feel safe in themselves.

"It's why I keep showing up—because I see what parks can do when schools can't."

Malik nodded. "And as someone living this, not studying it —I appreciate being at the table. Not after the decisions are made. From the beginning."

Joe D. continued, "The committee has reviewed a dozen proposals ranging from shoreline resiliency to biodiversity mapping, but one recommendation stands out in its capacity to do more with less—TrailMind.

"With the loss of federal funding and the retirement of senior NPS partners, we are facing both a staffing and mental health crisis—not only among visitors, but among our own rangers and volunteers. "

He clicked to the next slide on the screen:

TrailMind Deployment as Operational Relief Model.

"TrailMind reframes this challenge through user-experience design. Three key factors stand out.

"First, TrailMind embeds wayfinding and behavioral nudges into trail use, reducing direct staff burden.

"Second, it integrates trash pickup, trail maintenance reporting, and ecological data collection into the visitor journey.

"And finally—and most critically—it uses tech to reduce—not increase—anxiety activation. It is cost-effective nervous system stewardship."

The governor raised an eyebrow. "And the budget ask—does it include equitable access to the cost of the ferry?"

"The state's budget is coming in at twenty percent of what federal agencies had requested for the Harbor Islands Park. As you know, that amount was already submitted to the Massachusetts Legislature in the governor's budget in January.

"The line item has cleared the State Senate and is with the Conference Committee for reconciliation. We're cautiously optimistic—bipartisan support is strong, and the timing is aligned.

"In addition, the Harbor Islands Advisory Committee, with support from the MIT Quantum Health unit, has negotiated for free ferry fare for anyone with a prescription from a provider—so far Mass Blue Cross Blue Shield, Harvard Pilgrim, and Tufts are all on board to reimburse the ferry operator as part of a pilot program to measure cost avoidance using MIT's quantum analysis capability.

"And the ferry operator will honor the MBTA Link Pass. It is a homegrown Commonwealth solution, but it makes us a national model."

The governor turned toward the table.

"Speaking of national models ..." Her gaze landed on Darren Katsaros.

"Dr. Katsaros. You've made the federal AMC model famous for medication access. If low-income and rural communities can't reach public spaces, we've failed before we begin.

"I want to mobilize our Massachusetts health equity community to advocate the U.S. Congress for an AMC structured to guarantee equitable transport to public lands—state and national.

"Can I count on you to lead an advocacy strategy workshop at our 2026 Health Equity Trends Summit next week?"

Darren gave a faint smile. "If we frame access as therapeutic necessity? Absolutely."

The governor nodded. "Good. Thanks to Joe D. and the advisory committee's excellent private sector outreach, the Commonwealth can afford to pilot Motion as Medicine.

"But every state in the union needs this right now ... and I don't see Manchester-by-the-Sea voting to subsidize access to The Badlands."

That line earned a barking laugh from Joe D.

The governor raised a brow. "And TrailMind?"

Joe looked to Maya and Matthew, then back to the governor.

"We propose a TrailMind Implementation Fellowship— twelve months, five embedded sites, and a co-led youth advisory council.

"We don't just want tech pilots. We want healing environments."

"Then," the governor said, standing, "let's build them."

HANNAH LANDED A COVETED, digital "above the fold" slider spot on the *ClearFrame* website again.

Unprescribed Blog, June 5, 2026
"Flex the AMC. Fund the Ferry." By Hannah Oak

This morning, the governor convened the Boston Harbor Islands Park Advisory Committee under an expanded mandate already drawing national attention. And yes—before you ask—the real story isn't just about parks. It's about access, nervous system sovereignty,

and how we define public health in an age of rising
anxiety and shrinking trust.

And for once, policy isn't lagging behind lived
experience.

From Pill to Path

On Tuesday, June 2, I hosted Darren Katsaros—mental
health systems architect, Advance Market Commitment recipient, and famously allergic to microphones—
for a live *ClearFrame* conversation. I asked Katsaros to
justify why the AMC should favor pharma.

Darren offered this instead, "If we want scale, the
AMC has to flex. Innovation isn't always a pill—it's
sometimes a path."

That quote sparked thousands of shares—and a quiet but
unmistakable ripple through Beacon Hill. Two days later,
staff for Massachusetts' senior U.S. Senator confirmed she
is reviewing proposed directive language for the federal
Labor-HHS and Transportation-HUD Appropriations
Bills. The draft would frame equitable transit not just as
infrastructure—but as part of a therapeutic protocol.

Or, as one insider put it to me, "Not just access to
clinics—access to the commons."

The Senator's team is expected to coordinate with
Massachusetts House members to ensure the language
finds footing on both sides of the Capitol.

In plain terms? As Congress completes its mark ups of the federal FY27 budget, there is a narrow but real window to secure federal funding to guarantee ferry access, bus service, and trail linkages to national and state parks—not just as recreation, but as public health infrastructure.

Voices on the Ground

The story of how we got here belongs not to lawmakers or think tanks—but to those already doing the work.

When I visited the Inner Harbor Youth Alliance on Wednesday afternoon, a group of teens gathered in a side room with views of the herons and salt marshes near Chelsea Creek. We talked about TrailMind, about the Boston Harbor Islands, and about what it means to feel safe in your own body.

"We don't need another app telling us to breathe," said Laila, 16. "We need places where we can breathe without asking permission."

"I've never been on a ferry," said Tomas, 14. "It always seemed like something for tourists. Not for us."

The governor seems to get that.

She welcomed four new appointees to the Harbor Islands Park Advisory Committee:

* Janey Jones, well-known advocate for policies to end gender-based violence.

- Alexis Kim, educator and trauma-informed curriculum designer.
- Kris Barsa, Marine veteran and field coordinator for the Ranger Assist Peer Network.
- Malik Spencer, youth mental health advocate and community co-designer with the Inner Harbor Youth Alliance.

Here's what they told me about their writ:

Alexis: "This is not about designing content. It's about designing consent. Parks can model how public space teaches safety—and TrailMind shows us how."

Kris: "Some of us never learned to regulate. We learned to perform. But these islands offer a chance to retrain—not just veterans, but anyone whose body forgot how to rest."

Malik: "They didn't ask me to join because I had a degree. They asked because I've lived this. And I think the system's ready to stop managing our symptoms and start listening to us."

Janey: "Survivors don't just need exits from danger—they need entrances into public life. Every bus route, every ferry line, every open trail is another way back into themselves."

What's Next

Whether this becomes the new model or just a hopeful moment depends on whether the policy catches up to the practice. But right now, the map is expanding—and the story isn't over.

I'll be back Monday with a full recap of the advisory committee's first public agenda and a closer look at what the governor means when she says Massachusetts is "putting motion into medicine."

Stay tuned. Stay present.

IT WAS Friday evening and the Inner Harbor Youth Alliance conference room smelled faintly of pizza and floor wax, the way all good youth meetings do.

Folding chairs circled a low table stacked with notebooks, markers, and half-drained bottles of Polar seltzer. A hand-painted banner from a past rally still hung on the wall: "TRUST IS A PRACTICE, NOT A POLICY."

Nia stood at the front, sleeves rolled, tablet on the chair beside her. Maya, Sam, and Hannah had tucked themselves quietly along the back wall, notebooks closed, trying to follow Maya's rule: *listen first, interpret later.*

"Alright," Nia said, glancing around the circle.

"Tonight's not a focus group. It's not a beta test. It's just a conversation about what you trust—and what you don't—when someone says, 'we've built an app to help with anxiety'."

Laughter flickered through the group.

"Okay, who wants to start?"

A girl in a red hoodie raised her hand. "Depends who built it. If it's some dude in California telling me how to breathe, hard pass."

Several nodded.

"Why?" Nia asked.

"Because they don't know us," the girl said simply. "They don't know what it's like when your panic's not just school stress—it's rent, or cops, or your little brother getting deported. An app can't hold that."

A boy leaned forward, elbows on knees.

"Sometimes I trust tech more than people, though. Like, an app doesn't judge. Doesn't look at me weird. I can type what I'm feeling without seeing someone's face twist."

"That's real," Nia said quietly. "So for you, the screen gives space, not distance?"

He nodded. "Yeah. But I still want to know who's reading the data. 'Cause if it's going to my counselor, cool. If it's going to some company, nah. That's surveillance, not support."

From the back, Sam scribbled a note, *Transparency as safety*.

Another voice added, "I want tech that helps me feel my body again, not disappear from it. Like when TrailMind makes you notice your breathing? That's dope. But I don't want it deciding if I need meds or not. That's my call."

Maya watched Nia nod—slow, deliberate—letting silence do half the work. Nia, the one who had synthesized Trail-Mind's framing into *Calm, Curious, Courage*. This was it in practice.

A younger teen spoke up. "My mom says therapy's for rich people. Pills are free at school. So what do we do?"

The question hung heavy. Even the air conditioner seemed to pause.

"That's why we're here," Nia said gently. "To build tools that don't make you choose between help and agency. Between silence and stigma."

From the doorway came a soft shuffle. Maya turned—

Michelle Venable slipped in beside Matthew, who gave a faint nod of greeting. Behind them, Darren Katsaros.

Nia caught their arrival but kept going.

"What would make you trust a system that listens through sensors or apps?"

A girl with braids twined in copper wire answered. "When it tells the truth. Like—don't pretend it's therapy if it's not gonna cure me. If it provides temporary relief, say it that way."

Hannah glanced over to see how that landed with Darren, but his face was unreadable.

"Let us see our own data," another youth called out. "If my heartbeat's wild, I should know before a dashboard in D.C. does."

A murmur of agreement rippled around the room. Hannah whispered to Maya, "They're drafting the ethics for you."

Maya nodded. "And doing it better."

Then a quiet boy in the corner spoke for the first time.

"You know what I'd trust? Something that didn't start by assuming I'm broken. Maybe it could ask how I'm already surviving."

Nia smiled.

"So you'd be OK with answering that question—how you're surviving? Because that would give us resilience data. We can learn from it."

He met her eyes. "As long as you learn fast. We're tired."

Maya glanced at Matthew—his jaw tight, eyes damp. Michelle reached over and set a hand on his arm, grounding him.

Darren looked away, face still unreadable.

Nia closed the circle.

"You all just wrote the brief I wish Congress could hear.

"So before we wrap, one word from each of you—what real care feels like."

"Listening."

"Consistency."

"Safety."

"Honesty."

"Patience."

"Belonging."

Maya wrote each word in her notebook, then underlined them twice.

The youth hung around long enough to eat the pizza, then left for the bus stop.

The adults lingered, still half-hushed by the honesty that had just filled the room.

Matthew spoke first. "That—right there—is what co-regulation looks like."

Darren cleared his throat. "They'd eat me alive on the Hill if I said half of that."

Maya smiled faintly. "Then maybe that's your cue to start listening, not pitching."

Hannah dictated her blog into her phone. "Headline: 'They Said They're Tired'," she began.

Michelle overheard her and said, "Let's hope the governor reads this."

TWENTY-FIVE

Hannah's piece had dropped before sunrise on Saturday with the headline "They Said They're Tired".

By 8:00 a.m., it was trending under #RealCare and quoted in the governor's morning briefing.

Elspeth scrolled through it on her tablet as the ferry cut a smooth path across the harbor under early summer skies.

Darren stood at the bow, sunglasses in place.

Elspeth, hair secured in a Jackie O-style scarf, asked him, "You read this yet?"

He nodded. "Three times. I was there, and it still hit different seeing it written down. The words land harder in print—like a mirror you can't dodge."

Elspeth glanced at him. "Were you uncomfortable last night?"

"I was." Darren exhaled, rubbing his temple. "I thought I'd hear another round of platform complaints.

"But they were ... surgical. They didn't reject tech—they rejected the premise that they need fixing."

"Welcome to Generation Z," Elspeth said, jotting a note.

"They've watched our institutions overpromise for twenty years. They speak fluent skepticism."

He nodded, staring out at the harbor.

"One of the girls said, 'Let us see our own data before a dashboard in D.C. does.' It landed harder than any oversight hearing I've been in. Made me realize how much of our transparency talk is just theater."

Elspeth looked at him carefully. "So what do you do with that realization, Dr. Katsaros?"

He gave a small, rueful laugh. "Try not to weaponize it into another framework. Maybe just—listen."

"Careful," she teased. "That sounds dangerously unmarketable."

"They were talking about safety like it's a living thing," Darren said. "Not something you legislate—something you earn."

"Exactly. You translate that. Don't call it therapy—call it agency, participation, stewardship. Same soul, different syntax."

"You think that language—belonging, resilience—actually registers with Boomers in policy seats?" he asked.

"It can, if you stop dressing it in therapy talk. Give them civic words they recognize," Elspeth advised.

She smiled faintly. "That'll play well with the governor. Her generation equates safety with control.

"These kids equate it with transparency. That's a translation job waiting to happen."

He nodded. "Guess I'm the interpreter now."

"Then start with this sentence," Elspeth said, tapping the screen. "'As long as you learn fast. We're tired.'"

She looked up. "You think we can?"

Darren took a long sip of coffee. "Ask me after today."

The ferry horn sounded low and steady as Spectacle Island

rose through the mist. Nia and two teen co-designers from her field team waited at the dock, standing beside a simple easel that read: "TrailMind Adaptive Demo: Calm + Curious Modules in Field Testing. Self-Directed. User-Controlled. Consent-Based."

"Welcome to Spectacle," Nia called, extending a hand. "Thanks for coming out."

Elspeth shook it, polite but skeptical. "Appreciate the access. I'm interested to see how this feels beyond the slide decks."

"We've kept today's demo simple," Nia continued, handing them each a slim notecard.

"It's a user-led adaptive module. Just you, the environment, and sensory options you control."

Elspeth glanced at the card: *Notice your breathing. If you feel steady, choose one additional sense to engage: sound, texture, or motion. At any time, you can dial back or pause. Your pace, your call.*

Elspeth's eyebrow twitched. "You're testing informed micro-dosing of attention."

"Exactly," Ravi said, stepping forward.

"Unlike exposure therapy, where you deliberately push people into discomfort to desensitize them, this lets users titrate their own emotional load—moment to moment.

"No system intervenes. No default escalation. It's like giving them guardrails they can move or remove as they grow. That's how we protect against accidental overwhelm."

"Agency-centered," Darren said approvingly.

"Sovereignty," Nia corrected, simply.

They walked slowly up the winding Summit Trail. The harbor shimmered behind them. Soft breeze, distant gulls, and the smell of summer beach grass surrounded them.

At the first demo station, a small, laminated sign beneath a windswept pitch pine read: "Three Listening Paths Available. Choose based on your current state."

Next to it, a tablet interface offered: "A lightweight haptic vest is nearby, available but entirely optional."

Elspeth studied the menu. "No baseline assessment? No pre-screen?"

Nia shook her head.

"That's the point. The user self-assesses. They decide what feels right, or if nothing feels right at all. They can even just sit here and listen to the wind."

Elspeth hovered, then selected Curious Path and slipped on the headphones. A soft chant in Wôpanâak began—layered with the steady wash of waves and wind chimes synced to real-time breeze data.

After two minutes, she touched the tablet to lower the volume slightly. Another thirty seconds, and she gently unstrapped the haptic vest without saying a word.

When the track ended, she removed the headphones and sat still for a beat longer than anyone expected.

Farther up the trail, one of the teens quietly approached Darren and handed him a similar card, inviting him to try the paths himself.

He hesitated, then sat on the low bench and slipped on the haptic vest. He selected Pulse Path, leaned forward, and closed his eyes.

The soft percussive heartbeat rolled up through the vest's actuators. It wasn't overwhelming. It wasn't guided. It simply was. He exhaled.

When the track faded, he removed the vest, stood, and placed it carefully on the table.

"You know what's disorienting?" he said softly, half to Elspeth, half to himself.

"Nothing tried to fix me. I didn't realize how loud my head was—until I sat somewhere that didn't try to optimize it."

Elspeth said nothing but scribbled that line almost verbatim in her notebook.

"That isn't therapy," she finally said.

"No," Nia answered quietly. "It's pre-therapy. Or post-therapy. Or maybe not therapy at all. It's what happens when you let the nervous system feel what safe stillness tastes like—on its own terms."

Elspeth tapped her pen against her notebook.

"And if someone experiences distress during this?"

"They stop," Nia answered, straightforward.

"No badge lost. No failure logged. No auto-SMS from your pharmacy because your daily dose is still sitting in the sensor-lined blister pack."

"The data's anonymous," Ravi explained. "We're training comfort with self-awareness, not compliance with a regimen."

"We are in the process of expanding the design of the haptics for a broader spectrum of neurosensitivity," Nia explained, then added carefully, "And I'm sharing this with permission."

She glanced toward Maya, who gave a slight nod.

"Early in the pilot, we noticed a cluster of biometric feedback that didn't match any of our calibration profiles," Nia continued.

"It turned out to be from one of our own team leads. Dr. Venkataraman wasn't registering the standard comfort responses—not because she was disengaged, but because her sensory system speaks a different dialect."

Maya smiled faintly. "Turns out the tools I was designing weren't speaking to my own body."

Nia picked up the thread.

"That realization was pivotal. If even our lead researcher—

someone fluent in the language of design, intention, and data—was being misread by the system, then the system wasn't broken. It was incomplete."

She paused just long enough to let it land. "So we built new protocols. Ones that don't treat divergence as distortion. The neuroadaptive track came directly from that moment—from a need to design for inclusion not just as an ethical layer, but as a foundational one."

"After Nia found the outlier data," Maya said, with a dry little shrug, "I had to face the reality that I was the outlier. And it's kind of freeing.

"Living with a somatic profile that isn't typical shouldn't mean you're invisible to the tools designed to help you."

Darren watched Elspeth's face carefully. No sharp critique. Just ... engagement. Compassion?

As they walked back toward the dock, Maya fell into step next to Darren. "You brought her here to test our weaknesses."

He shook his head slowly. "She expected wellness fluff. What you're showing is consent-based nervous system recalibration. Harder to dismiss."

"And harder for NeuroEase to replicate," Maya added, voice low. "You can't pill your way to self-trust."

Darren looked out at the approaching ferry. He saw Michelle on the bow, wild black curls caught in the wind.

"No," he said. "But you can market the hell out of the illusion."

At the dock, Elspeth paused and turned back to Nia.

"This model presumes high user insight," she said.

Nia shrugged. "Or it builds it."

As the ferry drew closer, Elspeth remained on the dock a moment longer, notebook still in hand, watching the teens pack up the demo. Something in their ease unsettled her—a glimpse of safety not granted but claimed.

"THANK YOU FOR MAKING TIME, ELSPETH," Michelle said as Elspeth slid into the booth.

Michelle held up a thermos. "I brought some warm peppermint tea, hoping you'd share it with me—along with your impressions."

Elspeth replied, tightening her hold on the tea cup as the ferry lurched forward, settling into its route, "It was ... instructive."

Michelle smiled faintly. "That was the intent."

They let a beat of silence pass, both measuring the opening.

Michelle broke first. "I promised you a story no one else would touch. But I was wrong."

Elspeth's eyes narrowed slightly. "Go on."

"You know Josh Sterne has stepped in. Parachuted, really."

Michelle's tone was smooth, but not entirely forgiving.

"Apparently your column caught his attention. He told his staff not to leave this story to the 'legacy' outlets. He thinks you're giving your Boomer subscribers easy narratives that harden the pharma versus wellness binary."

Elspeth said nothing but allowed the irritation to show in the set of her jaw. Josh Sterne was known for shaping narratives with brutal clarity—and limited nuance.

Michelle continued softly.

"I think you may understand what matters even more than our Golden Boy publisher."

She let the thought sit there, unfinished.

Elspeth glanced down at her notebook, but didn't open it. The implication hung in the space between them.

Michelle kept her voice steady. "You saw today what consent architecture can mean—not just for these kids, but for people who rarely get to choose when the world overwhelms them."

Another pause. Not pushing. Waiting.

"They said they're tired," Michelle murmured. "What you saw today is what recovery looks like when people are finally allowed to rest."

Elspeth finally looked up. Her voice was quieter. "My son isn't on the registry."

Michelle said nothing.

"Technically he doesn't meet the full diagnostic threshold. Sensory integration atypicalities. Social hyperfocus. Auditory hypersensitivity. Brilliant, but fragile.

"He's learned to mask better than any kid should have to."

She let the words hang for a beat, then added with a dry edge, "And, professionally, it's easier for everyone if I remain objective."

Michelle nodded, not with pity, but with recognition.

"The luxury of objectivity is rarely offered to those of us with skin in the game."

Elspeth gave a faint smile, tinged with something closer to exhaustion than amusement. "You want me to rally the Boomers for TrailMind?"

"I want you to write the piece only you can write," Michelle said gently. "One that understands that not every metric of efficacy is a flat line on a clinical trial chart. One that understands what you saw on that island isn't simply about access—it's about autonomy. About designing for dignity."

She let her words soften. "And I suspect you already know how few interventions truly offer that."

Elspeth closed her notebook slowly. "If I write it, I'll write it clean. No angles. No puff."

"I wouldn't expect anything less."

They sat quietly sipping peppermint tea. Two women navigating the dissonance between loving fiercely and speaking carefully.

ON MONDAY MORNING, E14-647 in the Media Lab was humming—an organized chaos of shared documents, live feeds, color-coded walls, and screens showing split Zoom windows from rec centers, ranger stations, and school gardens across three time zones.

Maya had just stepped away to refill her tea when the door opened behind her.

"Was looking for you all at the Steam Café ..." Darren said, stepping in with his laptop bag slung over one shoulder.

Heads turned. Hannah, sitting cross-legged on the floor with a pile of printouts, didn't miss a beat.

"Steam's been closed since 2024," she said, deadpan.

The tension popped like a soap bubble. Laughter rippled across the room.

Maya turned, amused. "Darren Katsaros, welcome to the storm. This is what a neurodivergent co-design hackathon tiger team looks like."

A few heads swiveled. A couple of field-based co-designers blinked—either at his name, or at the idea of someone expecting to find a team *in real life*, on purpose.

Matthew gestured to a spare chair. "Find a flat surface. Or don't. We're boundary-light today."

Darren settled in, eyes scanning the virtual board.

"You're mid-flight, I can tell. I won't derail. I'm following up on a meeting I had with Thura Aung."

A murmur went through the room at the mention of the well-respected health policy advisor to Massachusetts' senior U.S. Senator.

Maya gave him her full attention.

"He said the Senator wants a memo. Not on pharma this time—but on a flexed AMC that includes mobility infrastructure as part of the mental health protocol. Transport, access, therapeutic thresholds. Ferries, shuttles, walking routes."

He looked around the room. "I need to know what this team knows——before anyone turns this into a framework.

"What are the actual access bottlenecks? What sensory and logistical needs emerge in motion?

"Because if we're going to pitch this as 'motion is medicine', we need field data to back it."

A twenty-ish young man haloed by the rising sun behind his tent piped in over Zoom.

"Are we talking just ferry access?" he asked. "Or things like scent overload on shuttle buses and platform noise thresholds?"

"Exactly that," Darren said.

Jackson, still at Glacier, raised a gloved hand.

"We've been logging ranger fatigue around group escort loads. Some of the stress transfer is nonverbal. The transition zones need redesign—what we call the ambient squeeze."

Maya's graduate assistant, Rafiq, typed in the shared doc.

Add: predictable route orientation, low-decibel holding zones, scent-neutral seating. And let's stop pretending transit is neutral—it's fully embodied.

Nia nodded. "And we need to document who's skipping the journey altogether. Not uninterested—just unwilling to white-knuckle their way through noise and crowd and expectation to get there.

"First time I boarded the ferry and that damn horn went off, I nearly dove straight into the harbor."

Alexis nodded and picked up the thread.

"Transit can feel like surveillance if the system doesn't give you rhythm.

"Our neurodivergent students are already working on transport maps that score routes by sensory exposure instead of speed. It's their idea of safety planning.

"And in the past eighteen months we're hearing more from first-gen students—especially undocumented families—who won't tap a Charlie Card or SNAP-linked transit pass because they're convinced it pings a database. Surveillance isn't just state—it's sensory and social, too."

Kris leaned forward. "For vets, too. We're trained to track exits and cues. If the path there feels hostile, we won't show up. Doesn't matter how good the programming is on the island.

"That's why I'm pushing ADA-plus design standards—dog-handler navigation under duress, bioswale buffers near transfer points, hydration nodes built into micro-climate corridors. I trained dogs for people. Now we need to design place to meet them both."

Darren was scribbling. "So you're saying that for the AMC to flex in the right way, it has to underwrite both cost and coherence. Access isn't just fare-free. Subsidy without sensory intel is just optics. It's stress-calibrated."

Ravi spun his screen around.

"We've already mocked up a ferry onboarding module that mirrors our Calm protocols—quiet, low-interaction, optional grounding narrative. You board into the experience, not just into the boat."

Darren looked impressed. "You're choreographing access."

"We're choreographing permission," Maya replied. "Movement as invitation, not requirement."

"It's the same principle we use in trauma recovery,"

Matthew added. "Predictability, pacing, the option to opt out without penalty.

"You can't heal if you're bracing the whole time."

Darren leaned back. "That may be the cleanest argument I've heard yet for why the AMC has to flex. And why it has to flex here first."

Nia looked up from her tablet. "Then take this to the Senator: The ferry isn't a bonus. It's the first gate to sovereignty. If you want nervous system equity, you have to fund the crossing."

The room was silent, but charged.

Maya looked up from her notes. "Title for your memo: 'To Get to the Commons'."

"Subtitle," Hannah added softly, "'Nervous System Equity and the Right to Arrive ... and Thrive.'"

Darren met her eyes and nodded.

BY THE TIME Maya and her team reached the meadow overlook, the governor's advance crew was already pacing it like a film set.

Danny Ruiz, the governor's chief of staff, pointed at the horizon through mirrored sunglasses. "She docks at 11:08, handshakes with rangers, quick walk to the demo site."

Grace Tuazon, director of outreach, adjusted the mic clipped to her collar. "Light's good for about ninety minutes. Let's keep the shot lines clean."

"We'll need background chatter—families, maybe a vet or two in TrailMind shirts. It has to read public benefit, not pilot project," Ruiz added.

Maya, Nia, Ravi, and Matthew joined them, wind pushing the scent of pine across the bluff.

"This is Nia, field co-designer and incoming MIT freshman," Maya said evenly. "Ravi's sensory-pipeline lead. Matthew and I handle the clinical framework."

Danny shook hands without looking up. "Perfect. Thanks for the heavy lift."

Nia smiled. "We're not lifting. We're tuning."

Grace caught the edge in her tone and gave a brief grin.

"You should know the frame here: public-sector innovation. We're showing that government can work. Smart tech plus public infrastructure equals high return."

Matthew raised an eyebrow. "Return in what currency?"

Danny didn't blink. "Trust. And, ideally, votes."

They began walking toward the demo station, Grace taking photos of sightlines as she moved.

"The governor's narrative is: smart tech, healthy public. We just need clarity."

Maya glanced at her. "Clarity or control?"

Grace hesitated, and winced. "Preferably both."

At the bluff's crest, the Curious zone shimmered—pine needles humming with the adaptive pulse.

Nia crouched by a sensor pad, adjusting calibration.

Danny studied the node. "This is where she'll do her trial?"

"Not a trial," Nia said. "A participation."

Grace crouched beside her. "Can we have her enter from the right? Backlight gives that halo effect."

"She's not a saint," Nia murmured.

Danny chuckled. "She's an executive. This visit's about legs, not hearts—how far this model can scale."

Ravi gestured toward the interface. "It's pre-loaded with the adaptive overlay. Syncs to breath and pupil shift. Designed to slow, not dazzle."

"Fine," Grace said. "We just need B-roll of her doing something. Maybe a kid handing her the gear. Youth empowerment sells."

Matthew's tone stayed mild. "Then shoot her listening. That's the story."

Danny made a note on his tablet.

"And the advisory committee members? We need a spread that looks like bipartisan buy-in."

"They'll speak," Maya said. "They won't pose."

Danny gave her a quick grin that didn't reach his eyes. "As long as they land the message: not therapy, public asset."

They started back down the trail. The gulls cried above them, the harbor glinting bright and indifferent.

Grace slowed beside Maya. "Off record? This is good work. But people are starving for stories of competence. We don't have to sand off the rough edges—just choreograph the clarity."

Maya didn't answer. The Curious zone behind them pulsed once—low, steady, almost like a breath.

Grace followed her gaze. "That frequency—is it intentional?"

"It's adaptive," Maya said. "Responds to whoever's nearby."

"So it's ... listening."

"Exactly." Grace jotted something on her pad.

"Scene setter: governor arrives as an executive ..."

She looked up. "How should she leave?"

Maya's reply was quiet, but it carried. "Let her arrive somewhere she can't control the outcome."

Grace met her eyes, then nodded slowly. "That's clarity too."

TWENTY-SIX

At 6:00 a.m. on Tuesday Michelle Venable was already on her yoga mat in the sunroom, breath synced to the vital pulse of ocean waves. She gave herself a quiet mental high five—yoga first, headlines second. A personal milestone.

As she opened her heart to the first sun salutation of the day, a calmly modulated AI voice piped through a countertop speaker.

"Good morning, Michelle. Beginning Morning Digest: customized summary from *ClearFrame*, *The Boston Globe*, *The Atlantic*, and *STAT*. Estimated duration: six minutes, thirty-two seconds."

Michelle smiled as she moved into a warrior pose.

The voice reported: "*The Globe*'s editorial page praises a 'rare convergence of public sector vision and sensory justice design'. The governor will visit the Boston Harbor Islands today for a TrailMind demonstration."

Michelle arched an eyebrow, breath steady, arms extended.

The voice continued, "Columnist Elspeth Channing

writes, 'Massachusetts may be the first state to show what it means to fund the nervous system as public infrastructure—where regulation isn't a prescription, but a shared condition. And where a ferry ticket can be a frontline mental health tool.'"

Michelle dropped to her knees and folded into child's pose. She couldn't help wiggling her butt in the air in celebration of the perfect timing of Elspeth's column with the governor's visit to TrailMind.

Jack walked into the sunroom, waving a hard copy of the *Globe*.

He arched a brow. "That a new asana, or did Elspeth just score the front page for your revolution?"

The Boston Globe, June 9, 2026, 6:00 a.m. edition

"Rethinking Mental Health Infrastructure: What Spectacle Island Teaches Us about Consent" By Elspeth Channing, Columnist

We have spent decades building ever more elaborate systems for tracking, nudging, and medicating the mental health of our youth. Behavioral compliance dashboards. Digital adherence blister packs. AI-powered coaching bots. Federal tax dollars, through Advance Market Commitments, are underwriting the next wave of pharmaceuticals promising neural recalibration at scale.

And yet, anxiety rates continue to climb.

Yesterday, on a small island in Boston Harbor, I witnessed something radically different—precisely because it was so unambitious by conventional standards.

The TrailMind pilot site on Spectacle Island is not therapy. It does not administer treatment. It does not diagnose, prescribe, or even monitor participants in any clinically coded sense. Instead, it creates what its designers call "adaptive consent architecture." The system invites—but never compels—users to engage their own attention, sensory input, and pacing.

At each trail station, users select whether and how to participate. A notecard suggests simple grounding prompts: breathe, listen, notice. An interface offers optional layers—soundscapes, haptics, Indigenous oral histories—always user-initiated, always user-controlled. If a participant feels overwhelmed? They stop. No data point penalizes them. No pharmacy alert triggers downstream interventions.

It is, as one co-designer described to me, "pre-therapy. Or post-therapy. Or maybe not therapy at all. It's a practice ground for learning how to sit with your own nervous system."

This may sound modest. In fact, it represents a profound challenge to our current healthcare model, one that increasingly equates data capture with care delivery, and compliance metrics with well-being. TrailMind is designed not to extract more behavioral data, but to return a measure of agency to those who are often treated as passive endpoints in complex diagnostic systems.

Critics will note—accurately—that this approach demands high user insight. But that criticism presumes what TrailMind seeks to challenge: that external systems are inherently better judges of readiness than individuals themselves. The teenagers I observed that day, many of them neurodivergent, were not fragile subjects to be carefully managed by algorithms. They were active participants—learning, adapting, exercising judgment.

This is not the full answer to the youth mental health crisis. But it may be one indispensable part: a consent-based framework that respects neurodiversity, teaches self-regulation, and expands therapeutic capacity without requiring infinite clinical staffing or pharmaceutical escalation.

As public dollars shift away from federal mental health programs and new state-level advisory boards scramble to fill the gap, we should ask ourselves: What kind of infrastructure do we want to build? Systems that chase compliance? Or systems that cultivate competence?

What I saw on Spectacle Island was not another digital solution chasing engagement metrics. It was a quiet invitation to something rarer in today's public health landscape: autonomy.

Policy makers should take note. Some forms of healing

don't scale through optimization. They scale through
trust.

Elspeth Channing is a columnist for The Boston Globe
and a member of the Boston Foundation's Civic Innova-
tion Circle.

HANNAH HAD JUST LOCKED her bike at the entrance to
the Davis Square T station—her next leg to join Maya's team
for the 8:20 ferry to Spectacle Island to await the governor's
visit—when her phone buzzed.

7:52 a.m.
Josh: Need to talk. Darren's testifying.
7:53 a.m.
Hannah: Testifying where? To whom? And do I need
to wear shoes?
7:55 a.m.
Josh voice memo: Joint Senate Appropriations
Subcommittees on Labor-HHS and THUD. Capitol
Hill. Darren just got the call. They want him to speak
to the proposed AMC flex language for transport-to-
healing spaces. Motion as Medicine is becoming policy,
Hannah. And you need to be in that room.

Look, the Harbor Islands are in the bag. The gaggle's
already fighting over camera angles for the governor's
walk. We don't need another 'sensory justice makes for
good optics' piece. We need the national story. We
need the person who understood from the beginning
that TrailMind isn't about tech—it's about consent, and

tempo, and infrastructure that co-regulates instead of coercing.

Get to D.C. Cover the hearing. And after that, get out to the other TrailMind field sites—Glacier, Organ Pipe, Shenandoah. See how the apps land in wild space, not just urban-adjacent parks. You're not documenting anymore. You're framing the movement. This is nervous system equity on a federal stage. You in?"

8:01 a.m.

Hannah: So just a small gig, then.

8:01 a.m. Hannah: Also—Organ Pipe in July? You want me to melt?

8:02 a.m.

Josh: Sweat is sensory data, Oak. Pack light. Carry signal.

8:03 a.m.

Hannah: Did you just drop signal theory as a vibe check?

A MAKESHIFT COMMAND hub was taking shape under the pop-up canopies: folding tables, hydration bins, walkie-talkie stacks, laminated zone maps, and a whiteboard covered in trail rotation schedules color-coded by access need.

Maya stepped back to scan the board, pen tucked behind her ear. "We've got thirty-six confirmed participants—ages ten to sixty-seven. Most of them are co-navigating with a peer, parent, or support animal."

Nia was crouched nearby, sorting trail badges by sensory profile: red, yellow, green, and grey for observers.

"Three trail routes, each anchored by a grounding node.

Everyone rotates once per hour, always with the choice to opt out at any time. Break tent near the ferry dock is scent-neutral and noise-dampened," Nia asserted.

"Except for when the damn ferry horn blows," she muttered under her breath.

Alexis stepped into the circle, holding a clipboard and a soft smile. "Six of my students made their own trail maps based on emotional wayfinding. They're leading a 'routes that listen back' loop on the north side. One kid renamed the beach access path 'The Slow Hello'."

"You have five vet-partners in the Curious circuit, but you need to get on a plane. You okay pairing them solo?" Nia asked Kris.

Kris adjusted Lumen's harness. "Fine as long as they have dogs to triangulate with. Lumen already flagged two breath pattern anomalies on the approach trail. She's reading before I can."

Malik was setting up a low table with snacks, fidget tools, and QR-code field journals. "We've got eleven youth co-designers between Inner Harbor Alliance and Alexis' class. Some are non-speaking. Most prefer to sketch or voice-note.

"No worksheets. Just rhythm."

Janey Jones surveyed the trails, nodding in approval. "This is what community-led planning looks like. No stage. No mic. Just systems that let people come in at their own tempo."

Ravi walked alongside Maya, gesturing toward the bluff where the Indigenous Sounds v2 module was set up under shade netting.

"We've preloaded three sequences—earth percussion, water threads, and speculative hum. Governor can try any of them. The AR overlay is tuned to Calm zone rhythms, so she won't trigger anything too sharp unless she leans in."

Maya smiled. "She'll lean in."

"She always does," Ravi smiled. "We've also got a mirror trail for the media team. No gear, just the aesthetics. That way, her 'authentic engagement' can be both real and televised."

<hr>

AT 9:48 a.m. Nia radioed in from the sensory toolkit zone.

"Node Two is ready. We've got art supplies, trail journals, clay for imprint mapping, and audio recorders with one-tap capture. Malik's group is loading into their first loop now."

Matthew checked the pacing chart. "Governor's team arrives at 11:08. Let her watch one trail rotate, then guide her through the co-design tent."

"She'll want to speak to at least three youths directly—one verbal, one sketch-based, and one sensory-log preference."

Alexis added quietly, "Make sure the conversation is on their terms. Choice of format. Choice of timing.

"We don't build trauma-informed systems just to suspend them when a governor arrives."

Maya nodded. "Then let's choreograph clarity. No performance. Just practice."

As the first participants moved toward their trail entry points—batons in hand, hats tilted against the sun, dogs sniffing the air—a low hum of purposeful quiet settled over the team.

The island wasn't hosting a showcase. It was hosting a way forward.

<hr>

THE FERRY HORN sounded low and long as the governor stepped off the gangway flanked by Danny Ruiz and Grace Tuazon. Behind them came two aides, a GBH camera crew, and the bright hum of live coverage.

Maya, Janey, and Alexis waited at the dock in TrailMind vests—not formal, not unkempt.

"Governor," Maya said, "welcome to the island."

"I've been looking forward to this," the governor replied. "It's not every day I get invited to a hackathon run by people who know what their nervous systems need."

Nia murmured to Maya, "Curious loop first—we're tracking a wind shift."

A youth guide led them up the bluff. Cameras trailed at a respectful distance.

Near the trail's edge, a participant named Deja tapped her baton twice and settled cross-legged on the moss.

A producer whispered, "Mind if we film her sketching?"

Malik stepped in. "Yes, we do. Deja opted out of camera engagement. You can film her artwork later if she consents."

The producer hesitated. "But it's a good visual."

The governor turned toward him. "So is listening."

Silence fell except for waves and pencil strokes.

Farther up the trail, media consultant Todd Wexley eyed the mirrored-path installation. "How do you measure ROI on a kid tapping a stick near some trees?"

Malik didn't blink. "You measure it when that kid comes back next week. When they stay present in class because they learned to breathe between ferry horns."

"Doesn't sound scalable."

"It's nervous-system infrastructure," Malik said. "Different tempo."

Inside the demo tent, adaptive audio hummed softly. Nia stood beside a timeline labeled Soft No / Slow Yes.

The governor leaned closer. "What does that mean?"

"It means systems can't demand instant clarity from people who need to feel safe first," Nia said. "Consent isn't always verbal. Sometimes it's time-coded."

The governor nodded. "Policy language I haven't heard before—but I like it."

At a rest node, Ranger Joe Morales stood with arms crossed. "Governor, we're short six rangers. An app doesn't stop erosion."

"You're right," she said. "That's why the budget fills the gap for the National Park Service partnership funds. And because burnout's real, Motion as Medicine isn't just for visitors."

He hesitated. "You think this'll last?"

"Only if we keep listening."

He nodded once, eyes softer.

Back at the tent, the governor removed her badge and tucked it into her pocket. "I expected innovation," she said. "What I didn't expect was coherence."

Matthew handed her a printout from the synced trail logs. "Three dozen nervous systems in motion. Design serving regulation, not performance."

The governor scanned it, thoughtful. "Looks like policy to me."

Maya smiled faintly. "That's the hope. A ferry ticket. A trail node. And breathing room. All supported by the public like they matter."

The governor looked out at the water, then back at the humming sensors—listening now, not performing.

***

DARREN WAS SHOWN to his seat in a hearing room in the Dirksen Senate Office Building in Washington, D.C. The official placard read, "Hearing: Flexing AMCs to Support Youth Mental Health and Mobility Equity." Beneath that, "Senate Appropriations Subcommittees on Labor-HHS and THUD (Joint Informational Session)."

The hearing room was packed. This wasn't a standard budget review—it was styled as a forward-looking policy forum, signaling that something new was being floated. Reporters leaned forward. Staffers hovered at the margins, scribbling notes.

The witness table was pre-set with slim digital briefing books with the gold Senate seal embossed. Darren sat between Dr. Amina Kassam and Kris Barsa, and thought: *I've known these two people for 18 years.*

The chairwoman opened with her signature blend of policy grit and populist clarity. "We are losing a generation to anxiety—and we are losing public trust in our systems to respond. But we don't have to keep choosing between pharmaceuticals and despair. What if the next great public health innovation isn't a pill—but a pass?"

She nodded to Darren. "Mr. Katsaros, you were one of the early recipients of an Advance Market Commitment for neuro-therapeutics. But today you're proposing something bigger. Let's hear it."

Darren nodded once and tapped his screen to bring up a composite image: a trailhead kiosk, a ferry boarding zone, and a teen holding a sensory-friendly transit pass.

"Madam Chair, Senators—thank you.

"The tools we use to scale medical interventions can also scale access.

"I'm here today to propose how a tripartite commitment among the Departments of Health and Human Services, Transportation, and Education can flex the AMC model from a single-stream pharmaceutical intervention to one that accelerates innovation in treating movement as a regulated intervention."

"Specifically, this AMC would underwrite intermodal

passes—ferries, shuttles, and green corridors—designed not just for cost equity, but sensory coherence."

He turned to address the Senator from Washington State, who had just spoken publicly about the latest pediatric anxiety trends.

"We're finding that the highest dropout points in youth mental health programs aren't at intake. They're at transit. The journey to care is itself a stress test. If we want them to heal, they need to arrive regulated. Not braced."

Kris jumped in smoothly. "For our veterans and our neuro-divergent kids, the point of failure isn't intention. It's naviga-tion. We've designed onboarding protocols for low-interaction ferry access, ADA-plus trail interfaces, even service-animal hydration nodes."

Senator Baldwin raised an eyebrow. "And you believe this qualifies under HHS prevention guidelines?"

Amina Kassam smiled. "The data suggests it does. We're not talking leisure. We're talking embodied regulation. Evidence-based, repeatable, cost-suppressing."

Senator Schatz, chair of the THUD subcommittee leaned in. "But who owns the farebox? Who sets eligibility?"

Darren didn't flinch. "The farebox is the old frame. What we're offering is a risk-tiered access layer, integrated with private insurers, Medicaid, SNAP, and school-based health systems. And unlike traditional transit subsidies, this model doesn't just get people to work. It gets them to safety."

The chairwoman tapped her pen. "And if we don't act?"

Darren's voice was steady. "Then we will continue to pay more to treat what we could have prevented. We'll spend billions on neural sedation while our parks empty and our kids disappear into their rooms."

He looked out over the chamber. "The AMC model was built

to bring vaccines to our nation during the lethal and disruptive COVID-19 pandemic. Today, we have to bring coherence to the most dysregulated generation. Same logic. Different frontier."

There was a moment of charged silence. Then the chairwoman nodded slowly, turned to her staffer, and whispered, "Mark that for report language. Underline it."

In the audience, Hannah Oak tapped a new headline into her notes, "Senate Considers 'Pass to the Commons' as Next-Gen Public Health Infrastructure."

TWENTY-SEVEN

The last ferry was still twenty minutes out, and the island had settled into soft birdsong and sea breeze. Folding tables leaned half-dismantled against the tent poles. Sensor batons rested in bins. Trail flags fluttered like quiet applause.

Maya stood at the bluff, the harbor gleaming beyond her, the day's adrenaline dissolving into a kind of reverent fatigue.

She watched Nia standing barefoot near a pitch pine, recorder still in hand.

"I'm logging my own nervous system for once," Nia said aloud, not to anyone in particular. "And it's ... not spiking. It's humming."

Beside her, a non-speaking teen named Rio lifted their journal for Maya to see. They'd drawn a grid of feeling states. One box was shaded in green and labeled safe–excited. Their finger tapped it twice, proud and certain.

Malik walked up beside Maya. "I thought I was here to rep. But I think I was here because I needed to reset."

He rubbed the back of his neck, looking out at the water. "Something in me ... unclenched today."

Maya nodded, eyes damp but smiling. Their words landed with more quiet authority than any briefing or headline.

This—youth attunement, unsupervised coherence—was the validation she hadn't known she was waiting for.

A warm, weightless sensation ran up her spine, like relief sneaking in to take in the scene. For the first time in a long while, she felt the work had stopped performing and started belonging.

She glanced toward the fading horizon, already imagining Matthew's face when she told him what she'd seen: that joy could register on a dataset, that safety could hum, that maybe this was what coherence looked like in the wild.

***

WHEN DARREN ARRIVED at Gate B12, Hannah moved her messenger bag to free up a seat for him.

"You know, I hate admitting this, but you keep surprising me."

Darren chuckled. "That's the nicest thing you've ever said to me. Should I worry?"

"Nah. It's not flattery—it's data.

"You run smoother than most of the execs I write about. And you're more agile than I gave you credit for. Your policy brief this morning? That was not C-suite boilerplate."

Darren smiled. "That's because you keep pushing me to keep the framing real. You're basically a live-in gut check at this point. And I don't even subscribe to your blog."

"Liar. You read every post. You even quote me in committee meetings. I have sources, remember?"

Darren smirked. "Fair. Guilty. Your reach is growing—*ClearFrame* suits you."

"Yeah ... it's weird. I used to think staying indie was the only way to hold on to integrity. But now? With their resources, I can actually chase the bigger story. TrailMind pilots across the country, ranger mental health initiatives, a few state-funded experiments in grief mapping."

"So you're going full National Parks correspondent? Trading hearings for hot springs?"

Hannah laughed. "I'm trading hearings for humans. And honestly, I think the edges are where the real shifts are happening. Policy is lagging. People aren't."

"I envy that, a little. I spend so much time making Neuro-Tech legible to investors that I forget what it was supposed to feel like."

"That's kind of the heart of it, right? You built a tool meant to help people feel again—and the machine that sells it numbs the mission."

"Not sure how much longer we'll be selling it," Darren said soberly. "Looks like NeuroTech might get squeezed out of the distribution side of NeuroEase. Not our lane."

"Oof. You okay?" Hannah asked gently.

"Honestly? I think I am. The Board will scream, but I've made my peace with it. We made our impact. Maybe the next move is less about scale and more about alignment."

"There you go again," Hannah raised her eyebrows in mock surprise. "That's not the answer I expected.

"So what's next?"

"I've been poking at the Flex AMC proposals. The ones that prioritize modular, responsive systems—hardware, wear-ables, ambient tech. Less prescription pad, more adaptive systems. NeuroTech could be useful there."

"You thinking TrailMind-adjacent? Co-regulation modules?" Hannah asked, intrigued.

"Maybe. But first I need to stop thinking like a pharma guy. I've been wondering if I should be out there—touring parks, like you. Not to lock up contracts. Just ... to see. What regulation looks like without a product pitch."

"Maybe don't wear the startup fleece. Or do. It might be good friction." Hannah shrugged.

Darren smiled. "You think there's a place for me in that landscape?"

"It's not a club, Katsaros. There's a place for everyone in nature."

A ground crew member invited passengers in group one to board.

"Well. Back to Boston. You flying out again soon?" Darren asked.

"Next week. Olympic Peninsula. After that, Joshua Tree. Want me to send you postcards from the trail?"

"Only if they're brutally honest. Like you."

THE GOVERNOR HADN'T CHANGED out of her field jacket. A faint ring of salt clung to the hem, a reminder that she'd stepped straight off the ferry into this meeting.

The conference table was smaller than usual, the lights dimmed to half. Danny Ruiz sat opposite her, tablet at the ready. Grace Tuazon had a yellow legal pad filled with shorthand notes and half-sketched arrows. The hum of the city came through the windows—a low, electrical heartbeat.

The governor turned a printed sheet between her fingers. "The youth feedback summary," she said. "Listening. Consistency. Safety. Honesty. Patience. Belonging."

She let the words breathe in the air. "They sound almost liturgical."

Danny glanced up from his tablet. "Not exactly Key Performance Indicators."

"Maybe they should be." She set the paper down beside her mug. "If our metrics don't measure what people actually feel, then we're auditing noise."

Grace hesitated. "Do you think voters care about belonging? It polls soft. They want outcomes—jobs, coverage, relief checks."

The governor smiled faintly. "Exactly. They call it relief. We call it belonging. Same sensation, different syntax."

She leaned back, eyes half-closed. "When that girl—Deja—refused the cameras, I caught my own breath slowing to hers. That wasn't optics; that was coherence. For ten seconds, everyone on that bluff was tuned to the same frequency."

Grace looked down at her notes, almost whispering, "It read that way on camera too."

Danny exhaled, tapping his pen. "So what do we do with it? You want a task force? Another blue-ribbon panel?"

"No," she said. "A budget line."

She opened her notebook—plain, spiral-bound, edges frayed from field use.

"TrailMind doesn't need another think tank. It needs breathing room—funds for ranger training, adaptive access, peer-led modules. If we treat the nervous system as public infrastructure, we start by paying attention to it."

Danny frowned. "We'd have to rename the appropriation. Health and Human Services won't carry it."

"Then we reframe it."

She jotted something quickly, underlining twice. Motion as Medicine—Pilot to Program. She looked up.

"Let's build the language backward from feeling: start with relief, end with policy."

Grace tilted her head. "Listening, consistency, safety,

honesty, patience, belonging," she recited again, slower this time. "You think we can budget for that?"

The governor smiled. "Not line-item by line-item. But we can design for it. You saw that island. That's what functioning government feels like."

For a moment, no one spoke. Outside, sirens threaded through the night, distant and thin. The governor rose, stretching slightly, the chair legs scraping against marble.

"Tomorrow," she said, "we draft the listening bill."

Danny blinked. "That's not a real thing."

"It will be," she said. "Call it what you need to for the docket, but that's what it is."

She slid the printout toward them—six words circled in pen. "Those are the first line items."

Grace looked at the paper, then up at her boss. "You realize you just turned a therapy vocabulary into state policy."

The governor smiled, tired and genuine. "Maybe we finally stopped pretending the two are separate."

She reached for her jacket, still flecked with sand, and turned toward the window. The harbor lights pulsed faintly in the distance, rhythm matching the ferry she'd just left behind.

For a brief moment she let her eyes close, listening—not to the city, not to the data—but to the low, steady signal of her own breath.

<hr>

THAT NIGHT, the harbor light pulsed faintly beyond the glass, matching the rhythm of the TrailMind nodes Maya imagined were still glowing on the islands. She stood barefoot by the window, hair loose, watching the slow sweep of the ferry beacon as it crossed the harbor.

The security chime sounded once, soft and familiar. When she opened the door, Matthew was already smiling—the tired, incredulous kind of smile that follows relief. His tie was gone, sleeves rolled.

"She listened," he said simply. "The governor actually listened."

Maya stepped aside to let him in. "You sound surprised."

"Not surprised," he said, setting his bag down. "Just ... recalibrated. For the first time in months, I don't feel like the hypothesis is outrunning the human data."

She poured tea, steady hands.

"Today, something built with the neurodivergent community crossed into policy. That's what integration looks like."

He laughed softly. "You mean coherence."

"Same soul, different syntax," she said, echoing his own words from earlier.

He looked at her—really looked—as if trying to measure the distance between the professional triumph they'd just lived through and the quiet of this room.

"When we started, I thought intellectual intimacy was the safest version of connection." He shrugged.

"No risk of misreading signals, no vulnerability hangover. But tonight I realized—"

"—it's the same system," she finished. "Cognition and affection. Feedback loops."

"Exactly." He smiled. "We regulate each other. And that's ... not theoretical anymore."

She crossed to the couch. "So what happens when the model works?"

He joined her, close enough that their shoulders brushed. "Then the experiment ends and the practice begins."

They sat for a while, quiet except for the hum of the city outside.

Maya turned to him. "We said we'd build it together—one evening at a time."

He nodded. "Maybe now we can let mornings happen, too."

She closed her eyes and reached for his hand, interlacing her fingers through his, feeling the low, syncing pulse of two nervous systems finally at ease.

A PREVIEW OF UNPRESCRIBED

Between 1999 and 2020, more than 500,000 people died from opioid-related overdoses in the United States.

But that's not the number that broke me. This is:

In counties like the one I grew up in—where the median income is below the national average and the nearest mental health clinic is two bus routes and a favor away—prescription opioid deaths weren't spikes.

They were slopes. Slow. Quiet. Respectable even, until the body gave out.

Like my dad's did.

He didn't get high. He got tired.

He didn't want to disappear. He wanted to stay at work. Pay the mortgage. Avoid scaring his only kid with a hospital bill.

And that's how the system let him die.

Not as a statistic. As a sacrifice.

There's a phrase in pharma circles: *adherence.*

It's how long someone stays on the drug. How reliably they refill it. Whether they "comply" with the protocol.

My dad was 100% adherent. He took the pills exactly as prescribed, even after the refill rejections started. He rationed. Bought generic when he could. Cut pills in half to stretch them.

He was what the system would call "a good patient."

And then, when the insurance stopped covering it, and his doctor started deflecting, he stopped asking. Started improvising.

My dad was an introvert, a man who thought therapy was "for people with more words than problems." He never told me he was addicted. He never said the word "pain." But he left a note.

Not a letter.

A sticky note.

Tucked in the shoebox.

"Don't let this be the story."

So here I am, dad.

Telling the story anyway.

Because it's not just yours.

This week, Congress is holding hearings on the $200 billion Advance Market Commitment for NeuroEase—a next-gen anxiety pill that's already being framed as "a moonshot for mental health."

But I can't help thinking: we've been here before.

The first moonshot was OxyContin.

And the rocket burned out in neighborhoods like mine.

So here's my question, to the policymakers, the biotech founders, the journalists parroting efficacy stats:

What happens when the pill runs out?

Unprescribed *follows Hannah Oak as she traces the human cost of systems designed to optimize compliance instead of care.*

ABOUT THE AUTHOR

Robin Johnson writes fiction about systems under pressure—where technological ambition, environmental limits, and civic institutions collide with ordinary human lives.

The Quantum Feelings series follows an ensemble of engineers, journalists, policymakers, and organizers grappling with climate disruption, housing instability, and institutional breakdown. The novels return often to questions of generational collaboration and responsibility across time.